**"Wa   to forget   ?
Did you go as willingly to Thornson's
bed as you did mine?"**

"Do not be crude. What choice did I have?"

"You could have said no. We'd exchanged vows."

Marguerite had expected this. But the deadly tone of his voice brought a breathless gasp out of her lips. "I spoke but a promise to you. Not all promises can be kept."

"It was much more than a simple promise." Darius stepped towards her. "It was a vow made to me, before God, before witnesses. A vow to be my wife."

She pushed him away. "Do not do this, Darius. We were impetuous children who acted on a whim. Nobody, not the King nor the Church, would hold us to those vows."

"Children? Impetuous children?" He grasped her arms. "Did you love Thornson?"

She nodded, then thought to turn the tables. "What about you? Do you not care for your wife?"

"I care   for my wife. To my
mi

M   lked
ab

FALCON'S LOVE

Denise Lynn

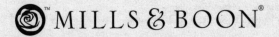

All the characters in this book have no existence outside the imagination of the author, and have no relation whatsoever to anyone bearing the same name or names. They are not even distantly inspired by any individual known or unknown to the author, and all the incidents are pure invention.

First published in Great Britain 2010
Harlequin Mills & Boon Limited,
Eton House, 18-24 Paradise Road, Richmond, Surrey TW9 1SR

© Denise L. Koch 2005

ISBN: 978 0 263 87565 2

Harlequin Mills & Boon policy is to use papers that are natural, renewable and recyclable products and made from wood grown in sustainable forests. The logging and manufacturing process conform to the legal environmental regulations of the country of origin.

Printed and bound in Spain
by Litografia Rosés, S.A., Barcelona

Award-winning author **Denise Lynn** has been an avid reader of romance novels for many years. Between the pages of books she has travelled to lands and times filled with brave knights, courageous ladies and never-ending love. Now she can share with others her dream of telling tales of adventure and romance.

Denise lives with her real-life hero, Tom, and a slew of four-legged 'kids' in north western Ohio, USA. Their two-legged son, Ken, serves in the USN, and comes home on occasion to visit and fix the computers, VCRs or any other electronic device Mum can confuse in his absence. You can write to her at PO Box 17, Monclova, OH 43542, USA, or visit her website, www.denise-lynn.com

Recent novels by the same author:

FALCON'S DESIRE
FALCON'S HONOUR

For Mom, with love.

Prologue

Falcongate
Normandy, Late Spring 1142

A small brazier provided light in the one-room hunter's cottage. They would supply their own brand of heat to warm the tiny chamber.

He slid beneath the furs on the narrow cot, then gathered her close. She came to him willingly, pressing the length of her body against his.

Her head rested just below his shoulder, her shaking breath blew hot against his chest. Stray curls from hair as bright as the summer sun tickled at his neck.

Her skin was so soft and smooth, like the fluffy softness of a rabbit. He stroked her slender naked limbs, reveling in the knowledge that she was his. She trembled beneath his touch, her nervousness making him feel bold and protective at the same time.

The thought humbled him and he silently swore to protect her always. Had he not recently vowed to keep her safe, to honor her, to love her for all time?

This night they would learn of passion and desire together. They would bind the vows they'd shared with love.

"You would think a Faucon would know not to let down his guard."

Darius of Faucon jolted out of his dream at the statement. He'd fallen asleep while fishing and had not heard the men approach. His first instinct was to grab the weapon lying at his side. But the tip of a sword steadily pressed to his neck kept him in place against the tree he'd leaned against earlier this day.

He squinted against the blazing sun and counted eight blades pointed at his chest. He glanced toward the next tree and saw Sir Osbert in the same predicament. Darius felt a measure of relief knowing that the aging captain of his guard had come to no harm.

From the tenseness of the man's stout body and the bushing of his near-white eyebrows, Darius doubted if Sir Osbert shared that relief. One thing was certain, had these armed men wanted either of them dead, they'd already be conversing with those in the afterlife.

Darius stared at the man leaning closest to him and asked, "Who are you? What do you want?"

The man stood, sheathing his blade as he did so. "King Stephen and Queen Maud wish a favor."

Though Darius was thankful to have been awoken from a dream that had haunted him nightly for nearly six years, he asked, "They could not simply send a missive?"

"They did. No one responded."

Obviously the request had been sent to Faucon Keep. He'd not been on his brother's property for a fortnight now. Instead, he'd taken up residence at the smaller and more secluded holding of Falcongate. Situated along a lazy river, it suited his needs for the moment.

Darius informed the man, "Comte Faucon is recently married and has not yet arrived home. The king knows this."

"Aye, and your other brother is encumbered elsewhere. That is why Queen Maud sent us directly to you. She thought you might be here instead of at the main keep."

"Obviously, she was correct." Darius rose, silently cursing the queen for remembering this holding. "What do they want?"

"An exchange."

The humor evident in the man's voice gave Darius pause. "Exchange of what?"

"A favor for your traitorous life."

"Traitorous?"

The man shrugged. "It seems proof has been given to place you in league with Empress Matilda."

The possible repercussions of that statement brought Darius's heart to a near standstill. "Who makes this wild accusation?"

The man's smirk widened. "Queen Maud."

Darius gritted his teeth to capture a shout of frustration. This false accusation was nothing but a game. A game the king and queen would play to ensure his immediate cooperation. A game where his life would likely be the only prize.

A game he obviously had no choice but to play. "And what…favor causes King Stephen and Queen Maud to employ such extreme measures to gain my assistance?"

The man nodded. "Good. You seem to understand the

importance of this request." He waited until Darius was joined by his captain before continuing, "It is a simple task."

Sir Osbert snorted in disbelief. Darius shared his man's opinion. *Simple* would likely translate to a mission requiring much gold, men and risk. He motioned for the man to explain. "Define what this simple task entails."

"Lord Thornson has died. He leaves behind a widow."

Likely a widow requiring a new husband. Darius swallowed before asking, "And they wish me to do what?"

"You are to take and hold Thornson Keep until the king and queen can find a man suitable to be a husband for the lady and a master for the keep."

Darius's exhale of relief escaped in a rush at the knowledge that he was not this suitable man. Then he realized that Thornson Keep was near the border of Scotland. It would put him not only weeks away from Falcongate, but on the edge of the enemy's territory. "A *simple* task to be sure."

The man's wicked chuckle preceded an ominous warning. "There is more."

Of course there would be more. Darius closed his eyes briefly and shook his head. "I am not surprised."

Chapter One

Thornson Keep, Northeast coast of England
Early summer, 1142

He had never found much pleasure in killing another, but Darius of Faucon was certain that battle would provide more engaging action than tracking down smugglers for the king. If nothing else, at least he'd be on the back of a sturdy warhorse and not lying on his belly in the cold mud staring over the edge of a cliff.

To keep the hilt of his sword from digging any farther into his flesh, he shifted his position on the ground. After two nights of this, nothing he did helped much. With the coldness of the earth, the hardness of his chain mail and the cursed dampness of the night, he doubted he'd ever again find comfort, warmth or even a measure of dryness.

He peered over the edge of the cliff, down at the flickering torchlight below. The figures on the beach hustled to meet boats landing on the shore. They lifted trunks and bags out of the four small vessels, carried them across the beach and disappeared into the cliffs. Only six men guarded the operation on the beach. The guards appeared to stand close to each other, instead of spreading out to keep their cohorts safe. Judging by this lack of concern for safety, he doubted there were any others farther up the shoreline.

Darius glanced up at the position of the moon. Each night at the same time, men had lit torches on the beach to guide the boats to those standing at hand to unload the cargo. King Stephen's fears were valid—a smuggling operation existed in Thornson.

And Darius had but a month to root them out.

No sense in waiting. They'd confront the smugglers this night. He scooted back from the edge of the cliff, rose and motioned to Sir Osbert. At least one of his "simple tasks" could be completed on schedule. First one mission and then the other.

Sir Osbert had the men ready for action when Darius met them a short distance from the cliff. Without a word, he led the men along the edge of the cliff as it sloped down to meet the beach.

Once on the pebbled shoreline, they kept their backs to the rocky wall as they moved closer to the smugglers. Just as Darius had surmised, the outlaws kept no guard on the outskirts of their operation, so certain were they of their safety. How long had they enjoyed free run of Thornson?

One of the many questions he'd have answered before his missions were completed…

When they neared the smugglers, Darius nodded to his men, drew his sword, stepped away from the rocks, then shouted, "For King Stephen!"

Men scattered. Those closest to the vessels jumped

inside the boats and quickly rowed away, taking the remainder of their cargo along. Those on the beach who did not run into the mouth of the cave dropped their loads, grabbed their weapons and raced toward Darius and his men.

Three of the smugglers fell with the first clashing blows from Darius's men; the criminals were no match for armed warriors. Those who'd been standing guard gave but a halfhearted effort to defend themselves. When it soon became obvious that Darius's men had gained the upper hand, one of the outlaws shouted, "To the lady!"

At the man's command, the remaining smugglers and their guards turned and raced into the cave. Certain the man who'd shouted must be in charge of the others, Darius pointed at him and ordered, "Take him alive."

He wanted all the information he could gather to take back to King Stephen, along with the name of the person backing this operation.

Sir Osbert quickly nabbed the man and held him at sword point. "Milord, shall I make him talk?"

Darius took one look at the unholy gleam in Osbert's eyes and shook his head. "Nay, it would be easier to discover what he knows while he can still breathe."

At that moment, the captured smuggler yelled, "Never." Then he threw himself at Osbert's sword.

Caught off guard, the captain had no time to move his weapon before the man impaled himself on the blade. "Good Lord, man." Osbert pulled his sword free and let the man fall to the ground.

Darius cursed, then knelt beside the dying man. "Give over. Tell me who you serve."

The man's laugh gurgled through his parted lips. He shook his head. "No."

"Which lady do you seek to protect? The Empress Matilda? The Lady of Thornson?" Darius frowned. Determined to gain any scrap of information he could, he grasped the man's shoulders and offered, "Go to your maker with a clean heart. Tell me and I will see you are buried with the blessing of the Church. Matilda or Thornson's lady?"

"Aye." The man's whispered answer was barely audible.

"Who?" Darius leaned down to better hear the answer, but the only sound that met his ears was the lapping of water at the edge of the beach. The man heaved one last breath and died.

Darius released the body. What could have been the end of one task was now reduced to a gain of nothing.

"Milord, shall we follow the others into the cave?"

Darius glanced from Osbert to the approaching sea. The incoming tide would soon crash against the rocks. Any caught between the sea and the cliff would be crushed.

He glanced at the steep rock face. The darker waterline high above them was visible in the moon's light. The height made following the smugglers into the cave dangerous: water would soon flood the unfamiliar escape route.

Since the possibility of a watery grave was not to his liking, he answered Osbert, "Nay. There is no more time this night." Darius rose and waved toward the dead bodies of the smugglers. "Gather the dead."

"Why not leave them here for the sea to bury?" Sir Osbert shrugged. "Let their death befit their deeds."

"I will not have that on my soul." Darius stared down at his captain. "Gather the dead. Take all but this one to the church in Thornson and let the villagers deal with them in whatever manner they desire."

A solitary figure backed farther away from the mouth of the cave, into the safety provided by the network of tunnels. He clenched his jaw with helpless rage, then whispered, "Fools."

These strangers knew not with whom they dealt. Swift and deadly justice would be their prize for interfering in things they did not understand.

He was sick unto death of serving another. It was time he answer only to the king. He deserved that privilege. Surely none would disagree. He would see to the strangers' deaths himself. He had already risked much—even murder—to get this far. It would be only right that he be the one to hold the sword to their necks.

The sea pounded against the rock cliffs, echoing like thunder across the open grassy land between the forest and Thornson Keep. On such a clear, sunny morning the rumbling echoed ominously.

From the cover of the trees Darius stared up at the great stone keep. The sound of the crashing waves reverberated through him, providing the perfect setting for the coming attack.

The king had given him the men, arms and gold needed to complete this part of his task—to take and hold Thornson Keep. After studying the keep's layout, he had assumed his force would be more than enough—he couldn't have been more wrong.

They'd rushed the keep repeatedly yesterday to no

avail. As far as he could tell, Thornson's force had been decreased by four men. But Darius had lost one of Faucon's men when the scaling ladder was pushed away from the wall and the man hit the hard earth, snapping his neck. Hopefully, his brother the Comte would take the situation into consideration when he learned the news.

Darius took another look at the parchment with the building plans before crumpling them and tossing the useless information to the ground. He stared back up at Thornson. It was more fortress than keep.

Continued battling would be a waste of time and lives. He and his pitiful band of men could batter at the gates until the world ended and it would make no difference to those inside.

The thought of laying siege crossed his mind—briefly. Darius's instincts warned him that he and those with him would die of old age before Thornson's stores dwindled.

How was he to *hold* the keep if he could not find a way to gain control?

And why did the king seem not to know of this situation? Perhaps he did know and simply did not care, or think it worth mentioning.

Sir Osbert joined him at the edge of the clearing. "Milord, have you done something to anger King Stephen or Queen Maud?" Osbert's stare remained on Thornson.

"Besides the false accusations they lay at my feet, nothing I am aware of comes to mind."

"How do they expect you to take and hold this keep?" Osbert swung around and looked at Darius. "We would need more than twice the manpower we have."

"I know." His captain was correct. Thirty men would not be able to breach Thornson's thick, stone walls. "I thought we would try the direct approach next."

"The direct approach?"

"Aye." Darius stared at his captain, waiting for the objections sure to come.

Osbert widened his eyes. "You think to just ride up to the gate, accuse them of being traitors and demand they hand over the keep?"

"It is worth a try." In truth, Darius held little hope that the tactic would work. While it would be an easy thing to lay the smuggling operation at Thornson's feet, it might not prove as easy to place that burden on the traitor's widow.

However, he had a gut feeling that someone at Thornson might want the dead body currently draped across the back of one of Darius's horses.

"But, Milord…"

"Even if we do not accuse them outright, Thornson died months ago." Darius cut off his man's further objections. "His widow holds the keep. Do you think she enjoys the work and responsibility something that size requires?" When Osbert said nothing, Darius continued. "If that isn't enough incentive, surely someone wishes to lay claim to the body we possess."

Osbert sat back in his saddle, contemplating Darius's explanation. Finally, the man nodded. "Aye, it is worth a try."

"I am glad you agree." His sarcasm was clearly lost on the captain. Darius pulled a rolled parchment from a strap on his saddle. "And if either of those ideas fails, perhaps the king's written orders will help convince Thornson's lady to see reason."

Sir Osbert nodded, then turned his horse around. "I will gather a few men to join us."

"Four archers will be enough." While Darius held little hope that this would work, he was not foolish enough to think it held no risk. The archers could provide the cover needed if they had to beat a hasty retreat. "And we'll take the body with us to the gates."

Osbert and the archers joined Darius in a few minutes. Darius led them out of the woods wondering if it would be a bad day to die. He squinted against the bright sunlight and hoped the Saints would be for him and not against him this day.

He, the four archers, Osbert and the horse with the body slung over its back crossed the expanse of open land toward Thornson.

The wind howled, buffeting them with a force that threatened to knock them from their mounts.

Darius kept his gaze trained on the wall. Though Thornson's men peered between the crenellations, none had aimed arrows at Darius or his companions. Still, he did not relax his focus. They were only halfway to the keep and anything could happen. In less than a heartbeat circumstances could reverse. A single, well-placed arrow could change everything.

Not that any would mourn his death. His father had disowned him years ago when Darius had foolishly taken his future into his own hands.

He blinked. What had brought that thought to his waking mind? Until this moment, the memories of his young wife and the wrath of both fathers had plagued him only in his dreams.

Darius rolled his shoulders, seeking any action that would take his mind off the insanity of the past. There was plenty to concern him right now. Smugglers to rout, a keep to hold, and now, less than a full month to complete his missions.

And his mind wished to dwell on things long dead?

He never should have returned to Faucon. He should have stayed away and let the rumors of his demise flourish and grow unchallenged. That would have been the easier thing to do.

But when had he ever chosen the easier way?

Darius silently cursed his womanly concerns into nothingness.

They drew nearer the walls of Thornson. He motioned to Sir Osbert to lift his banner. It was time to see if his direct approach would succeed or fail.

The brilliant green silk unfurled and whipped in the strong winds. Would those on the wall recognize the black falcon? And would they realize the folded wings and closed talons were a position of peace, not war?

Lady Marguerite of Thornson leaned against the saw-toothed wall surrounding the keep, fighting to keep her wits about her. Whenever she thought it was not possible for life to get worse, it somehow did.

Two nights ago they'd lost Matthew on the beach, along with at least three of the villagers. Yesterday, four of Thornson's guards had died while fighting off this force attacking her keep.

All knew the day would come when King Stephen's men approached their gates. In truth, she was surprised it had taken this many months.

Thornson Keep was too strong, too rich and far too strategically located for King Stephen to ignore for long. The keep was a veritable fortress near the border of Scotland. He needed the men and the gold this property could supply. Little did he know that these men were loyal to Thornson alone. And Thornson's loyalties had been bought by Empress Matilda.

If Stephen would investigate the rights he'd issued, he'd soon realize that Thornson far exceeded what had been granted. This adulterine holding was no tower keep constructed of timber, with useless wooden palisades to protect those inside.

By the good graces of Empress Matilda and her uncle, King David of Scotland, just a short two days' ride to the north, Thornson had quickly grown and prospered.

And while they had not denounced King Stephen outright, they openly remained loyal to those who had helped them. It was a game Thornson played. A dangerous game to be sure, but one he'd seemed to enjoy. It had kept him out of Stephen's useless battles until the end.

She wrapped her arms about her waist. She'd not thought of his death for many weeks now and had no wish to revive that nightmare. It was better to remember her husband alive.

The Lord of Thornson had been old, so nobody had deemed him worth notice. A foolish mistake. She shifted her gaze toward the pounding sea. It thundered with an intensity that had fired her elderly husband's blood. His passion had been poured into completing this keep before he left this world…for her.

She'd arrived at Thornson with naught but the naivete of a girl ten and five. The keep had seemed more of a guardhouse for the men and stables for the horses, than a keep. Now, a little over six years later, Thornson had become a fortress built to keep her safe.

She turned and surveyed the work Henry had seen completed. Two thick stone walls surrounded Thornson. An enemy could batter away at them for a lifetime and not gain entrance.

The inner courtyard housed the men, their horses and practice grounds. The grounds had seen much use since their completion.

The outer courtyard served as a gathering place and a market of sorts. Here, the villagers came to buy and sell wares, and to share the local gossip and news.

At the northeast corner rose the keep itself. Steep, jagged cliffs served as the back wall to the keep. With the constant surging of the sea, nature had created a safer, more secure wall than man. None could scale the slippery, sheer rock face.

"Milady."

Jerked out of her thoughts, she looked at Sir Everett, Thornson's captain of the guard. "Yes?"

He nodded toward the field. "They approach."

She gasped and turned. She'd expected them to once again charge full strength toward their certain death. Instead, only six men rode forward. Six men and one riderless horse.

She swallowed an unladylike curse. *Matthew.* There was little doubt in her mind that the body draped across the back of the horse was he. When the others had returned the night before last they'd recounted the battle on the beach and how Matthew had foolishly called out for them to return to her.

How many times had she begged them to cease their nighttime activities? She'd warned them that eventually this would happen. Now it had.

When she'd received word from the villagers about

the bodies left at the church, Matthew hadn't been among them. She'd hoped he'd somehow escaped.

Sir Everett asked, "What do you think they are about?"

Marguerite shrugged. "You would know the minds of men better than I." After Thornson's death, she'd received no word from King Stephen. She'd assumed that he'd send someone to become the new Lord of Thornson when he saw fit.

Which warmonger had the king sent?

Even though it was his right, she bristled at the thought of a king's man taking possession of her husband's keep.

She could not stop him from taking the keep any more than she could stop what the future would hold for her. Nor could she prevent this man from doling out his form of justice to those he found to be outlaws.

Still, she chafed at the ever-present certainty that King Stephen could and would control her destiny.

Oh, would that her husband had been an earl, or that she'd been rich or powerful in her own right. Then none would determine her future. She'd determine her own. She'd also be able to protect those in Thornson who thought they were doing the right thing.

Marguerite slapped the skirt of her billowing gown in frustration. What good was *if only*? Wishing for what could not be only served to pass the time, nothing more.

She focused on the men approaching. Would one of them become the new master of Thornson? Or would they only hold the keep in Stephen's name until a more suitable man could be found?

She studied the men closely. It was not hard to determine who led whom. Obviously, the tall man riding in the center of the group would be the leader. His outward appearance of calm belied everything she'd learned about warriors.

Contrary to what her father and his men had taught her as a child, she'd found that the calmest was always the most alert, the most attentive to detail, the most dangerous.

It would be best for all if this was the king's chosen man. It would be easier to learn the ways of one man and be done with it, than to learn his ways only to have yet another man to deal with later.

Marguerite narrowed her eyes. Dangerous or not, she'd soon learn his weaknesses. Everyone had at least one, and she'd discover his quickly enough.

A movement from one of the other approaching men caught her attention. Curious, she stared as he lifted and unfurled a brilliant green banner.

Her heart lodged in her throat. Curiosity quickly became horror. She had wondered if life could get worse? Here was her answer.

Yes. It could, and had.

Of all the men serving King Stephen, why did the king have to send *him* to Thornson?

The man seated in the center of the approaching group could be none other than Darius of Faucon. The green banner, bearing the black falcon at rest, whipped in the stiff breeze above his head. If it did not scream his identity to anyone else, it did to her.

Against all common courtesy, Rhys, the Comte of Faucon, would display a royal golden eagle on his banner. Gareth, the second brother, would fly his deceased father's falcon with talons extended in a posture of war. But she knew Darius's standard well—the falcon at rest had a double meaning to her, one she'd not forgotten.

She no longer had the option to defend her keep. Marguerite could not, would not be responsible for this man's injury or death.

Marguerite raised her voice so the men gathered on her walls could hear her order. "Hold your weapons."

"My lady?" Sir Everett made no effort to conceal his disappointment.

She pinned him with a stare, silently daring him to disobey. He motioned the others to hold.

Certain they would follow her orders, she gestured to the men at the gate tower. She lifted her fist in the air, with her thumb pointed down. All at Thornson knew the signal to surrender.

Whispers raced from man to man along the walls. The murmurs of disbelief and disgust reached her ears. She wanted to apologize to each and every man who'd pledged to protect her from harm. But she could not.

She held firm to her orders, but even she cringed as the plain white flag rose slowly above Thornson keep.

Marguerite wrapped her arms about her stomach, in an attempt to quell the sudden spasms. If any discovered the secret she and Thornson had so carefully hidden, her whole world would shatter. Her future would be lost before it began.

This could not be happening. Not Faucon. Not now.

"My lady?" Sir Everett stepped closer to her. "Shall we raise the gate?"

"No!" She nearly choked on her shout.

The men on the walls turned to stare at her sudden contradictory order. She wanted to slap herself for her sudden outburst. Instead, Marguerite slapped at the skirt of her gown again. She needed to be more careful. It could do much harm to let all know how nervous she felt.

"No, not yet." She took her time and kept her voice steady. "Let us see what they want first."

She already knew what they wanted; her men probably did, too. But she needed a way to gain time to think, and this was the only tactic she could devise at the moment.

Darius and his men stopped within shouting distance. The man next to Darius yelled up at the gate tower. "Darius of Faucon demands entrance."

Marguerite bit her lower lip to stop the unbidden smile from crossing her mouth. Sir Osbert's voice was a little deeper, a little older, but it still carried true and strong—an ability that had helped earn him a place at Darius's side.

Sir Everett, the captain of Thornson's guard asked, "On what authority?"

Faucon held up a rolled missive. "On the authority of King Stephen."

"For what purpose?"

"To hold this keep for your future lord."

"My lady?" Sir Everett looked to her for his orders. "Do you wish to grant them entry?" A wicked smile lit his face as he grasped the hilt of his sword. "Or do we send them away?"

She shook her head. "No, we have already cried truce. Sending Faucon away will do no good." Marguerite spoke more to herself than to the captain of Thornson's guard. "He would only find another way to gain entry." She frowned, desperately seeking a way to protect herself and those in Thornson.

She could not deny Faucon and his men entrance—no matter how much she wished to do so. Everyone would then know she had something to hide, and she could not permit that to happen.

All was not hopeless or lost. Her stomach calmed and her racing heart slowed to a more normal rhythm. There was something she could do.

She gave Everett his answer. "Nay. Do not send them away. Tell them to hold for a time."

"Are you certain, lady?" Sir Everett sounded incredulous, as if he could not believe what his ears had heard. "You know what this will mean for Thornson? For all of us?"

Marguerite narrowed her eyes and stared pointedly up at him, refusing to have her orders ignored. "It means Stephen's men will have charge of the keep…for now." She pushed passed Sir Everett. "If it does not happen today, it will happen tomorrow or the day after. Let us see this through now. Tell them to hold. Permit them entrance only after I send you word."

"And how do I keep them at the gates until then?"

She paused before descending the ladder to the bailey. "I care not. Discuss the weather. Just do as I say."

Everett nodded in acceptance of her wishes, but his wide eyes gave away his doubt at her wisdom. "Aye."

Marguerite paused on the ladder. "It will not be for long. No more than a few moments. Once they are inside, direct them to the hall. I will greet them there."

Chapter Two

After delivering the body to the captain of Thornson's guard, Darius strode up the stairs leading to the Great Hall. Each step made him wish he'd left his helmet and mailed gloves on. Right now he was more than ready to do battle. If the Lady of Thornson thought to try his patience, she'd succeeded thus far.

She knew full well that he was here on the king's business. Yet for most of the morning, she'd kept him and his men pacing outside Thornson's walls like unwanted beggars.

King Stephen was right. Someone did need to take charge of Thornson. It was obvious by the way the men on the walls acted. No guard in his right mind would have thought to use trite conversation about the weather as a ploy to detain a company of men from the king.

And no guard who possessed even the minimum knowledge of warfare would have kept them waiting after hoisting a white banner signaling surrender. Their notion of surrender needed much revising.

Darius wondered if the men, arms and gold supplied

by the king would be enough to complete the missions he'd been assigned. If King Stephen's concerns had been left to stew for too long, Darius knew he could find himself in more danger than they'd imagined.

He stopped outside the door to the Great Hall and took a deep breath. One item on his long list of tasks was to take control of Thornson. He'd do that through the widow. She'd already played him for a fool once this day, and he'd see to it that little game was never repeated.

Darius turned the metal rod and pushed the door open with enough force to slam the iron-studded oak against the inside wall. He stepped through the doorway more than ready to put the Lady of Thornson in her place—and met the shocked gasps of servants with a glare.

He swept the hall with a searching look and found—nothing but servants and a few guards.

His temples throbbed. Livid, Darius clenched his jaw to keep from shouting in rage. Instead, he grabbed the closest man by the front of his tunic and dragged him forward. "Where is your lady?"

The man raised his hands in a useless manner to protect himself. "I do not know, my lord."

"Find her and bring her here now." He pushed the man away and watched in satisfaction as his order was carried out.

The other servants and guards scurried out of his way as he crossed the hall. His spurs jingled with each step on the hard earthen floor. A guard quickly grabbed a chair and pulled it over to the long trestle table before making good his escape.

Darius tossed his helmet on the table, then threw his gloves alongside of it before taking the seat. A female servant approached hesitantly, carrying a tray of food. Another brought a jug and a goblet. Neither said a word as they placed the items on the table, then left.

Within a few heartbeats the hall was empty save him. Which suited Darius just fine. He poured himself a draught of wine and leaned back in the chair to await the Lady of Thornson.

Marguerite made certain to keep to the shadows as she leaned on the railing and peered down into the hall at Darius.

"My lady, he seems to be in a fine rage."

Marguerite laughed softly at her maid's statement of the obvious. "Of course he is, Bertha. Considering how long I have kept him waiting, I am surprised he is not roaring about like a wounded bear."

"Do you think this wise?"

"Ah, Bertha, this is not Lord Thornson whose anger flared in fists and shouts. Darius of Faucon is slow to anger and quick to forgive."

"You know this man?"

"Aye, from when we were children."

Bertha glanced over the railing, then faced Marguerite. "I beg pardon, my lady, but he does not look like a child any longer. You could not have seen him in the time you have been here. So you cannot be certain of his temperament now."

Marguerite knew she'd already said far too much. "You are right. It has been a long time. I do hope the man is as close as possible to the child in temper."

"From your lips to the angels' wings, my lady." Bertha nodded down toward the hall. "Do ye think it might be best to join him?"

While it might be best, it wasn't something Marguerite looked forward to doing. "Has Marcus's welfare been guaranteed?"

"Aye. He will remain in the village until plans can be made to take him north. Everyone in the keep and the village have been informed of your wishes. None doubt your wisdom in this matter."

Marguerite's chest tightened around her heart. She grabbed the railing to keep from falling. *Oh, Marcus, my love, know my heart goes with you always.* There was nothing she could do to alter what must be. But that knowledge did little to ease the pain of facing yet another loss so soon.

"Thank you." She gently grasped Bertha's hand. "What would I do without you?"

The maid patted her shoulder. "My lady, you know full well that I would do anything for you and his lordship."

Marguerite straightened her back. "I need see this done."

Bertha wrinkled her nose in distaste and shrugged before asking, "Do you wish me to accompany you?"

"No."

The maid's relief was audible in her sigh. "Very well, my lady."

"I should do this alone. But I thank you for the offer."

Marguerite waited until Bertha took her leave before glancing down at Darius one more time. To her, he'd been a breathtaking boy, and he'd grown into a fine-looking man. From what she could see, the years had been kind to him. They'd blessed him with broader shoulders and muscular arms. His dark hair still waved about his head in riotous disorder. She knew it would run through her fingers like a rabbit's silky fur.

After smoothing the skirt of her dark green gown, Marguerite headed toward the stairs. Would he remember her? Would his memories speak kindly of her? She shook her head. What matter to her what he did or did not remember?

After what she'd done to him this day—crying truce, then making him wait—she doubted if any man, friend or foe, would look upon her kindly.

No. Between those slights and making him enter an empty hall with none to greet him properly, she'd more than likely dealt quite a blow to his pride.

No matter. It meant little whether he looked upon her kindly or not. She'd had a life away from Darius. A full, good life. One that would live in her mind and her heart forever. One that she had to protect at all costs.

She paused halfway down the steep winding stairs and looked at him. "My lord, pray forgive my tardiness in attending you."

He rose and stared up at her, his visage angry and impatient. No, it was plain that he did not remember her. Marguerite realized suddenly that his remembering and securing his kindness mattered a great deal to her, but she knew not why.

Darius's heart seemed to halt at the first word that had left her lips. *It couldn't be. Dear Lord above, let me awaken from this dream.*

He rose and stared speechless at the vision in green coming toward him. Even though he'd have thought it impossible, Marguerite was lovelier than the memory he'd carried in his mind.

He knew Marguerite had wed, that had been made quite plain to him. He'd not known whom she married and he'd not asked, afraid the knowing would prompt him to further rashness.

The years had softened her girlish body to womanly curves. From the swell of her breasts and the fullness of her hips, she was a sight that could stir a dying man's passion.

And he knew full well what passion lay beneath the silken softness of her skin.

His only regret was that he'd not been here to watch her grow into such a fine woman.

Darius lifted his gaze and stared into the sea-blue eyes he'd missed for so long. She stared back at him. Confident. Proud. Not even a small smile of welcome crossed her face. She looked upon him as if she were meeting a stranger.

He swallowed. Surely she remembered him. How could she have forgotten?

Did Stephen and Maud know of his past relationship with the Lady of Thornson? Had they devised this mission for him intentionally?

She approached the head of the table and took a seat in the high-backed chair. Once he'd regained his own seat, she said, "My Lord Faucon, I understand you are here from the king."

What game did she play with him now? Torn between the desire to tear the covering from her head and run his fingers through what he knew would be unruly blond tresses and a sworn responsibility to his king, Darius chose a third option instead.

He handed her Stephen's written orders. "Yes, Lady Thornson, I am here on the king's mission."

If she wished to toy with him, he'd see it through. And in the end he'd beat her soundly at her own game.

Marguerite smoothed the missive out on the table. Her hands remained steady; never once did her fingers tremble with suppressed nervousness. After reading the orders, she rolled the parchment carefully into a scroll and handed it back to Darius.

"So, I am to surmise that you will see to the care and security of Thornson until a suitable replacement for the lord can be found?"

"You surmise correctly, yes."

"Excellent." She rose. "Then I shall retire to my chambers and leave all to your capable hands."

Darius hooked a foot around the leg of her chair and jerked it beneath her. "Sit back down."

Except for the widening of her eyes and the thinning of her lips, she gave no outward show of emotion.

Darius waited until she resumed her seat before stating, "I will see to the safety and defense of Thornson and you will continue to oversee the daily activities while awaiting the arrival of your new husband." Suddenly the thought of awaiting a new lord for Thornson left a bitter taste in his mouth.

She folded her hands atop the table and stared intently at them. "I have yet to mourn my first husband."

That wasn't precisely true, but he only offered, "The king obviously thinks three months has given you plenty of time for mourning."

Marguerite looked up, her eyes flashing like uncut gems caught in the sunlight. "I care not what your king thinks." Her voice rose with each word. She gripped the arms of the chair until her knuckles turned white.

"*My* king?" Were the rumors true? Had Thornson been loyal to Empress Matilda or King David instead of to King Stephen?

"I have sworn allegiance to no one. Thus, he is your king. Not mine."

"Your husband swore an oath for the both of you. You and Thornson's men are bound to honor that oath, or be held as traitors to the Crown."

"My men are not traitors."

"Lady Marguerite—"

"My pardon?" She interrupted him and leaned forward. "I gave you no leave to make use of my given name."

Had she cracked an open palm across his face, Darius would not have been any more shocked. A sword to his chest would not have brought as much unbidden pain as her sharply spoken words.

He wanted to yell, to demand she explain not only her actions of six years ago, but her coldness now. Darius swallowed against the building tightness in his chest. He would not permit her the power to once again hurt him.

Instead, he drew on the memories still fresh in his mind and willed his heart to harden against her. Before she could read his thoughts, he schooled his features to remain frozen in a mask showing as little concern as she displayed.

"Forgive me, Lady Thornson, but they are not *your* men. They are King Stephen's men and will be expected to act as such."

"And if they choose otherwise?"

Darius smiled. "Then they will die."

She gasped. "How dare you."

He leaned across the table, until they were nearly nose to nose, before warning, "I will dare much more if you unwisely insist on playing out this charade any further, Marguerite."

She opened her mouth, but before she could say anything, the door to the hall creaked open and Sir Osbert crossed the chamber.

The captain's soft curse heralded his arrival at the table. Darius turned his attention to Sir Osbert. "Yes?"

"My lord, the men are settled in, orders have been given." He tipped his head at Marguerite. "You are looking well, my lady. The years have been kind to you."

"I cannot say the same for you, Osbert. You look a might older."

Darius whipped his head around and glared at her. "And here I thought you'd forgotten."

She smiled. "Darius, how could I ever forget a childhood friend?"

Childhood friend? What an odd way to refer to their relationship when last they'd parted. He silently invited Osbert to join them with a wave toward an empty seat.

Marguerite shrugged. "Would you care to start over?"

Start over? No. Unless murder had been declared legal. What he really wanted to do at this moment would brand him a criminal. Darius leaned back in his chair.

"Oh, yes, by all means, let us begin again." His sarcasm was rewarded by the arching of her eyebrows. Certain he had her attention, he continued, "Let me go first this time, shall I?"

It took a few moments, but Marguerite nodded her consent.

"To make this transfer of power easier for all concerned, give me the names of the smugglers operating on your beach."

Marguerite's already pale complexion lightened further. She looked from him to Sir Osbert and then to the door before saying, "I know not of what you speak. What smugglers?" Finally, she brought her wavering attention back to him. "If you know of any such criminals in the area it is your duty to bring them to justice."

She had always been a terrible liar. He was grateful that much had not changed. At one time his touch had driven her to distraction, making her say and do things she'd otherwise not.

Would that have changed?

Darius smiled before leaning his arms on the table and taking her hands between his. "Oh, my lady, fear not. I intend to bring them to justice."

He lifted one of her beringed hands and studied it intently, tracing the blue spiderweb of veins on the back of her hand with a fingertip. Her skin was soft beneath his touch.

He turned her hand over and lazily traced the lines on her palm. A tremor coursed up her arm. When she tried to pull free, he tightened his hold, keeping her firmly in his grasp.

"My lord, what are you—"

He cut off her question by placing a kiss on the palm of her hand. "In the East, there are palm readers who would tell you that your life line is broken."

When she knitted her brows in confusion, he explained by tracing the jagged line. "Here, see how it stops and starts again?"

She leaned forward to peer at her palm. "Yes."

"'Tis broken." He traced the line again, ever so lightly. Darius bit the inside of his mouth to hold back his smile at her shiver. He still had the power to shake her reserve. That could only work in his favor.

Marguerite inhaled sharply before asking, "What does that mean?"

Darius raised her hand and brought it to his mouth. Before she could react, he trailed the tip of his tongue along the line on her palm. At her gasp, he brushed her hand across his cheek, leaning into the forced caress.

He kept his gaze locked on her face. "What it means is that you have had more than one husband." When just the lightest shade of pink colored her face, he added, "At the same time."

Marguerite tried unsuccessfully to jerk her hand from his hold. "How dare you."

"At the risk of repeating myself, I dare much and will dare much more before you and I are through."

This time when she tried to free her hand, he let her go. Without another word, she rose and headed toward the steps.

She thought it would be that easy? That she could just walk away and be done with him? Not this time. Darius remained seated, but called out, "If you walk away before you are excused, I will find the smugglers myself and they will be executed in your bailey."

She halted and turned around to face him. "Who are you to excuse me in my own keep? Who are you to decide the life and death of Thornson's men?"

Darius rose. "Who am I?" He picked up the missive from the king. "In case you have forgotten, I am your lord and master for now. I alone have the power to decide life and death over those at Thornson."

Marguerite returned to the table and stood across from him. "What has become of you, Darius?"

He placed his hands on the table and leaned forward. "My dear wife, I am everything you ever dreamed of, everything you ever desired." He tossed her own words, spoken long ago, in her face. Then he added his own. "I am every nightmare that ever pulled you from your sleep."

"I am *not* your wife." She straightened her spine, lifted her chin and stared back at him. "I will beg you to remember that. I will do as you order, Faucon, but no more."

We will see about that. He kept his thoughts to himself, nodded and said, "Good. Then I order you to take yourself to your chamber and remain there until I say otherwise."

Her eyes widened, but she said nothing before leaving the hall.

Darius's heart beat so hard he thought it would burst. He lunged back down into the chair and rubbed the throbbing in his temples.

Sir Osbert had remained silent through the conversation with Marguerite, but now he cleared his throat and asked, "My lord, if I might speak out of turn?"

Surprised, Darius peered up at him. "If you have to ask, this should be interesting. Please, feel free."

"Do you not think that was a little rough?"

"Perhaps. Should I have sweetened every word so she felt at ease? That way, she would have thought herself free to continue on her merry way as if nothing were amiss."

"'Tis not what I meant and you know that well."

"Then what do you suggest, Osbert?" Darius lowered his hands and sighed. "She made fools of us at the wall. She called a truce and then kept us waiting for

God only knows what reason. She pretended not to know me, then lied to my face."

"You do not think she does that to protect herself?"

"She does that to protect not only herself, but the secrets she's hiding."

"Lord Darius?"

He shook his head. "Osbert, there is much more going on here at Thornson than even what the king was aware of, and I intend to ferret out all I can. To do that, I need her to know she cannot trust me. To realize that she cannot use what was once between us to her benefit."

"I see your point." Osbert scratched his head. "I am just not certain this is the best way around the problem."

"And you suggest?"

His captain shrugged. "I suggest I follow your lead and see where we end up."

"Good." Darius rose, picked up his helmet and gloves, then headed toward the iron-studded door. "For now, let us take stock of this keep."

He needed to know how many men currently served at Thornson. It would also be to his benefit to discover the type and number of arms available.

Since the keep itself was more than what it was supposed to be, there was no telling what other details had not been reported to King Stephen. Darius would sleep better knowing what he faced.

Chapter Three

Once she heard the great oak door thud closed, Marguerite cracked her chamber door open wider. Had Faucon left the hall? She crept out onto the landing and peered down into the Great Hall.

Her shoulders sagged with relief at finding it empty. Stay in her chamber, indeed. How did he think she was going to oversee Thornson if she was confined to her room like a wayward child?

There were many tasks requiring her attention. Tasks that no one else could complete.

Marguerite sighed. She gritted her teeth and squinted her eyes. She would allow no further complications in her life.

"My lady?"

Marguerite jumped. She'd not heard Sir Everett's approach. She forced herself to ignore her musings and looked at her captain. "Yes?"

He made an exaggerated point of slowly looking from her, down to the door of the Great Hall, then back to her before inquiring, "Is anything amiss?"

She wasn't certain if it was the arrogant tone of his voice, the disapproving tilt of his brows or just his demeanor overall that set her teeth on edge. Thornson's captain had become increasingly harder to control of late. This was something Marguerite knew she needed to stop—now. If she did not see to his demeanor, Darius would.

Straightening her spine did little to bring her face-to-face with the man, but the action fortified her strength of will. "Nay, Sir Everett, nothing is amiss." She kept her voice steady, and was rewarded when the arrogance momentarily left his face.

He took a step back. "Is there anything you require?"

Marguerite shook her head. "Not at this moment. Why do you ask?"

"You were overlong with Faucon and I feared you required assistance."

Her chest tightened with her anger. He had been watching her. How dare he spy on her in her own keep. "I was not with him overlong. Faucon is here on the king's business. Would it not appear strange if I did not greet him?"

"Well, yes it would, but—"

She gave him no time to complete his sentence before asking, "And since I was the one who kept him waiting for so long, is it not right that I spend a little time assuring him of our welcome?"

Everett tugged his forelock and dipped his head. "You are correct. Pray, forgive me."

He gave in far too easily, but unwilling to pursue this any further at this time, she relented. "Fear not, Sir Everett, I will do nothing to bring shame or disgrace to Thornson." To herself she added, *Especially not with*

Darius. We've shamed ourselves more than once in the past. I'll not repeat my childish mistakes.

Marguerite nearly laughed at Everett's loud sigh of relief. She waved him away. "Go. See that Faucon's men have all they require. Let them have no reason to question our hospitality—or loyalty to King Stephen."

She knew that Everett fully understood what would happen if Faucon discovered Thornson's loyalty to Empress Matilda. Her captain would be the last person that would let that happen.

After Sir Everett left, she headed toward the alcove at the back of the Great Hall, mentally ticking off the tasks still needing attention this afternoon.

The cooks would need an accounting of how many more mouths would require food. And she needed to assure herself that everyone understood her odd request of silence about Marcus. To do that, she would have to travel into the village, and while there it would be a sin not to visit with Bertha's sister, who was due with her fifth child any day now. Sally Miller had mentioned that her husband's joints ached him to no end of late; she should see how he fared. Then, she could spend some time with Marcus. He would be gone from her soon and she wanted to spend every moment possible in his company until they were parted.

And when all of that was done, she would need to conjure some womanly type of excuse to give to Darius for disobeying his orders. Marguerite rolled her eyes. Orders, indeed. She was the Lady of Thornson and she'd not seen anything in King Stephen's missive that changed her status.

Darius already knew she'd lied. He just didn't yet realize it had been intentional. She needed his attention focused on her.

With a little subterfuge on her part and a lot of luck, *she* would be Darius of Faucon's weakness. If he spent most of his waking hours concentrating on what she was doing, or not doing, he'd not notice the activities of her men.

"Pray tell me, how did Faucon come to be inside Thornson?"

Sir Everett flinched at the smooth tone of his inquisitor's voice. He'd learned that the calm hid a violent temper. "Faucon and his men were sent here on King Stephen's orders. They tried to capture the smugglers, and then attacked the keep."

A twig snapped beneath the man's boot when he stepped closer. "I saw what happened on the beach. And I heard about the attack." Like a snake attacking its hapless prey, he wrapped his fingers around Everett's neck. "I asked you how Faucon came to be inside the keep."

Everett swallowed. His throat strained against the deadly grasp. "Lady Thornson cried truce and let them enter."

The other's loud curse sent a nearby rodent scurrying beneath the leaves on the forest floor. "No one will be permitted to thwart my plans. No one. Keep an eye on both of them. Make certain the lady does nothing further to jeopardize our plans, and find out all you can about Faucon." He released his hold on Everett's neck and stepped back. "I will return tomorrow. Have some news by then."

Still gasping to draw air into his burning chest, Everett could do little but nod.

* * *

Marguerite slipped into the kitchens through an oft-used tunnel door. The cook and her helpers merely nodded and carried on with their duties.

This afternoon's tasks had taken longer than she'd expected. She had little time left to make herself presentable before the evening meal was served.

The servants were in the process of setting up the long trestle tables in the hall when she passed through on her way to her chamber. She had less time than she had thought. Since she'd used the maze of tunnels to exit and return to the keep, it had wasted more time than usual.

But it wasn't as if she would have been permitted to simply walk through the gates. She'd had no other choice but the tunnels.

At least her day had not been wasteful. Even during this trying time it had been filled with joy. She smiled at the memories.

She and Marcus had ventured into the forest seeking yarrow for one of Bertha's concoctions. They'd laughed and danced about the forest as if not a care in the world beset them or Thornson.

And when she'd forced herself to part from him to return to the keep, their shared tears of sadness at the coming separation had mingled. *Not long, my love. Our parting will not be for long.* It was a vow she would sooner die than break.

Would that Faucon's departure came soon. She needed things at Thornson to return to some semblance of normalcy. Even if they found another man for her to marry, a stranger's presence would be better than Faucon's. Someone who knew her not.

Bertha joined her at the foot of the stairs. "How fares my sister?"

"Other than being anxious for the babe to arrive, she is fine, Bertha." Marguerite glanced about the hall before heading up to her chamber. "Have you seen Faucon or his men?"

Bertha followed. "His men guard the walls and the gates."

"*His* men? What about Thornson's guards?" Marguerite was thankful she'd not approached the gates.

"Our men have been relieved of duty, my lady. I am not certain what, but something happened earlier that seemed to anger Faucon."

"I wonder what it could have been?" No doubt he'd found her missing.

The women paused at the top of the landing. Marguerite noted Faucon's guards flanking the stairs. She raised her eyebrows at their presence, but said nothing as she and Bertha walked by them.

She pushed the door to her chamber open and frowned at the warmth rushing out from inside the room. "Bertha, did you—"

Her maid's gasp effectively stopped her question. Marguerite spun around.

Sir Osbert smiled at her from behind the maid. He had one hand covering Bertha's mouth and his other wrapped around the maid's arm. He nodded toward the chamber before leading Bertha away.

"Get in here and close the door."

Marguerite's heart thumped against her chest. She turned toward the stairs, only to see both guards waiting for her. Escape would not be an option.

After taking a deep breath, she entered her chamber and shut the door behind her.

Darius stood by the lit brazier—the source of the heat she'd felt. He held out a goblet. "Here, join me."

"Join you in what?"

"Our evening meal. Since it seems you cannot follow even the simplest order to remain in your chamber, I thought I would see to it myself."

Marguerite swallowed a curse. She'd expected his anger, not his personal attention. What game did he play? She took the proffered goblet and sat down on a stool. "I am certain you have many other responsibilities to keep you busy."

He shrugged before walking to the narrow window and staring out at the now darkening sky. "I thought so, too. But, obviously, my main responsibility is seeing to your safety."

"My safety? There is no danger for me at Thornson."

"No?" He turned and looked at her. Golden flecks glittered in his hazel eyes. "Just earlier today you intentionally lied to me about smugglers and criminals, knowing full well that I'd see through your fabrication. Then you reminded me that it was my duty to bring those men to justice. A duty I will not shirk."

She couldn't deny his accusations, so she remained silent.

"Do you think the years have addled my wits and made me a simpleton?"

"No."

"Then how could you even begin to imagine that lying to me would not arouse my suspicions about everyone at Thornson? Did you really believe for one moment that I would ignore all the others because of your falsehoods?"

Her heart raced. She gripped the edge of the stool with one hand to keep from bolting to her feet.

"Need I remind you, I had two brothers? It was an easy game for one of us to draw our father's attention, so that one of the other boys was free to do whatever he wasn't supposed to do. How could I not suspect Thornson's men of being up to something nefarious?"

Wonderful. Not even one day had been completed, yet he was full aware that she toyed with him.

And by the glint in his eyes, the stiffness of his stance and the tic in his cheek, she knew he was furious. Marguerite had to admit the years had taught him to restrain his anger remarkably well.

"Your obvious lying was so out-of-character that I could come to no other conclusion but that you were doing so to protect your men. Now I need discover what they need protecting from."

She took another swallow of the watered wine before asking, "And what do you plan to do with me?"

"I have not yet decided. When I first made my rounds of the keep and started putting the pieces together, I had planned on hanging you from the tower. But I realized that would only find disfavor with the king."

She completed that thought for him. "And heaven forbid that a Faucon incurs the king's disfavor."

He raised his goblet toward her. "True. Or at least let it not be on *this* Faucon's head."

"So, after that realization what did you decide?"

Darius walked away from the window toward her. "I thought to drag it all out into the open. But alas, you were not in your chamber."

Marguerite swallowed. Lie? Don't lie? Darius grasped

her chin, tipping her head back and stared at her. Her mental debate found a quick death under his piercing attention.

She jerked her chin out of his grasp. "I have responsibilities, too, Faucon."

"So you used the tunnel in the kitchen building to sneak out of the keep."

How in Hades did he know that?

"Do not look so surprised, Marguerite. My men are good at their jobs. It took all of a few hours to find at least three tunnels. And the kitchen one brought them closest to the village."

A knock on the chamber door stopped their discussion. Marguerite rose, but Darius pointed to the stool. "I will get it—you stay right there."

She sat back down and fumed. Her mistake had been in forgetting that Darius of Faucon was not a stupid man. He knew her well, and it would be an easy thing for him to deduce her motives and then actions.

She would simply have to become much cleverer than he. And quickly.

He came back from the door carrying a tray laden with thick slabs of bread, cheese, fowl, two apples and what Marguerite hoped was a pitched of cider. "I assumed after your full day that you would be hungry." He put the tray atop a wooden chest.

"No, I find my appetite is quite small this evening." Actually, she was famished, but she was also tired of his assumptions on her behalf. "But please, feel free to eat your fill."

"I plan on it." He broke off a piece of bread and handed it to her. "You are going to eat, too. I'll not have you getting sick."

"I said I am not hungry." Her rebellious stomach picked that moment to growl. Marguerite sighed, then took the bread from Darius. Before taking a bite, she looked up at him and said, "I could easily learn to hate you."

He reached out and stroked her cheek with his finger. "I know from experience that it is not quite as easy as you might think."

Not wanting an explanation for that cryptic remark, she concentrated as best she could on eating, her cheek still tingled from his brief touch.

As she reached for a small eating knife, Darius plucked it from beneath her hand. "Let me."

She leaned back. "Let you what?"

He speared a small bit of the hen and lifted the meat to her mouth. "Feed you."

"I am capable of feeding myself, thank you." She reached for the knife, only to have him wave it away.

He drew the morsel before his face and make a grand play of inhaling. "Ah, I detect a trace of cumin beneath the garlic sauce." He again offered the tidbit to her. "It does smell appetizing."

He was right. The aroma made her mouth water. "I would prefer—"

Darius stopped her complaint about feeding herself by sliding at bite between her open lips. She hadn't realized how hungry she was until she swallowed the tender fowl. From the self-satisfied look on Darius's face, it was apparent if she wanted to eat, she'd have to let him have his way.

It wasn't as if they hadn't done this before. Feeding each other with pilfered food used to be a regular occurrence—one they'd both enjoyed.

She held out her empty goblet. "Is that cider or wine?" Would he remember that she didn't like wine?

"Cider, of course." He filled her drinking vessel, took a sip and handed it back to her.

Marguerite took the proffered goblet, knowing his full attention was focused on her, she lifted it to her lips, and drank from the same spot as he.

It would be all too easy to let the years slide away. From somewhere deep in her heart she could almost hear the gurgle of a rushing stream, smell the freshness of newly harvested hay and feel the softness of the grass beneath her. The sparkle had always come quickly to Darius's eyes, and her smiles had come gently to her lips. Everything was simpler then—back when love was new.

What was she thinking? Marguerite banished the nearly forgotten memories before they bore fruit. She had a keep, men and promises to worry about. The luxury of simpler days and newly forged bonds were beyond her grasp.

Darius offered her another bite of hen. Garlic sauce dripped off the end of the knife and ran down her chin. Before she would wipe it away, he removed it with a swipe of his finger.

As he lifted it to his mouth, time seemed to come to a standstill again and Marguerite knew, by the faraway look in his eyes, that he, too, was remembering another time, another shared meal. She wondered if his stomach knotted while a sudden warmth heated blood, or his pulse quickened the same way hers had.

Darius cleared his throat, then handed her the knife. They ate the rest of their meal in silence.

Once they'd finished eating, Darius asked, "Where were we?"

"I do not remember."

"Ah, yes, what am I going to do with you?" He frowned, mimicking intense concentration. "Since hanging you is out of the question and truly any form of physical punishment would also be unthinkable, I can only think of one thing."

She dreaded his answer, but asked all the same, "And that is?"

He flashed her a smile. The same one that used to set her blood racing and reduce her limbs to little more than jelly.

"I will remain at your side at all times."

That would not do. Not at all. It would be impossible to carry out her duties and responsibilities with him underfoot. How would she see to the weekly shipments? Worse, how would she spend what precious time she had left with Marcus?

Marguerite shook her head. "I do not think that is wise."

"No?"

He was enjoying this far too much. "No."

"And why is that?"

"It will make it difficult to meet my love each day if you are always about." Now that was not exactly a lie.

"My, my. Two husbands and a lover." He paced the chamber before her. "What a busy woman you are."

"I do not have two husbands." Nor had she said *lover,* but let him think what he wanted on that score.

"I stand corrected. One of your husbands is dead."

"My *only* husband is dead."

Darius walked behind her. Before she could turn around, or move out of his way, he placed his hands on her shoulders. Marguerite knew the taste of fear. A cold dread snaked its way down her spine, all the way to her toes. The hairs on her neck rose.

But it was not Faucon she feared. It was herself.

It was fear of the memories that had surfaced when he'd held her hand earlier and again when he'd fed her. Fear of the bubbling passion his obscene caresses of her palm had created. Fear of the way her memories had returned with such ease. Fear of wanting his steady warm touch to continue.

He kneaded her shoulders, stroked his thumbs along the back of her neck. More than six years disappeared…and they were once again in the hunting lodge.

Marguerite tipped her head forward, letting him work the kinks out of her neck and shoulders. Not having the strength or the will to fight him, she sighed.

Darius's breath was hot against her neck. His kiss on the sensitive flesh beneath her ear brought a soft moan to her throat. Unable to stop herself, she let it escape.

He answered the sound with a low, gentle laugh before pulling her to her feet. "I am your husband, Marguerite." He kicked the stool out of the way, slid his arms around her and held her back against his chest.

She pressed into his embrace, grasping his forearms for support. "Those vows were not binding."

He rubbed his cheek across the top of her head before returning his lips to her ear. "They were as binding as the actions in our marriage bed."

He slid a hand up her stomach, scorching her skin through the layers of her clothes. He cupped one breast, thumbing the nipple to a hard peak, drawing a breathless gasp from her lips.

"Darius, do not do this."

He turned her around in his arms. As he lowered his

head to hers, he asked, "Do what?" before running his tongue along the line between her lips and easily parting them to delve inside.

His kiss stole the slim remainder of her will. She curled her arms around his neck and ran her fingers through his hair. She had remembered correctly, his hair was still as soft as a rabbit's fur.

And his kiss still had the power to make her hungry for more.

Darius lifted his head. "Will one husband and one lover be enough, do you think?"

His question was like a punch to her stomach. She lowered her arms and pushed him away. What had she been thinking? Was she little more than a whore willing to put her entire future in danger for a kiss?

He retrieved his goblet and downed the contents before turning back to face her. "Tell me something, Marguerite, was it easy to forget our marriage? Did you go as willingly to Thornson's bed as you did to mine?"

"Do not be crude. What choice did I have?" She crossed the chamber, putting as much distance between them as possible.

"You could have said no. We'd exchanged vows."

From the moment she'd recognized him from high atop the wall, she'd expected this, but the deadly tone of his voice made her gasp. "I spoke but a promise. Not all promises can be kept."

Shards of gold sparkled in his angry eyes. There had been a time when she'd been content to lose herself in his gaze. A time when no secrets lay between them. A time so long ago.

"I remember that vow, Marguerite. It was much more than a simple promise." He stepped toward her.

"It was a vow made to me, before God, before witnesses."

He stood before her, close enough that his warm breath caressed her cheek. "A vow to ever be my faithful wife."

"No." She pushed him an arm's length away. "Do not do this, Darius."

"Do what? Do not remind you of vows made and broken?"

She closed her eyes. She did not need to see his face to recognize the anger in the tightly controlled tone. Even though she'd come to love Henry Thornson, the years that had separated her from Darius had never dimmed the memories she'd carried in her mind, in her heart.

But she could not allow fleeting whims of childhood to mar her recent past, or destroy her future. No matter the cost to her soul, Faucon had to be led to believe how little those vows meant to her.

Marguerite silently prayed for the strength to lie to him yet again this day. Certain her riotous heart would withstand the self-inflicted pain, she stared up at him and hardened her voice. "We were children, Darius. Impetuous children who acted rashly on a whim. It was more childish folly than binding oath. Nobody, not the king nor the Church, would hold us to those vows."

"Children? *Impetuous children?*"

She flinched at the fury in his voice.

He grasped her arms, his hold tight and unyielding. "Childish folly? Were we not of an age to wed? Had we not been promised to each other since birth?"

"Yes, but it was not what my father wanted."

"And you did not argue with him?"

"Argue with my father?" She swallowed an unbidden laugh. "Be reasonable, Darius. You know it would have been easier to argue with a boulder."

"Did you go willingly to Thornson's bed?"

Marguerite paused before answering. He was not going to like this at all. "Not at first. At first I wanted only you."

"And then?"

"When I knew that you and I were never going to be reunited, I had to choose what kind of life I wanted."

"And you chose…?"

"Safety. Security. Warmth and love." If he knew the whole truth, would he be angry, or would he understand? Uncertain, she could not take the risk.

He looked at her. "You loved Thornson?"

She nodded, then thought to turn the table by asking, "What about you? Do you not care for your wife?"

He made a noise that sounded like something between a cough and a snort before answering. "I cared a great deal for my wife. To my misfortune, she cared not enough."

She was stunned to realize he talked about her. She found it hard to believe that he had never married another.

Darius walked toward the door and ordered, "Get ready for bed. I will return anon."

"Return? For what?"

He looked at her, his smile more of a smirk. "I was not jesting. I am not leaving you alone."

Chapter Four

Bertha stood next to Marguerite in the garden. "How do you fare, my lady?"

It was all Marguerite could do not to shout in frustration. But with Darius not more than ten paces away, shouting was unthinkable. She'd not give him the satisfaction of knowing how much his presence unnerved her.

She kept her voice low and admitted to her maid, "After two days of his constant company, I am ready to run his own sword through him." She jerked another clump of wayward grass from the herb bed and tossed it on the growing pile of weeds.

"Is there anything I can do?"

"Nay. Just tell me how Marcus fares." Marguerite's heart ached at the limitations of this forced separation. If she could not abide two days without Marcus's sweet smile, what would she do when he was completely out of her reach?

"He fares well, fear not on that score. He misses you, of course."

"And I him."

"But we received word that the men from King David will be here to take him north by the end of the week."

Marguerite nearly choked on a strangled sob. "That is only three days from now."

Bertha leaned down and placed a hand on the younger woman's shoulder. "I know, child, I know. You have to find a way to see him before he leaves."

"How?" She wanted to scream. She needed desperately to cry. Faucon's all-too-knowing stare caught her eye and she knew she could do neither.

Intent on making her sham of weeding look earnest, she yanked more of the wild greenery from the herb bed, while she mulled over the situation. While tugging on a stray runner of yarrow from between the fragrant lemon balm, she got an idea.

Marguerite cursed aloud. "This blasted yarrow. Bertha, would you aid me, please?" When the maid knelt next to her, Marguerite talked fast; she knew Faucon would quickly join them.

"Are all the tunnels guarded?"

"They seem to think so. But, my lady, the ones in the stable and the well have not been found."

"Good. I will use the stable exit." It would bring her out just beneath the edge of the cliffs. The weather had been dry of late, so climbing the handholds up to solid ground would be manageable. Risky, but manageable. Right now, the level of risk was not an issue. She had to see Marcus, or die trying.

Marguerite wiped her arm across her forehead, giving her the chance to take a peek at Faucon. He watched them closely, but had not yet moved. "I need a diversion in the bailey. But it has to be something big."

"Our men could attack Faucon's. Would that be diverting enough?"

Marguerite blinked at her maid's unusually bloodthirsty suggestion. "No. I want a diversion, just long enough so I can make my escape. We do not need a battle ending in deaths." She laughed, more to keep Faucon from becoming overly curious than anything else, and asked, "What about a nice little fire?"

"The men would be willing to do that. It might serve your purpose."

"It *has* to work. And it has to be done immediately. The longer we wait, the more time Faucon will have to realize we have something planned." Footsteps behind them alerted her to his approach. Under her breath, so only Bertha could hear, she quickly ordered, "Tell Everett to see to it now. Failure will rest on his neck."

Marguerite sat back on her heels and brushed her hands together, dislodging as much dirt as possible before lifting one hand in the air toward Darius. "What excellent timing, my lord. I am done here."

He assisted her to her feet before offering the same help to the maid. Bertha thanked him, then addressed Marguerite. "By your leave, my lady?"

Marguerite nodded. "Yes, do see to your sister. Give her my regards and best wishes."

Once the maid left the walled garden, Darius asked, "Is the babe come yet?"

"Not yet." It amazed her that he kept up with the villagers' comings and goings almost as well as Henry Thornson had. Her father had never concerned himself with those in the village, or in the keep for that matter. She'd first thought Henry's outward display of concern odd.

Where Henry's display was explainable—after all, these were his people—Darius's concern was downright disturbing. She could not determine his motive.

He pulled her hand through the crook of his arm and led her toward the keep. "Has the midwife been summoned?"

"Yes, Sarah gathered her supplies yesterday and took up residence near the mother-to-be."

"Good." He patted Marguerite's hand. "Then all will be well."

These were the things that drove her to distraction. His touch and the way it made her flesh tingle. His concern and the way it fluttered against her heart. His nearness that she had so easily come to accept.

Since that first night, as far as anyone could tell, he had been the very vision of decorum. He escorted her everywhere—to meals, outside in the bailey, on visits to the village, even to the chapel. He and no one else guarded her chamber door at night. From the outside.

What those observing this display did not realize was that he had her under complete and total guard. He wasn't protecting the Lady of Thornson, as they thought. He kept her prisoner.

Granted, her invisible cell was lined with the softest of furs and many bags of gold, but she still chafed under the confinement. And her heart fought valiantly to not take his show of tender care seriously.

They walked out of the walled garden and into the courtyard. Marguerite willed her pulse not to race with anticipation.

"My lord!"

Darius stopped at Everett's frantic shout. Both Everett and Osbert ran toward them.

Osbert reached them first. "My lord, there is a fire in the main gate tower."

Darius released Marguerite's arm. "How did this happen?" He pinned Everett with a glare.

"I don't know, my lord. It was just now discovered."

Marguerite took a step away from the men, but without even looking, Darius reached out and grasped her wrist. He held her arm out toward Osbert and ordered, "See that she returns to her chamber and stays there."

With obvious reservations, Osbert nodded and took her hand in his own. "My lady?"

When Darius bolted toward the main gate, Marguerite took one look at Osbert's frown of worry and offered, "Go with him. Darius needs you, Osbert. Let no harm befall him."

To her surprise, her play on his worry for Darius worked.

The captain stared hard at her before asking, "You vow to return to your chamber?"

After silently asking forgiveness for the lie she was about to voice, she pushed at his shoulder. "Yes, I promise. Go. Hurry." Surely God would understand the necessity.

He did not wait for further urging. Once he was out of earshot, Everett shook his head. "That was easy enough."

"You need to join them before they notice your absence." Marguerite pointed a finger at him. "Hear me well, Sir Everett. Let no harm come to anyone from Faucon, or from Thornson—do you understand me?"

His expression hardened, but he nodded. "Yes."

"Go."

As he headed toward the main gate, she raced across the bailey toward the stables.

"And what have you discovered for me?"

Sir Everett nearly fell off the cliff at the unexpected question. Since Faucon's arrival, he had met King David's man in the woods, not out here in the open.

"Nothing with any meat."

"No? Then you are not giving your responsibilities enough attention."

The man stepped closer to him, knowing full well that if Everett moved, it would take him to the beach in one long fall.

"Faucon's men are a closed lot. They fear giving any information away, so they say nothing at all."

"Let me make this easier for you. I want to know how many men are in Faucon's company, how well armed they are, how long they plan to remain at Thornson." He grasped the front of Everett's tunic and continued. "And I want to know their plans for Thornson's replacement."

Everett fought to ignore the chill racing up his spine. He glanced to his left, down at the beach far below, and answered, "Yes, my lord. I will see to it."

The man released him. "You do that. And quickly, before the next shipment arrives."

Darius wiped the sweat from his brow. The fire hadn't lasted long, but the damage was much more than minor. It would take a few days to repair the gate tower. In the meantime, he would assign more men to this gate.

"How do you think it started?" Osbert asked from behind him.

Darius turned around and glanced at his man's side. "Where is Marguerite?"

"In her chamber."

"Are you certain of this?"

Osbert shrugged. "Aye. She vowed to go there and remain while I assisted you."

"You have been here this whole time?"

"Yes, my lord."

"And she has been alone this whole time?"

Osbert's eyes widened. "Oh, no. You don't think she would…she wouldn't dare."

A curse escaped his mouth before Darius sprinted toward the keep, Osbert right behind him. "Get two horses ready in case she did dare."

Osbert veered toward the stable as Darius continued on to the keep. He raced through the Great Hall and up the stairs to Marguerite's chamber.

Before entering, he paused to catch his breath. If she was not inside this room, he would need all the patience and strength of will he possessed to keep from strangling the first person he encountered.

He pushed the door open and stepped through the entry way into the chamber.

His shouted curses at finding it empty brought Bertha to the doorway. "My lord?"

Darius whipped around and grabbed the maid by the arm. "I thought you had gone to be with your sister."

Bertha shook her head. "Not with the fire. I might have been needed."

He did not believe her excuse for a heartbeat. "Where is your mistress?"

Bertha peered around his body "She is not here?"

"Woman, do not play games with me. Where is she?"

"I do not know, Lord Faucon." The maid shrugged. "The last time I saw her, she was with you."

Her attitude bordered on nonchalance and made him realize that Marguerite had obviously told the maid not to be afraid of him. A normal servant would be cowering beneath the glare he directed down at her.

Darius needed this woman to understand that while she did not need fear for herself, perhaps she should fear for her charge. He grabbed her other arm and shook her. "Tell me where she is, or I swear to you I will beat her senseless when I do find her. I am sick of her lies and will tolerate them no longer."

Bertha's eyes widened. "You will not harm her if I help you?"

He choked. The maid dared to make a deal with him? "I promise you only that she will live."

Bertha chewed on her lower lip and stared up at him. Finally, she nodded. "She is in the village. She does nothing wrong, my lord."

"In the village where?" He released her.

"She will be either in the cemetery, or in the woods nearby."

That made little sense to him, so he asked, "What is so important there that she risks my anger and possibly her own life to thwart me?"

Bertha shrugged. "Since you are going to discover it for yourself, I do no harm by telling you. She goes there to be with Marcus."

He thought he'd been angry before. He'd been certain that he'd reached the limits of his ire a time or two in the past.

He'd been wrong.

What filled him now was a pure rage so hot, so vio-

lent that it clouded his vision, and his thoughts, with a
red haze. He strode toward the door, adjusting his sword
belt and vowing, "Your lady may live, but her lover will
not."

Bertha rushed after him, shouting, "No, my lord
Faucon, you do not understand. Marcus is not—"

Darius slammed the door in her face, cutting off the
rest of her words.

Without stopping, without a single glance left or
right, he marched out of the keep, into the bailey and
silently swung himself up on his horse.

"My lord?" Osbert met his hard gaze and shook his
head. "Nothing. It will wait."

The two men rode through both baileys and out of
the gates. They crossed the open field, following the
narrow road toward the village.

With each fall of his horse's hooves, Darius willed
his anger to cool. It would do him no good to be blinded
by rage when he met this Marcus. Battles were not won
by those who lost their senses.

And he *would* win this battle. He cared not what
Marguerite, her father, the Church, or even the king
thought or said about the matter. As far as he was concerned, their marriage was fully binding, and with
God's grace he would end this charade tonight.

He knew the how of it. What he could not understand
was the why.

It was not for love. That had been killed and effectively set aside years ago. It had nothing to do with lust.
That was something any woman could provide.

He needed to understand the why—else it would be
nothing more than another charade perpetuated by his
own pride.

While he had missed her gentle touch, the taste of her lips on his, the sound of her voice, the very scent of her skin, there was something else that drove him to this madness. Something inside of him ate at his gut, tore at his heart. And he knew not what.

It was as if his soul was aware of something that he had yet to discover.

Something he needed to uncover before he went completely mad.

Darius raced through the village, thankful those in his path quickly gave way. He slowed his pace only when he reached the hilly fields on the other side of Thornson's demesne lands.

With a hard yank, he brought his lathered horse to a stop, pulled his sword from the wooden scabbard hanging at his side and looked across the field, to the cemetery.

Osbert caught up with him and stopped alongside. "Darius."

His captain's winded voice held a note of censure. Darius looked at him and tried his best to reassure the man. "I will not harm *her*. But I cannot promise to let her lover live."

The captain reached out and briefly touched Darius's shoulder. "I cannot stop you from doing what you must. But think on this first. Do not let jealousy rule your sword arm."

"It is not jealousy that eats at me." That was the plain and simple truth. Not one speck of jealousy flowed through his veins.

"Then what is this?"

Darius shook his head. "At the moment I do not know. But before this day is out, I will."

A movement at the edge of woods situated on the far side of the cemetery caught his eye.

Osbert saw it, too, and gasped.

Darius sheathed his sword. "For the love of God." He flicked the reins and started toward the two figures. They walked hand in hand to a spot in the cemetery where they sat down.

Marguerite put an arm around her companion and drew him into her lap. Darius's heart twisted with pain at the obvious display of love between mother and child.

He and Osbert reined in their horses at a slight distance from the edge of the cemetery. Marguerite's attention was so focused on the child that she had not noticed him.

Osbert broke the deafening silence by softly stating, "You did not know."

"Nay." Darius shook his head. "How could I? No one has said a word about Thornson's child."

How had she hidden this from him? Where had the child been? Why had no one at the keep mentioned a word about a child? Not even in hushed whispers. They didn't so much as ask about his whereabouts.

At that moment the child jumped up from Marguerite's lap and drew her to her feet. They danced around a few of the crosses, before Marguerite pulled the child into a hug.

Darius's horse whinnied, catching the attention of Marguerite and the child. The youngster turned around and stared at both men.

Osbert swore. Darius nearly fell from his horse, the blood draining from his head in shock. He now knew what his heart and soul had been hiding from him.

Chapter Five

Marguerite heard the horse's whinny. With her heart in her throat and a silent prayer on her tongue, she looked up at the men. Her first impulse was to swoon, her next to run. But where would she go? She and Marcus were out in the open on foot. Darius would catch them long before they made it to the cover of the forest.

Osbert's curse rasped against her ears. She cringed and tightened her arms around Marcus.

Too soon. Darius had discovered her absence too soon. Just a few more precious moments and she'd have taken Marcus back to Hawise and John in the village.

Surrounded by Hawise's six raven-haired children, the boy would have been safe, hidden in the open, Faucon none the wiser.

What would he do now? She studied Darius intently. At first he'd appeared to be shocked. His complexion had paled, his eyes had widened.

Now, as he held her steady gaze on his approach, he

narrowed his eyes. When he was close enough, she could see the unsteady tic in his cheek.

As he drew nearer, his attention shifted to Marcus. Marguerite could not help but wonder at his thoughts as his gold-flecked hazel eyes met the gold-flecked hazel eyes of her son—*their* son.

Oh, dear Lord, she'd sworn not to break this vow to Thornson. Her entire adult life had been built on a lie of her husband's making. And she'd never once objected.

How could she object, when keeping the lie meant security, safety and love?

The men stopped their horses little more than an arm's length in front of her and Marcus.

"Well, I'll be damned."

Osbert's near whisper mirrored Marguerite's thoughts. In the end, her lie most likely would damn her. *Merciful Lord, let it not condemn Marcus to damnation, too.*

Marcus tipped his head and looked up at Osbert. "Do you not know that swearing is a sin?"

"Is it, now?" Osbert acted surprised. "Thank you for making me aware of that, Master…what is your name?"

The boy lifted his chin a notch more. "Marcus. I am Marcus of Thornson."

Osbert slid down from his horse. He studied the boy from head to toe, then a broad smile lit his face.

His easy recognition only strengthened Marguerite's resolve to keep anyone else from seeing Marcus and Darius together.

Osbert squatted to Marcus's level. "Well, Master Marcus, I am honored to meet you."

"Who are you?"

"I am Sir Osbert of Faucon. And how many years are you, Marcus?"

The boy held up all the fingers on one hand, while looking at Osbert's horse. "Is that your horse?"

"Why, yes, it is."

"He is big."

"Not that big." Osbert straightened and snapped his fingers. "Why, I bet a fine young man like yourself could sit atop him with no trouble at all."

Marcus twisted against Marguerite's hold and looked up at her, his eyes alight with anticipation. Marguerite sucked in a shallow breath before pleading, "Osbert, do not harm him."

Osbert jerked upright as if he'd been struck. "You know me better than that, my lady."

She pulled her son tighter against her.

Marcus struggled briefly against her hold. "Mama?" He stared up at her, fear replacing the anticipation.

"Do not frighten him." Darius leaned forward. "It is unnecessary."

Frighten him? Nay, Marcus had no cause to be afraid. It was her own fear that held her back. If she let him go with Osbert, would she ever see her son again? Marguerite shook her head.

"No. I cannot let you take him."

"Take him?" Osbert's dismay was evident in his voice. "I only offer to let him ride my horse, that is all." He looked at Darius. "My lord?"

Darius dismounted, wrapped his reins around a wooden cross and held Marguerite's stare. "We need to talk. Let the boy go with Osbert." When she made no move to release her son, he added, "Do not make me force this issue."

He was right. They did need to talk. Marguerite took her arms from around her son and ran her fingers through his long black waves before releasing him completely.

Darius looked down at Marcus, then motioned toward Osbert. "Go for a ride. Sir Osbert will see that you are safe."

Marcus dashed to Osbert's side, obviously eager to get atop the horse. The captain swung the boy up into the saddle and walked alongside, one hand on the boy's waist and the other with a firm grip on the horse's rein.

Marguerite and Darius stared at each other in silence. Darius wondered if the thoughts and emotions running through her mind and body were as confused as his own.

Osbert and Marcus completed two circles around them, and when they came by Darius the second time, Osbert cleared his throat. "Obviously the two of you would like to be alone to share this moment of total silence together. Master Marcus and I will be over in the field teaching this horse a thing or two."

Marguerite wiped at her tears and turned away.

Darius stepped forward and pulled her hard against his chest. Countless words rushed to his throat. He swallowed, trying to decide what to say, what to ask first.

Finally, he choked out, "What have you done?"

She shook against him, her sobs muffling her voice. He cradled her head against his chest.

"Marguerite, crying will not help."

When she heaved a sigh and regained control of herself, he asked again, "What have you done?"

She remained in his arms, speaking into his chest, "I thought only to protect my son."

"*Your* son? I am fairly certain you did not create him alone. I do not think anyone could deny who fathered him."

"Thornson is his father."

"Why do you lie? Thornson is dead. And that boy is Faucon through and through."

She stiffened against his chest. "He is Thornson's son." Her voice rose with each word. "He is Marcus of Thornson."

"Shh. Hush, Marguerite." Darius ran a hand down her back, seeking to calm the hysteria apparent in her voice.

Odd, now that he should be angry with her and at all that she had taken from him, Darius's main thought was that she did not feel threatened. He rested his chin on her head and gently swayed from side to side.

"Why did you seek to hide him?"

"I promised Henry that I would keep our son safe."

"He was safe at Thornson, was he not?"

"Until you came, yes."

"Marguerite, what did you think I would do to a child? Is your opinion of me so low that you would believe me capable of harming a child?"

Her head shook beneath his chin. "No."

"Then why hide him?"

She shrugged. "I was afraid...I thought that..." She sucked in a big breath of air. "I thought that if people saw you and Marcus together that they would think... they would assume..." She paused and buried her face in the folds of his tunic. "They would know he was yours."

Darius closed his eyes. The pain behind her words tore at his heart. "And why would that be so bad, Marguerite?"

"I promised Henry to never let anyone know the truth. In exchange, he raised Marcus as his own and made sure both of us wanted for nothing."

"So, he knew?"

"Of course he knew. I was not a virgin on that wedding night. I was already carrying your child."

"From *our* wedding night."

"Yes. Henry protected my child and my honor."

"And in exchange he gained a son he could no longer conceive on his own. *My* son."

She pushed him away. "It was not as if he stole him from you."

"Heavens, no. He could not steal what I did not know I had. How clever of him."

"Clever? You talk as if he devised some great plan for his benefit."

"Did he not? You think Thornson held your honor and well-being above his desires?"

"Desires?" Marguerite fisted her hands at her sides. Her face flamed with anger in the midday sun. "Desires? What desires? What evil plots do you lay at a dead man's feet?"

Before he finished his missions and returned to Faucon, he'd lay a great many evil plots at Thornson's feet, but this was not of that caliber. "I did not say his planning was evil, only clever."

"Clever, how?"

"Please, Marguerite. Do not seek to convince me you have become blind or addled. Tell me the people of Thornson did not look upon your elderly husband in a different light once your condition was known."

"Different?" Her forehead creased while she searched for an answer. "No. I do not think they did."

"They did not whisper about his renewed manhood? His increased vitality with his young wife?"

The redness in Marguerite's face deepened, but not with anger. She looked away, obviously embarrassed.

"Ah, I see I am correct. And you do not think this made him feel as giddy and proud as a puffed-up peacock?"

"Does not every man experience some measure of pride in the same situation?"

"I would not know, would I."

Marguerite rolled her eyes and shook her head. "Tell me, Darius, are you not feeling a small increase in your own pride at the moment?"

She had no inkling, but of all the emotions racing through his head and heart, pride was not among them. "Pride? No. Some anger perhaps. Definitely a sense of loss."

"Loss?" She turned around and walked amongst the crosses. "What did you lose? A Faucon could never understand the meaning of loss."

The pain in Darius's chest grew. His anger increased. Not understand loss? "Why do you think that? Because of the size and wealth of the holdings? Do not forget, those belong to the Comte, not to me."

"As if Rhys would let one of his brothers go without."

"Rhys was not the Comte six years ago." Darius paused to swallow the bile flowing toward his throat. "He had no say over others in the family."

"Your father was a good man. He would never have let his sons suffer any loss."

"Under normal circumstances, perhaps. But when angered, his fury knew no bounds."

Her short laugh of disbelief singed his ears.

"I find it doubtful that anything could anger him that much outside of battle," she said.

"His son's secret marriage to a traitor's daughter would."

She stopped midstep, frozen. Finally, she slowly turned to face him. "Traitor? Are you referring to my father?" While her voice was soft and steady, her thinned lips, furrowed brow and narrowed eyes gave lie to her outward calmness.

Darius shrugged. "Yes, and you well know that. Was that not the reason he became so angry at what we had done?"

"No. He had already made arrangements for my marriage to Henry."

"Ah, yes. It is only natural that a staunch supporter of Empress Matilda marry his daughter to another of his kind."

"Now you call Thornson a traitor, too?"

Darius laughed at her question and then laughed more at the outrage evident on her face. When he controlled his mirth, he asked, "And the men I interrupted on the beach were not smugglers?"

She tossed her head. "No. They were gathering a shipment of supplies."

Sometimes he actually enjoyed the way she barefaced lied to him. It reminded him of an inept warrior banging a sword on his shield as a call to battle. The lie was an open invitation to prove the folly in her brashness.

"When next I catch these men in action, I will be successful in capturing them. Then we shall determine whether their activities are nefarious or not." His warning garnered no response, so he added, "But fear not, their payment will be small compared to what their leader suffers." Her gasp was enough reward for the moment.

Marguerite threw her hands up in the air. "We could argue this all day. What would it change?"

"Nothing. It would change nothing. In the end, I still lost my home, family and name, along with the first five years of my son's life."

She looked at him in total confusion. "I do not understand. How did you lose your home and family?"

"Simple." He kept his voice as even as his memory would allow. It had not been simple. In truth, it had been the worst day and night of his life. "My father ordered me from the keep and had my name struck from all records."

"What?" Her voice rose in shock.

"You heard me. Your father's men took me from that cottage, slung me naked from a pole—secured like a trussed stag—and dropped me at my father's feet in the center of Faucon's bailey. While providing much entertainment for the guards, this did not please the Comte."

"Oh, dear Lord, I did not know." She stepped toward him. "How could they have done that?"

"Since at the moment they found us I was not armed, nor clothed, it was an easy matter."

She blushed. "Ah, yes, it was an inopportune moment."

Darius glanced toward Osbert and Marcus in the distance. "I would say that single, inopportune moment was enough."

She took another step closer and touched his arm. "Darius, I beg of you, do not take my son's name from him."

He looked down at her. What did she expect him to do? "I cannot permit him to be raised as a traitor to the Crown."

"He is but a child."

"Aye. Surrounded by those loyal to Matilda. He will page and squire where, Marguerite? Where will he learn how to be a man? In King David's court? Who will teach him of honor and loyalty? One of Matilda's barons?"

"What does that matter to you? By the time he is of an age to be sent away, you will have been gone for years."

"He is my son. It matters a great deal to me. Answer me. What arrangements, what promises have already been made for his future?"

She turned her head and whispered, "He will go north."

Darius grasped her arms. "Only over my dead body."

"It is none of your concern." Marguerite wanted to scream. Instead, she gritted her teeth and did her best to not give in to the pressing urge. "Do not waste your time fretting over what you cannot change." She winced at the tightening of his grip on her arms.

In keeping with his family's trait, Darius's eyebrows rose like wings over his glittering stare. "If I have a mind to, I can change everything—and well you know that."

"You cannot prove Marcus is not Thornson's son." She knew the weakness of her response, but she had to believe she had some semblance of control over Marcus's future.

"I do not—"

"Lady Marguerite!" Hawise's shout cut off whatever Darius had been about to say. She and her husband John approached.

"It seems you are saved—for now." Darius's tone

and pointed look made it clear this conversation was far from finished.

"My lady, when you did not return, we were concerned."

Marguerite briefly touched Hawise's arm to reassure the woman. "Nay, I am fine." She turned to John and explained her delay. "Lord Faucon and his man came upon us. So, we were quite safe."

John looked about. "Where is Master Marcus?"

Marguerite swallowed a groan; she should have said nothing to draw attention to her son.

"He is with my man." Darius pointed across the field toward the figures in the distance. "Sir Osbert is giving him a riding lesson."

"Ah, 'tis certain the boy will enjoy that, my lord." John's forehead creased as he stared at Darius. The man glanced at his wife, then toward Osbert and Marcus before bringing his attention back to Marguerite.

Hawise pursed her lips. "Upon my word, Lady Marguerite, Lord Faucon and Master Marcus could be related." In her usual forthright manner the woman spoke what was on her mind.

Darius watched Marguerite closely. He wondered if Hawise and John noticed the slight tremble of her chin, or the paling of her face.

He'd barely had time to sort through the truth himself; he was not ready to deal with others.

To disabuse the couple of their opinion, Darius gasped, then said, "Related? Heavens above, if the color of one's hair spoke of a family tie, I would be related to all of your children."

John laughed first. "My lord, you are welcome to a few of them if you would like."

After a few moments of awkward silence, Hawise nudged her husband with her elbow. "Speaking of children, we have left ours alone long enough, I think."

Obviously married enough years to know a hint when delivered, John nodded. "By your leave, Lady Marguerite, my lord."

Marguerite glanced at Darius before saying, "I will be along later."

She waited until Hawise and John were well out of hearing range before letting loose with a string of curses aimed mostly at herself, then covered her face with her hands. "Oh, God, what have I done? What will I do now?"

Darius had wondered the same thing. While he still did not understand Marguerite lying about Marcus's sire, he fully understood her recent motives.

Taking the lie into consideration, she had been right to hide the boy. Not so much from him, but so that people could not see them side by side. Marcus looked so much a Faucon that it would take an imbecile not to notice the likeness.

She was also correct in her last question—what could she do now?

He ran a hand through his hair and looked up at the sky. An answer to her dilemma struck him out of the blue. *Marry her.*

He shook his head, hoping to clear the sudden insanity.

But the action only served to strengthen the madness.

He stared at her. Marguerite had turned toward the open field. As she watched Osbert and her son, a frown wrinkled her forehead. She worried her lower lip with her teeth. Her concern would only be expected. He had the power to ease her troubles.

What about his own?

What would King Stephen do? What would his own brothers think, or say?

Darius sighed. When had he ever taken the easier way?

He placed his hands on her shoulders. "Marguerite?"

When she turned her face to look up at him, he saw the unshed tears gathered in her eyes before she lowered her gaze.

"I have a solution." Suddenly he knew what everyone would think—they'd swear he had lost his ability to reason.

"What?" The hopeful look on her face gave him the strength he needed to complete his moment of insanity.

"Marry me." Almost as an afterthought he added, "Again."

Shock instantly replaced the hopefulness. "*Marry* you? Faucon, you are surely addled to even suggest such a move."

"Perhaps. But it would solve much."

"How? How would it solve anything?"

"Thornson will be given to a new lord. Like it or no, you will be required to remarry. Why not let it be to the monster you know instead of a stranger?"

Marguerite could not believe what she heard. There were countless reasons the unknown would be better. Reasons she wished not to voice to Darius. Then, there was also the obvious. "Pray tell me how our marriage could possibly keep people from seeing you and Marcus together and not guessing the truth?"

"Simple. Once we are wed I will publicly declare Marcus to be Thornson's sole heir."

"You would do that?" She could think of no man in her acquaintance who would do such a thing.

"Falcongate may be nothing more than a minor holding attached to the keep. But it is more than enough for me and a son or two."

"That son or two includes Marcus?"

He took her hands in his. "Since we will never come to an agreement, it will be up to him when he is old enough to understand. I see no reason to change his memories of the man he considers his father."

It started as a small, gentle tug in the region of her heart. But it grew warm and insistent. As hard as she wished to deny the sense in his solution, she could find no fault with it as far as her son was concerned.

"What about us?"

Darius looked genuinely confused. "What do you mean?"

"Us." Where did she begin? "Darius, I mean not to have this come between us. I did love Henry. I still do, and a part of me always will."

He clenched and unclenched his jaw, but he finally said, "I will have to learn to live with that. Can you honestly tell me that you will never have room in your heart for me again? Is there nothing of what was between us still there?"

He was so serious, so intent. He would never understand. She could only repeat, "We were but children."

He released her hands, tipped her chin up and lowered his mouth to hers.

In the heartbeat before he touched her lips, Marguerite knew what would happen, so the war that raged with her heart and mind was not in the least unexpected.

His lips were warm against hers. His touch chased away the chill brought about by the rising ocean breeze.

Darius slid his arms about her and drew her against his chest. The embrace, pressing her against the hardness of his chest, provided a place of refuge. For the first time in months she knew a measure of safety.

He broke their kiss and asked, "Will you marry me, Marguerite?" His words brushed across her lips like fragile fairy wings.

Without a single doubt Marguerite knew she could place the safety of her son in his hands. But what about Thornson and the men? Darius was King Stephen's man and that would never change. Thornson rested in Matilda's hands and neither would that ever change.

Darius rested his forehead against hers. "You hesitate far too long in your silent debate. What concerns you more, Marguerite? Your son's welfare, or that of your men?"

Had he never lost the ability to know her thoughts? "I…" God forgive her, but she could not lie to him again. Nor could she speak the truth.

"You what?" He trailed kisses across her forehead, down the side of her face, then along her jaw. "You know I will not harm Marcus."

He teased at the corner of her mouth, knowing full well that his touch threw her thoughts into pure chaos.

Darius traced her lips with the tip of his tongue, sending a shiver down her back. "I am well able to deal with your men. Have no fears on that score."

When she opened her mouth to respond, he captured her words with a kiss. An insistent caress that stole her thoughts and urged her to cast caution aside.

She sighed and felt his lips briefly curve into a smile against her own.

Aye, her actions led him to believe he had won, she'd grant him that much. She leaned tighter against him, wanting more than just his lips on hers. And knowing that *more* only increased the desire.

He pulled back a hairsbreadth from their kiss. "Marry me."

Before she could catch the breath needed to respond, he once again took her mouth, her tongue, with his own.

Marguerite knew he thought to seduce her into giving him the answer he wanted. But she was no longer ten and five, and no longer ignorant of the ways of men.

She slipped one hand up to run her fingers through his hair. He held her tighter in his arms.

Marguerite pulled away from their kiss. She stared into his eyes and for a moment regretted what she was about to do. "Darius, I cannot decide something this important on a moment's notice."

He lowered his arms and stepped back. A stranger would not have noticed the hurt and anger race across his features before he dropped his mask of indifference into place.

"You must decide quickly, else King Stephen will take the matter out of your hands."

"A few days is all I require." She reached toward him, but he moved away. "Darius, give me but three days to think on what will determine the rest of my life."

Marcus's laughter drawing nearer prompted her to

add, "Marcus stays with Hawise and John until then. I'll not have anyone spouting an opinion that he might overhear."

Darius's thunderous glare made her pulse quicken, but he only nodded, then said, "Three days."

Relief flooded her. That was all the time she would need. When Marguerite turned to greet her son, Darius grasped her arm.

"That is all, Marguerite. Three days and then this game ends."

Chapter Six

Darius leaned back against the wall surrounding the inner yard. This was the day. He blinked against the blinding sun. At least it appeared to be a good day for deciding one's future.

Marguerite had asked for three days and that time was now up. Not wishing her to feel completely forced into agreeing to their marriage, he'd intentionally left her alone.

While he had found himself quickly missing her company, it had given him time to investigate the oddities happening at Thornson. There were plenty of them to scrutinize.

A movement caught his attention and he watched as yet another one of Thornson's men entered the stables and did not exit from the front, nor the left side of the building. This made five men in just a short time. He shifted his attention to the opposite wallwalk, waiting for Osbert's signal.

Before long, his captain walked away from the stable section toward the main gatehouse. Darius curled

and uncurled his fingers at his man's silent signal—
Thornson's men had not exited from the rear or the
right side of the building, either. He headed toward the
gatehouse to meet Osbert.

He'd ceased guarding Marguerite because he'd
thought the secret she worked so hard to hide was Marcus. Now, he wondered if perhaps she had more to keep
from him than just her son—their son.

Far too many men had headed into the stable and not
reappeared for hours. Obviously, a tunnel entrance had
been missed during his men's initial search.

While planning and constructing mazes and tunnels
provided others with a great deal of amusement, the time
wasted discovering the hidden entrances and passage-
ways always proved to be little more than a nuisance.

Darius and Osbert descended the wall and met in the
bailey. "Have they been this busy before these last three
days?" Darius asked.

Osbert shook his head. "Nay. I would hazard a guess
something is in the works."

"Another shipment of *supplies,* I am certain."

Osbert snorted at the obvious sarcasm before asking,
"Shall I gather the men and go after them?"

"No…" Darius's answer trailed off as he watched
Marguerite leave the keep and head toward the currently popular stable. Just as he decided to follow her,
she turned and waved to him. After a stable lad brought
out a horse, she led the animal to Darius.

"How fare you this beautiful day, my lord?"

"Fine, Lady Marguerite. And where are you off to?"

"The village." She looked at him as if daring him to
tell her otherwise, then relented. "If that is permitted,
of course."

He wanted to tell her no, just to see her cheeks flame and eyes glitter. But he refrained from the churlish urge. "Do not let me keep you from your duties."

With Osbert's assistance, she mounted the horse and smiled down at Darius. "Thank you."

He stepped closer and touched her leg. "Three days have come and gone." She nodded, giving him silent assurance that she remembered what was expected of her this day. He asked, "I will see you at the evening meal?"

She reached down and stroked his cheek with the back of her hand. The light touch rippled like a warm shiver down his spine.

"Of course I will see you then." Marguerite prodded her horse with her foot and left the bailey.

Darius waited until she was through the gate before ordering Osbert, "Follow her."

He hated not trusting her, but what had she done to prove herself worth any measure of trust? Nothing so far.

He headed toward the keep and Marguerite's chamber. While she was out on her jaunt into the village under Osbert's watchful eye, he would discover what he could.

Once out of the keep and onto the open field, Marguerite urged her horse into a gallop. She laughed as the wind tore the covering from her head. It would take a great deal of patience to untangle all the snarls from her hair, but she'd worry about that later.

Right now, she just wanted to dwell on the changes this day would bring to her life. The men would take Marcus north tonight and she'd go with them.

Had she not loved Henry, the thought of wedding

Darius would not rest so heavily on her heart. Even dead, Henry Thornson held a place that no man could ever reach.

But…that wasn't quite true. She urged her horse to gallop even faster. She feared that Darius could very well touch the places she'd promised for all eternity to Henry.

Unbidden tears stung her eyes. This wasn't fair. Not to her and certainly not to Darius either. She'd been so certain that when the time came, Stephen would send a stranger—a man she would never come to love.

Then all would have been as she'd planned. She'd have been ever true to the husband the king sent, but she would have gone to her grave having loved only Henry.

Instead, Stephen saw fit to send Darius. His only task had been to hold Thornson safely until a husband could be found. But Darius would always be Darius. It was not in him to do only what he was told. He found it needful to go further. In keeping with his very nature, he offered what he thought would best suit the needs of the moment—marriage to him.

Now she could only hope that someday he would understand what drove her to run away. And perhaps, one day in the future, he might even come to forgive her for the grievous sorrow she'd caused him.

She'd done her best the past three days to try to leave him a missive that would explain all. But finding the words had not been easy. Marguerite had little hope that she'd explained it in a manner that he would understand.

She knew for a certainty that when Darius read her words, his first reaction would be one of great anger. Her only hope now was to leave Thornson before he found her odd message.

When she reached the edge of the forest, she reined

in the horse and turned to look back at the keep in the distance. Her heart pounded with regret and a sense of loss so great she thought it nearly unbearable.

"Lady Marguerite."

She forced her attention away from what she might never see again and looked through the denseness of the trees at Hawise.

"My lady, come." The woman held out her hand. "Do not torture yourself. Come, Marcus awaits."

Marguerite dismounted. After securing the reins to the bridle, she turned the horse toward Thornson. The beast would soon grow hungry and, without a doubt, find its way back to the stables.

"Are you certain the lady is joining us?"

Sir Everett answered, "Yes. She suddenly refuses to let her son go north alone."

"I do not see the reason behind her decision." The man in the shadows tugged at his short beard. "Did something that I am not aware of happen to bring her to this course of action?"

"Nothing I am aware of, my lord. She told me only yesterday that she would be traveling with Marcus. I am not in a position to question her. I simply follow orders."

"Ah, yes, the ever-obedient Sir Everett. I am quite certain you follow her every order."

"I—"

The man waved off Everett's reply. "Oaf, that did not require a response. See to it that the lady and her son remain hidden until I return."

"Hidden? Why, Lord Bainbridge, I did not realize I needed to be hidden on my own land."

Both men jumped at Marguerite's statement. She

smiled before continuing. "Ah, I see I have intruded. What grand plans do you so secretly discuss that I catch you unawares?"

Sir Everett backed away, letting the other man answer.

"My lady, this night's activities require great planning." He paused and glanced at the boy standing next to Marguerite. "This must be Lord Marcus."

"Yes, this is Thornson's son." She tried to move Marcus forward, but he hung back.

Surprised, Marguerite watched her son. Normally outgoing, the boy took one look at Bainbridge and ducked behind her. Something, motherly instinct perhaps, warned her to be leery of this man.

Lord Bainbridge appeared not to even notice Marcus's actions and continued their conversation. "Young Marcus would be quite safe with me. There is no need for you to accompany him to King David's."

His voice was too smooth, his tone too condescending, and his smile, while curving up the corners of his lips, never reached his eyes. Marguerite smiled back like the good and proper woman he mostly likely expected. "Oh, no, my lord, it is no discredit to you. I simply have not been to court in years and thought this would be the perfect opportunity to renew old acquaintances."

Though Bainbridge was distantly related to her deceased husband, they'd not been in each other's company enough for him to know how she would react in any given situation.

In this she had the upper hand. Henry had trusted Bainbridge only as far as he could see the man. Which is why Henry oversaw this final leg of the smuggling operations himself. Bainbridge was not stupid enough to cross King David, so there was never any doubt that once loaded, the supplies would reach Scotland. Especially considering that the manifest had always been carried by a courier on horseback, instead of being sent on with the boats. That way those unloading the boats in Scotland knew what to expect before the vessels hit their docks.

Henry's concern had always been whether or not the weapons and gold would make it out of the caves and into the receiving boats. He'd not permitted anyone else, not even Bainbridge, to oversee the loading.

Lord Bainbridge's ice-blue eyes narrowed as he studied her. Marguerite kept her smile frozen to her mouth. She hoped she did not look quite as foolish as she felt.

Finally, the man nodded and closed the small distance between them. "I understand. Now that dear Henry is no longer with us, you must hunger for company." He put his hand on her shoulder and gently squeezed. "I will be honored to escort you and Marcus to King David personally."

The man truly was a dolt. He'd misread her smile as some odd sort of invitation to take liberties with her. Only the fact that Marcus hugged her legs kept Marguerite from seeking to tear Bainbridge's arm from his body. She lowered her shoulder to remove his unwelcome touch.

"I apologize." Immediately, Bainbridge stepped back. "I meant no harm. My only motive was to offer comfort and what I hope will be the start of a fruitful relationship."

"Relationship?" Marguerite had no intention of starting any type of relationship with this man. She had already planned on petitioning King David to put someone else in charge of the Thornson-to-Scotland section of the journey.

"Lady Marguerite, while Henry and I were distantly related, it was by marriage only. His uncle married my mother after I was born."

She knew this much. She also knew of the rumors that his mother had not been married to anyone when he was born. He came by his name only because his mother had been in King David's court at the time of the conception.

However, she didn't share her knowledge of the situation. Instead, she said, "Yes, Lord Bainbridge, I am aware of your relationship to Henry."

He smiled at her and took her hand in his. "I wish for us to become well acquainted. There is much we could do for each other."

"Such as?" She resisted the urge to jerk her hand free from his sweaty hold. For the moment, she needed his assistance. But Marguerite could barely wait for the journey to be over and done so they could part company forever.

"Well…" He paused and looked down as if suddenly embarrassed. She knew better; his display was but a show.

Dear, dear Henry, bless you for warning me about this man. She held her tongue, waiting for him to speak what was on his mind.

"It is a well-known fact that Thornson needs a strong hand to guide its men and to oversee the king's business."

And he thought he was that man? Marguerite bit the

inside of her mouth to hold back a laugh. By the way Bainbridge fidgeted, she gathered he was not yet finished, so she remained silent while he conjured his next admission.

"Young Marcus needs a guiding hand to grow into manhood." He lifted her hand and pressed his lips to her fingertips. The stiff hairs of his beard and mustache prickled against her fingers.

He stared at her over their hands. "And I am certain that a lovely woman such as yourself is in need of a strong man as husband." Again, he touched his mouth to her fingers, then added, "I would be honored to be that man."

Only when her horse sprouted wings and flew would she consider this beetle-brained lack-wit for a husband. Even then, she'd not let him in her bed. She'd sooner leap off the cliff and commit herself to eternal damnation than share a bed with Bainbridge.

As gently as possible under the circumstances, Marguerite pulled her hand free. At the first opportunity she intended to scrub it clean. For now, she lowered her arm and hid her fist in the folds of her skirt.

"My Lord Bainbridge, I thank you for such a generous offer, but Henry has not yet grown cold in his grave. I am certain that when the time is right, King David will do what is best for Thornson and for Marcus."

"But what about you, my dear?" He reached out and tucked a wayward strand of hair back into place behind her ear. Marguerite shivered with revulsion at his touch.

"Me? I will be pleased to do as the king bids."

"Surely, since you were married to an obviously lusty warrior—" his glance briefly drifted toward Marcus, then back to her "—you have needs that are not now being met."

Lord above, what was this man going to suggest next? Marguerite lifted her eyebrows. "Needs?"

His smile was one of unadulterated lust. She found herself watching his lips to see if any drool slipped from between them.

Slowly, probably to be certain she would notice, he ran the tip of his tongue along his upper lip. Her stomach knotted. She swallowed to keep the bile from racing up her throat.

"Lady Marguerite, I am not a man of many delicate words. Thankfully, you have already had one husband in your bed, so plain speaking should not offend you over much."

"I—"

He placed his fingers over her lips and shook his head. "No, no, let me finish first. A union between the two of us would give us wealth beyond imagining. Thornson's lands added to my own would rival only King David's properties."

The man was insane. There was no other explanation for his addled behavior. He should be presenting this offer to the king, not her.

"Fear not, though. It is not only your property I covet." He lowered his overbright gaze to her breasts. To her astonishment and horror, his hand followed. "I must admit, the mere thought of having you in my bed to enjoy for a lifetime of pleasure makes me bold."

Marguerite tried to back away, but Marcus was still wrapped around her legs. When she moved her arm to reach behind her, Bainbridge grasped her wrist.

"Let me go. Do not act so foolish in front of my son."

He pulled her forward until she leaned against him. Quickly, before she could clear her muddled wits, he slid his hand from her breast and wrapped his arm around her, pinning her to his chest.

Over her shoulder, he ordered Everett, "Take the boy to the camp. We will be along…soon."

Everett peeled Marcus from her legs and pulled him away. When he yelled for Marguerite, his cry was stifled.

Marguerite pushed at Bainbridge. "If one hair on my son's head is harmed, I will kill you. Do you hear me?"

The man laughed. "I would never be so stupid as to let any harm befall Thornson's son. King David would have my head."

He lowered his mouth closer to hers and whispered, "The mother is another story, however."

Marguerite twisted in his arms. "Let me go, Bainbridge."

He moved back and forth, seeking to pin her lips with his own. Unsuccessful, he grasped the hair at the nape of her neck. "Hold still. Do not act the frightened virgin. It is unbecoming and will do you not a bit of good."

Fear drew the metallic taste of blood to her mouth. She thought she'd had the upper hand, but she'd not suspected the man's level of depravity.

Henry had painted Bainbridge as a brainless toad-eater. Never once had he described the man as dangerous. Henry had misjudged this man and, sadly, so had she. That had been a large mistake—one she needed to be sure she did not repeat.

She punched him in the side. "I am not acting the frightened virgin. I do not fear you." Silently praying her false bravado would make the man see reason, she continued. "If you wish to join our lands, this is not the way to go about it."

He leaned away but did not release her. "It matters not if you enjoy my methods. Crude or pleasant, you will be my wife."

"If that is what King David wishes, then so be it. But I want to hear that from him."

Bainbridge shrugged. "I am afraid the king does not see it my way."

Ah, so he'd already approached the king. That explained this man's actions now. He was obviously angry at being denied his request, and thought to take matters into his own hands.

She wondered why David had not granted permission. Perhaps it had something to do with what Bainbridge had said earlier—the combined property from their union would be immense. That in itself could prove a danger to King David.

"And you think force will convince me to see matters your way?"

"I had planned to woo you, to shower you with attention you could not ignore. However, since you have decided to go to King David's court, it is impossible for me to put my plan into action. Your decision forced me to act quickly."

Marguerite recognized an opening that could very well save her and took the chance. "Did you not think to come to me? Perhaps we could have devised a plan together." She arched one brow. "Maybe it is still not too late."

Bainbridge cocked his head and narrowed his eyes. "Why would you wish to fall in with me? What deviousness do you seek to develop?"

"Deviousness? Is it devious to seek my own future instead of the one King Stephen plans for me?"

"Stephen? What has he to do with any of this?"

If the man truly did not know, then he was every bit the dolt Henry had described. "Thornson may be loyal to King David and Empress Matilda, but the keep sits on King Stephen's lands. It is a fine line we have always walked."

He released her and twisted the ends of his short beard. "That is why Faucon is here, to keep control of Thornson for King Stephen."

Marguerite mentally reminded herself to tread carefully. She meant only to gain her freedom from this man, not cause a war. She shrugged, kept her tone light and said, "So he thinks. Since he is not the man King Stephen has chosen for me to marry, we pay little attention to him."

"King Stephen thinks to select the next lord for Thornson?"

"Yes. I wish not to marry one of the enemy." She pasted her fake smile back on her mouth. "So you see, I, too, can benefit from falling in with you."

Bainbridge returned her smile. And this time his expression of glee lit up his eyes. He held out his hand. "My Lady Thornson, if you can find it in your heart to forgive me, I would like very much to combine our plans for our mutual benefit."

She prayed he would not notice her trembling, and placed her hand in his. "My Lord Bainbridge, I would be more than happy to work together on this matter."

He led her toward his camp. She only half paid attention to his idle chitchat. Her mind was far too occupied with plans of escape for her and Marcus.

Chapter Seven

Darius sat on the edge of the bed in his chamber and stared blindly at the missive he gripped tightly in his hands.

How could she do this to him? How could she do this to herself—to them? If he did not know Marguerite better than she apparently knew herself, or if he could not read the meaning she'd tried hard to hide between her words, he would be livid.

Another man, one who knew her not as well, would be intent on destroying her keep, stone by stone, out of rage. But he was not another man.

No. Instead, he was a simple fool who would go to his grave still loving this woman. A woman who so feared returning his love that she would rather run away than take a chance.

So, instead of raging, he sat alone in his darkening chamber, listening to the sound of his heart shattering once again.

He wished it were possible for him to reach inside his body and pull his beating heart from his chest. He wanted to study it carefully, to discover if it would crack like a fragile egg dropped on the hard ground. Or perhaps the pulsing mass would burst like a ripe plum squeezed in one's fist.

All he knew for a certainty is that it felt as if it were cracking and bursting.

His brothers Rhys and Gareth had often accused him of thinking too much. He'd scoffed, but perhaps they were right.

The door to his chamber unceremoniously flew open. Osbert rushed in breathless and flushed. "My lord, it is Lady Marguerite—she seeks to run away."

Darius waved the crinkled parchment he held. "I know."

Osbert leaned against the door frame, one hand on his chest while he gasped for air. "I very nearly killed myself to bring you this news and you already know?" He scratched the end of his nose. "And yet here you sit doing nothing?"

Darius rose and tossed the note on the bed. "Exactly what do you think I should do?"

"Go after her?"

After readjusting his sword belt and taking his gloves and helmet from the top of a chest, Darius put them on while reassuring his man. "That is the first activity I will accomplish."

Osbert grunted, then stepped farther into the chamber. His eyes held surprise when he caught sight of the damage littering the floor of the room. "An odd summer storm sweep through here recently?"

With little more than a glance at the broken chest, and shattered goblets and plates strewn about, Darius shrugged. "Aye. Thankfully it was less intense and of a shorter duration than the one which swept through Lady Marguerite's chamber."

He'd left her bedchamber in an utter shambles. At the time he hadn't been certain what he was looking to discover. He'd just wanted information, some clue of what she'd been planning, or of the happenings here at Thornson.

He'd found nothing, only some tossed-away scribbles addressed to him. Once he'd read her brief attempts at explaining herself, he tore her chamber apart looking for more writings.

And when he found none there, he knew without a doubt where he'd find the finished message.

He had raced to his chamber and, once there, literally torn the hinged lid off his wooden storage trunk and pulled his standard from the bottom. Wrapped in the Faucon banner she'd made for him long ago, he found her garbled explanation.

If he knew Marguerite, and he was certain that he did, she would assume his first reaction would be one of anger. Although his anger was directed only toward her method and not her reasoning, he would do his best to fulfill her assumptions.

But first, he had to find her and bring her safely back to Thornson. He swore that if any harm befell her or Marcus, she would come to greatly regret the rashness of this day's actions.

He walked toward the door. Osbert stepped in front of him, took one look at his face and swore. "Do not let her do this to you again. Darius, my lord, it is not worth the renewed torment."

"You are wrong. She is worth everything to me, and well you know that. I am bringing her and our son back here only long enough to fulfill my duties to King Stephen and then I am taking them home."

"And if she will not go? What will you do then? Force her? That is not the way to a woman's heart."

Darius lifted one brow and looked down at his man. "Oh, she will go. Trust me, she will follow her son wherever he is sent."

Osbert blinked but moved out of the way. "As you wish."

The two men headed down the corridor toward the stairwell at the end of this hallway. The door to Marguerite's chamber stood open and the sound of a muffled voice drifted out of the door. Darius stepped inside the room and surveyed the damage he'd created.

Bertha stopped her task of cleaning up the mess and stared at him. "My lord? The lady is not here. Is there something I can do for you?"

"I know she has taken it into her head to run away." He paused, waiting for Bertha's reaction. She didn't disappoint him. Her face turned a dull red and she could not hold his gaze.

"Gather her personal effects and deliver them to my chamber. I will bring her back to Thornson, Bertha— as my wife. From this moment forward, if you do anything to assist her in leaving this keep, or in committing any type of treason against me or King Stephen, you will answer to me and me alone."

The flush drained from the maid's face, leaving behind a mask of sickly white. She swayed slightly on her feet.

"Am I understood?"

She remained silent, but nodded.

"Good. After you put her things in my chamber. I am

certain your sister could use your company in her time of need and I require some days alone with Marguerite."

Bertha dipped her head. "Thank you, my lord—" Her voice broke and she looked up at him with teardrops on her cheeks.

He crossed the room and took her hand. "Fear not. You will return after the baby is born. We will have need of you. I will not harm your lady, but I cannot permit Thornson to carry on as it has. It will be up to her to right the open acts of treason in this keep."

Certain she understood, he wished her and her sister well and took his leave. He brushed by Osbert, descended the stairs and headed out into the bailey.

Darius paused long enough to shout, "Faucon, to me!"

Once his men began running to answer his call, he crossed to the stables to meet his gathering force and lead them on what he hoped would not be a fruitless chase after a woman frightened by nothing more fearful than the thought of falling in love.

Marguerite rose from her seat on a log by the fire, leaned against a tree and picked at the dark bark with her fingernail. It was all she could do not to spit out a string of unending curses.

She and Bainbridge had still not come to any solid agreement. They had hiked to this small clearing deeper in the forest, then talked almost all afternoon without finding any common ground. She stared at the smoke curling up from the dying fire before glancing at the thick trees surrounding the clearing. Of course, it did not help that she really was not trying to find any common ground.

She absolutely refused to be married to him before they arrived at King David's court. He absolutely refused to go to court without the benefit of marriage between them.

A hand touched her shoulder. "Lady Marguerite, have you had a chance to think of another way around our disagreement?"

If he did not quit sneaking around in this manner, surprising her, Marguerite swore she would run a sword through his sleeping heart this very night.

Instead of voicing those thoughts, she turned to him and graced him with a half smile and a shrug. "No, not yet. I still do not understand why you insist on having such a secret marriage when I am certain I will be able to make the king see reason."

"And I am not so certain of your abilities to reason with him. He has already told me no once. I do not understand why you think you would be better able to sway him to our side."

"Because, you speak to him only of battle and defense. I would speak to him of the many added benefits the strong bargaining power of our combined holdings would provide for him."

Bainbridge shook his head. "Nay, what cares he for bargaining power? Who would he need to bargain with and for what reason? We are men. Fighting is what we do. King David has many who would willingly go into battle for him."

The absurdity of some men never failed to amaze her. Why did they think of battle first and negotiation only as a last measure? Were the lives of the men under their command and the lives of the villagers truly worth so little to them?

Marguerite swallowed her frustration. "My lord, he holds Northumbria from King Stephen. While the land itself is rich, he has no fortifications of any worth there. Thornson is his closest stronghold to those lands."

"Yes?"

It took every ounce of willpower not to slap him alongside his head. "Thornson is to the southeast. Bainbridge is situated to the northwest. Northumbria lies between us. We could provide a direct land route for supplies, or even men if required, in addition to what already travels by boat."

It was as if someone lit a candle behind his eyes. "I see. Yes, yes, you may be right."

He paced back and forth quickly. When she opened her mouth to say something, he waved her off. Finally, he stopped pacing and paused before her. "Stay right here. I will return anon. I find that I need a few moments alone to think on the merits of this plan of yours. It may work, but I am not yet certain."

She leaned back against the tree. "Take all the time you require. I will remain here."

Marguerite watched him leave without another word. She closed her eyes and rubbed her throbbing temples. How could he be so stupid and still live? It did not require someone well versed in the intricacies of war to realize that having one's borders protected by allies would be worth much.

It was no wonder Henry despised Bainbridge. The man was little more than an imbecile. A combination that suited any man for little more than greed and treachery.

Marguerite pursed her lips and looked about. Where were they keeping Marcus? She'd not seen her son once since entering this clearing.

Had she not been convinced that he was in no danger from Bainbridge, she would have been frantic by now. But the man was right: King David would have his head if anything happened to Thornson's heir while under his protection.

She patted her hair into place as best she could, smoothed the skirt of her gown and proceeded along a half-cleared trail. One way or another, she'd discover Marcus's whereabouts, even if she had to stand in the middle of the forest and scream like a crazed woman.

She found Sir Everett sitting on a log at the end of the trail. In the middle of the open area a tent had been pitched. Her son was most likely in there. Without pausing she walked past Everett toward the flap of the tent.

He bolted from his seat and before she could enter the abode, he grasped her wrist. A hold he quickly released when she turned an icy glare on him. "I am sorry, my lady, but you cannot go inside there."

She stepped back. "I am only looking for my son. Is he in there?"

"No." Everett shook his head—too quickly to suit her. "No, he is not."

"Then pray tell, where is he?"

"He…he is…" Everett paused, his faced scrunched into a mask of intense concentration. "He is playing with the other children."

"What other children?"

"From the village. They were playing in the woods and I thought it would be permissible for Marcus to join them."

Outside of herself, Marguerite did not know of a worse liar than Everett. "You lie. There were no children this far away from the village."

He cringed under her accusation and looked away. She took the opportunity to whip open the flap of the tent and look inside.

"Momma!" Marcus nearly flew into her arms.

She glared at Everett. "Would you care to explain yourself? Or would you rather find yourself without employ?"

"No, my lady, I did only what Lord Bainbridge asked of me. I would never take it upon myself to harm Master Marcus."

This much she knew was true. No one from Thornson would seek to bring harm to her son. Still, that did not excuse Everett for lying.

"We will discuss this later. From now on, I will keep Marcus by my side. That way I need not worry about his safety or whereabouts."

"My dear, I am afraid it will not be possible or even seemly to keep the child at your side."

Bainbridge stepped across the clearing. He motioned to Everett. "Take the boy away from here and do not return until I bid you to do so."

Everett glanced back and forth from Marguerite to Bainbridge. He finally fixed his attention on Bainbridge. "Where do I take the boy?"

"Must I think of everything? Is there no nearby hunter's cottage? Crofter's hut?"

Unwilling to have her son out in the forest without protection, or in a place she did not know about, Marguerite suggested, "Take him to the hut by the inlet. We will pass there on our way north."

Everett nodded. "Yes, my lady." He plucked Marcus from her side before the boy could react, and left the camp.

Bainbridge grabbed her arm. "I told you to stay put until I made up my mind."

"I only came to find my son. What harm was there in that?"

"If you cannot follow my orders, how am I to trust you will do as you say?"

"I did not realize it was an order. I thought it just a simple suggestion."

His hold tightened. "Anytime I tell you to do something, you will consider it an order."

The hairs on the back of Marguerite's neck rose at the tone of his voice. She plucked at his fingers, seeking to release herself from his bruising hold. "You are hurting me."

He laughed. "Good. I am glad I finally have your full attention. I have made up my mind. We will marry this very evening. By morning you will be left with no doubts as to who is the absolute master in this venture."

"You would not be so vile."

"No? You think not?" He pulled her closer so they were nearly nose to nose, the stench of his breath nearly choking her. "You need think again, Lady Bainbridge. The time for seeking a way to convince me to change my plans is at an end."

"Do not call me that. I am not Lady Bainbridge and no matter what plans you seek to enact, nothing you do will ever convince me to marry you."

The hissing sound of a sword being pulled from a wooden scabbard took both of them by surprise.

"Good Lord, Marguerite, exactly how many men do you plan to take as husband before you leave this earthly world?"

Chapter Eight

Never, in all of her years, had she been so glad to hear Darius's calmly spoken sarcasm. It was all she could do not to break down and weep with relief.

Bainbridge released her so quickly that she stumbled and fell to her knees on the hard ground. Immediately, Darius moved his horse between her and Bainbridge.

"Are you unhurt?"

"Yes. I am whole."

Darius reached down to her. Without looking up, she raised her trembling hand and placed it in his. He closed his fingers securely around hers while she scrambled to her feet.

She knew without even looking that anger filled him from head to toe. She'd heard it in his voice, behind the comment about taking numerous husbands.

"Look at me."

When she failed to respond to his softly spoken order, he gripped her hand a little tighter. She lifted her face and met his rage-filled stare.

Aye, he was angry. His face appeared to be carved

from stone. The sharp line of his jaw was more defined, more rigid than she'd ever seen it. His frown was so fierce that his eyebrows met like wings above his eyes. For a moment, Marguerite's eyes played a trick on her, making him look like the bird of prey he was named after.

But it wasn't his anger that worried her. It was his silence.

She wished he would rant, rage or even shout. Do anything except silently hold her stare hostage. Finally, when she thought she could stand no more of his wordless anger, he shifted his gaze to Bainbridge.

Without taking his attention from the other man, Darius spoke to her. "Lord Bainbridge and I have matters to discuss. Marcus is with Osbert at the trailhead. He will escort both of you back to Thornson. You will stay there until I return. Do you understand me?"

The urge to rail against his high-handed order died quickly. "Yes, I understand."

There was a time to fight and a time to retreat. And knowing full well the difference between the two options and having a good idea of each outcome, Marguerite released Darius's hand.

She turned toward the trail and gasped at the sight of Faucon's men surrounding the clearing. They opened a path, permitting her to exit the ring. Certain she need not fear for Darius's safety, she proceeded down the trail.

Darius waited until Marguerite was safely away before focusing his attention on Bainbridge. He wanted nothing more than to run his sword through the man's worthless hide.

However, all of the information he'd gathered thus

far, pointed to Bainbridge as the smugglers' leader. If he killed the man now, without proof, Darius would have nothing solid to hand over to King Stephen.

So, to his bitter regret, he'd have to let the man live— for now. In the meantime, Darius would do all he could to urge Bainbridge toward more acts of treason. What better way to assure that happened than to demand he cease? A loyal servant to King Stephen would follow the order—Darius was certain Bainbridge would not prove loyal.

He pointed his sword toward Bainbridge's chest. "Would you care to explain what you were doing with Lady Thornson?"

Bainbridge looked at the men encircling his camp before replying, "I was doing as she asked, that is all."

"And that would be what?"

"She wished an escort north, to King David,"

That piece of information surprised him only a little. He'd expected her to run away—but to King David? Why not to her father?

Darius leaned forward in his saddle. "Where does marriage fit into that task?"

Bainbridge backed away, his hands twitched nervously at his sides. "As a favor to Lord Thornson's memory, I thought only to keep his widow safe."

Daruis's men snickered at the lame response. He raised a hand, silently ordering quiet. "Safe? It seemed to me that you were prepared to do great harm to the lady. That is your idea of keeping her safe?"

"She can be a bit headstrong and sometimes needs a man's…strength to convince her of what is right."

Headstrong? Marguerite? Darius nearly choked on his own snicker. "And you think you are the man to do the convincing?" Before Bainbridge could answer, Darius ordered, "Leave Thornson's lands."

Bainbridge drew his shoulders back and gripped the sword hanging at his side. "Who are you to tell me this?"

Darius smiled, then urged his horse forward a step. Two of his men positioned themselves directly behind Bainbridge, effectively keeping the man in place. Darius lifted his sword and pressed the point against Bainbridge's throat. "I am Darius of Faucon, here on King Stephen's orders to hold and rule over Thornson."

He twisted the sword enough to draw blood, then drew it back slightly. "If I see you again, I will do more than just prick your flesh. Do you understand me?"

Bainbridge only nodded, but the look of rage on his face before he turned to leave promised that they would meet again.

An occurrence Darius would look forward to with pleasure.

As Darius had stated, Marcus and Osbert awaited her at the head of the forest path. Faucon's captain said nothing when she joined them. He only handed her the reins to her horse, waited for her to mount the animal and then led the way back to the keep.

To her greatest relief, Marcus appeared unhurt. Perched atop Osbert's legs, the boy was as happy as a puppy at play. He held the reins to Osbert's horse and chattered the entire way back toward Thornson.

Marguerite could not hold back her smile at the knowledge that he was unhurt and back to his usual self. Without being told, she was well aware that Darius's captain had something to do with the boy's demeanor. "Sir Osbert, do you have children?"

Her attempt at making conversation was met only by a brief cold stare shot at her from over his shoulder. Undaunted, she tried again. "You should have a house full—you seem to be good with them."

"Do you not have enough to worry about at the moment? You need not concern yourself with my life. You need consider your own, very carefully."

He kept his voice light, but she took the warning to heart. "Perhaps you are right. But I would think that as lady of this keep, I would not have to worry overly much."

Osbert snorted and shook his head. "You were not there when he discovered your message."

Marguerite's heart sank. She'd hoped that Darius had not found her writings. She was truly surprised that he had found her message so quickly. She had thought she'd hidden it well. "Is that why he came? To stop me from leaving?"

"No. He came because I had followed you and discovered that you planned to take this boy away. He was in the middle of reading your words when I went to him with the information I had found."

Marcus leaned over and peered back at her. "Momma, are we still going to see the king?"

She cringed at his question, but answered, "No, sweeting, not today. Maybe some other time."

Seemingly satisfied with her answer, he went back to the task of guiding the horse.

"Was he very angry?" Worry kept her voice to little more than a whisper.

"Angry? You of all people should have known what your words would do to him."

It had been years since she'd truly known Darius. If he was not outraged, then what?

"Lady Marguerite, he will not allow what you plan."

She frowned at Osbert's statement. "I have many plans. Which one do you speak of now?"

"The boy will not go north."

She bristled at the surety in Osbert's tone. "It is not his decision to make."

"You are right. You made the decision for him by forcing his hand."

Something in his words, in the way he said them, gave her pause. "What do you mean?"

"He does not trust you to do what is right."

"And exactly what is that?"

"Not raising the boy as a traitor to his king."

She gritted her teeth and clenched the reins. "I repeat, it is not his decision."

Osbert slowed his horse and waited for her to come alongside. When they were eye to eye, he looked at her, smiled and said, "The decision has already been made. You would be advised to do as you are told in the next few days. Otherwise, Marcus will go to visit his uncles in the south."

"What?" Her voice rose. Marcus jumped, startled by her shout. She took a deep breath and reached across the space between them. "Give me my son this instant."

Osbert laughed and spurred his horse, leaving Marguerite alone at the sparser line of trees between the dense forest and the open field.

She quickly cleared her head and raced after them, only slowing when she realized that Osbert would never have spoken to her in such a manner if he'd planned anything underhanded. In his rough way, he only sought to give her warning of what might happen.

At the moment, though, she truly had no time to worry about the near future. She needed to gather her mental defenses for Darius's return later this day.

No sooner had the thought formed in her mind than she heard the pounding of hooves from behind her. She turned around to see who approached at such a furious pace.

Darius broke free from the forest and Marguerite closed her eyes in a quick prayer. Dear Lord he looked like a rider come from Hades to claim his next victim.

Without slowing, he rode straight toward her, ripping the reins from her hands as he passed. Oh, aye, he claimed his next victim, all right—unfortunately she was that luckless person.

Jolted by the pace he set, she grabbed her horse's mane to keep from falling off the beast.

"Darius, stop this." To her utter amazement, he reined in his horse and came to a dead stop in the middle of the field.

He turned his horse around so they could look at each other. Never having been on the receiving end of such a cold, hard stare, she suddenly wished she'd kept her mouth shut.

He tore his helmet from his head, throwing it, his battle gloves and his sword to the ground with a force that made her wince.

Not wanting to see the full extent of the anger on his face, she closed her eyes tightly.

For more heartbeats than she could count, he said nothing. The only sound that broke the silence between them was that of his steady, even breathing and the roar of her own heart pounding in her ears.

When she could stand no more of his deathly quiet, she opened her eyes and asked, "You saw to Bainbridge without difficulty?"

He only nodded.

Again, the silence dragged on. Finally, in desperation to end this well of nothingness, she shouted, "What did you expect me to do?"

He said nothing, simply leaned back in his saddle, crossed his arms against his chest and stared at her.

"You left me with no choice."

Still no response was forthcoming.

"I must protect my son. I cannot marry you."

She wanted to scream at his silence. "Dear Lord, Faucon, can you not understand?" She answered her own question. No, he did not. How could he possibly understand what she herself didn't?

She thought she had explained all to him in her letter. Obviously not—otherwise he would not be seated on his horse glaring daggers at her.

Frantically, Marguerite searched for the right words that would make him see reason. Unable to find any she had not already used, she cried, "Darius, leave Thornson. Go away from here and let me live in peace."

The only sign that he'd heard a single thing she'd said was the slight upturn of one corner of his mouth.

"Damn you, say something. Anything. Good Lord above, Faucon, I know you are angry."

He slid off his animal and slapped its rump, sending it toward Thornson. "You know nothing."

Before she could react, he pulled her off her horse and sent that beast on its way, too.

"Anything?" He jerked her hard against his chest.

The metal links of his armor dug into her flesh through the fine linen of her gown.

Darius grasped the back of her head and brought his mouth down on hers. She struggled against his hold, to no avail.

To her dismay, tears of anger, frustration and embarrassment gathered and fell from her eyes.

He broke his harsh kiss and placed his lips against her forehead. "Cry all you wish, Marguerite. It will change nothing. You will marry me. This very day. I care not if you keep Henry Thornson in your heart forever. I care not if loving me fills you with a mistaken sense of guilt."

Without a doubt he had found her missive. She shook her head. "I cannot. Do not make me do this."

He held her head between his hands, forcing her to look up at him. Marguerite blinked through the tears blinding her and gasped at the pain etched on his face.

No anger glittered in his eyes, only hurt, and she could not bear knowing it existed because of her.

"Yes, Marguerite, you can do this and you will." He brushed the tears from her face with the pad of his thumb. "I will touch not only the hidden places in your heart that you hold sacred for Henry, but the places that used to be mine."

She tried to look away, but he would not let her. "Do you understand me? I care not that you love him still. He is no threat to me. He is dead."

She flinched. The truth in his harsh words pierced her like an arrow. "How can you be so cruel?"

Darius ignored her question and continued as if she'd not spoken. "*I* am here. I will be the one who keeps you safe from all harm. I will be your protection from any danger. And it will be my arms that hold you when you are cold or lonely."

Fresh tears fell anew. She shuddered under the weight of his words. "Why? After all I have done to you, why would you do this for me?"

"Because you are my heart. It was not childish folly that created my feelings for you. I have loved you since the moment I saw you. I knew then that you were my future. And when I read the unholy missive you left for me today, I knew that you resisted me out of misplaced fear."

He slid his arms around her, cradling her head against his chest. "Once, long ago, you knew that the chance for love was nothing to fear. You were willing to lay down all for that chance. I cannot—I *will* not—allow you to let that slip through our hands again."

She wished not to anger him, nor to cause him any further pain, but she had to ask. "And what if I cannot love you again?"

His chest shook lightly beneath her cheek. "Fear not, someday you will." He kissed the top of her head. "But for now, do you think you can at the very least like me a little?"

Marguerite shrugged. "Of course."

He caressed her back, ran one hand the length of her side, before lowering his lips to her neck. His breath against the sensitive flesh was hot, causing the beginnings of desire to stir in her.

"Do you think bedding me would be entirely unpleasant?"

She smiled and pressed closer to him. "No."

"Well then, that is where we shall start." He nipped

at her ear. "There is one thing you could do for me now, though."

"What is that?"

"Promise you will never leave me another message to read."

Marguerite's face burned. "I promise, I will not."

"Good." He leaned away and looked down at her. "My, what a nice shade of red."

She felt her cheeks grow even hotter. "I feel foolish enough. There is no need to make it worse."

"Aye, there is. Embarrassment will not kill you, but maybe the memory of it will make you stop and think before doing anything so foolish again. Bring me your fears and your anger. I can deal with them. We can deal with them together. Do not hide from me, Marguerite. Do not seek to run away. There is nothing we cannot discuss. Nothing. We may not agree, but that does not mean we cannot speak of it."

"Or shout about it?"

"So be it. So what if we do shout? Will the world come to an end?"

"Do not be silly. No, it will not."

"Will you cease loving Marcus the moment he disagrees with you on one thing or another?"

"No. Of course not."

"It is the same for me. I will never cease loving you simply because we cannot agree."

She knew this theory would be put to the test often, and most likely soon, but she nodded in agreement.

"Good, because we had a prior arrangement and your answer is due now."

Marguerite sighed. "It is not wise, but yes, I will marry you…again."

Darius lifted one arm over her head. Before she could ask what he was doing she heard the thunder of many horses approaching from the keep.

She pushed away from him and looked toward Thornson. Her mouth fell open at the sight. It appeared that every man, woman and child rode toward them. When she was able to find her voice, she asked, "What is this?"

"This, my dear, is your wedding."

"You had it all planned. How could you be so certain that I would say yes?"

He draped an arm across her shoulders and drew her against his side. He smiled at the approaching riders and said, "Even when you are not certain yourself, Marguerite, I hear the words your heart whispers to mine."

Chapter Nine

Marguerite stretched the kinks from her body before untying the laces of her gown. It was the end of the longest and strangest day of her life.

And now that it was nearly over, she found herself with a new name and a future she had never dreamed of having.

On a normal evening, Bertha would bustle around, nattering on about the day's events before retiring to her own bed in their shared chamber.

However, there was nothing normal about this night. Her maid was not present and they would not be sharing a chamber again anytime soon. Her clothing and personal items had already been moved into Darius's chamber—their chamber.

Marguerite was grateful for the move. She did not think she could bear sharing with Darius the bed she and Henry had occupied.

She had left the merrymaking below, seeking some time alone. Time to prepare herself for the night ahead. Everyone seemed to be happy for her; none had cried foul about her wedding Darius. Instead they had all drunk heartily to the union.

He would soon join her. But right now, she welcomed the quiet. Marguerite rose and snuffed out the single candle. The glowing charcoal in the brazier provided enough light. She undressed in the near darkness, the brazier helped chase away some of the chamber's chilliness.

Once naked, she shrugged into a fur-lined robe as she crossed to the narrow window opening, wincing as she stepped barefoot on the crushed herbs scattered about the floor. She peered out the window, looking up at the stars twinkling against the dark night sky.

They reminded her that once, long ago, she had made useless wishes upon those stars. Wishes destined to remain unfulfilled.

Even though those dreams had been crushed by her father's hand, Henry Thornson had patiently taught her to believe once again in wishes and dreams.

Her breath caught in her throat. Oh, how she missed him. Even tonight she could not set his memory aside. There'd been a time in the beginning when he'd frightened her nearly beyond bearing. But with his tender care, she'd come to realize that her burly, loud husband was as frightening and dangerous as one of his newborn hunting pups.

He'd encouraged her to speak her mind. Marguerite smiled at the memory: she could no longer remember what had started the row, but she'd never forget his vow to ignore her until she learned to say her piece.

Ignore her he did. For days on end. Until she was so livid and beside herself that she tracked him down at the practice fields and tore into him like a crazed woman.

The twit had laughed at her before hauling her over his shoulder and tromping across the bailey, through the hall, up the steps to their chamber.

By the time he had dropped her on their bed, they were both laughing and breathless. They didn't leave their chamber for two full days.

Marguerite drew in a shaking breath and wiped at the tears gathering in her eyes. "Oh, Henry, how could you leave me like this?"

It was unfair to blame him, but she did. It wasn't as if he'd had a choice. There'd been a skirmish at the border and Henry had taken an arrow from one of King Stephen's men.

He died the next day, in her arms.

"Cease." She clenched and unclenched her hands. Thoughts of years gone by gained her nothing but torment. A useless exercise when trying to deal with the uncertainty of the future.

Marguerite turned away from the window, away from her haunting thoughts. She needed to find a way to banish Henry from her mind. But right now, she was too tired to think. She slipped out of her robe and climbed into the bed to await Darius.

From his semi-hidden seat in the far corner of the hall, Darius stared across the nearly dark room toward the stairs.

By now she should be abed. After all that had occurred this day, he did not doubt that she had already fallen asleep.

What images filled her dreams? When she closed her eyes at night did the past haunt her sleep?

"My lord?"

Darius raised his half-empty goblet. "Osbert, I am glad you could find the time to rejoin me." He kicked a small stool, sending it skidding toward his captain. "Take a seat, have another drink."

"My lord, I..." Osbert fidgeted, looking everywhere except at Darius. "I tried to return to you earlier, sir."

"Zounds, I am surrounded by the worst liars." Darius pointed at the stool and waited until Osbert sat down before saying, "You came back as soon as you thought I'd consumed enough wine to put me to sleep."

The captain stared at his feet. "Well, yes." He sighed heavily before meeting Darius's eyes. "I thought perhaps it would be best for all concerned."

Darius leaned forward to retrieve the jug of wine from the floor. He poured some into another goblet that he handed to Osbert. "I have some very bad news for you, friend."

Osbert took a full drink of the beverage, sputtered, then made a face as Darius laughed out loud. "You do not like your drink?"

"It tastes as weak as water."

"That makes perfect sense, since it is water. I thought remaining in full control of my senses would be best for all concerned."

"After all these years, would it not have been better, for all concerned, to have left things as they were?"

"No." Darius shook his head. "It is my wedding night—again. Strange to think that the images in my mind cause me to fear this night."

Osbert shook his head. "Her father will not be dragging you from your bed."

"Thank the Lord for that much."

Osbert set his goblet down. "I have a thirst for something with a little more life."

The captain spied another pitcher and went to retrieve it. He sniffed the contents and smiled. "This is more to my taste." After returning and taking a long drink, he asked, "What good do you think will come of remembering things from years gone by? What is done is done. Let it go."

"I have tried."

"If I remember correctly, this union is what you wanted." Osbert poured Darius a goblet of stronger wine and handed it to him. "A toast to your marriage, my lord. Drink up and take yourself to bed."

Darius laughed. "Quit stalling? Be a man and all that?"

"Aye. You will feel better for it on the morrow."

After tossing down the contents of his goblet, Darius grimaced as he rose. "That stuff will kill you if you are not careful. I will leave you to your poison."

He headed up the stairs toward his chamber, all the while wondering what he should say to make this easier for her. Suddenly the thought of bedding her in her first husband's keep seemed wrong.

He paused outside the chamber door and swiped a hand down his face. She was his wife. In truth, she had been his wife before she was Thornson's.

He had gone to their first marriage bed with the same level of anticipation. Over six years later and again his palms sweated, his heart jumped around as if in preparation for battle, his legs even shook.

Under any other circumstances he'd recognize these symptoms as signs of cowardice or fear of the unknown. Tonight they were nothing more than an overactive memory dwelling on what had happened in their last marriage bed. Her father and his men were not here. A fact that did little to quell his nervousness.

He mentally shook himself. He was acting like an old doddering woman, frightened of his own shadow.

Darius opened the door and stepped inside. Light from the brazier cast a pale glow across the room. He glanced at the bed. "Marguerite?"

When she did not answer, he exhaled in relief and crossed to stand in front of the narrow window opening. A million or more stars dotted the night sky. He could not resist the urge to make a childish wish upon one of them.

"What do you wish for, Darius?"

He turned toward her. "I thought you slept."

"I did, for a time." She sat up, keeping a firm grasp on the covers, and rested her back against the mound of pillows behind her. "What do you wish for?"

Darius crossed the room and sat on the edge of the bed. He brushed a wayward strand of hair from her face before caressing her cheek. "I wished to have the right words, to do all the right things to make this night easier for you."

Marguerite closed her eyes and rubbed her cheek against the palm of his hand. "I think you just did."

Spoken on a breathless sigh, her words invited him to come closer—an invitation he could not have ignored even if he had wanted to.

He leaned forward and gave her a kiss. A gentle kiss meant not to frighten her.

Marguerite whispered against his lips, "I am not afraid." She slid one hand through his hair. "I will not break, Darius."

He found her boldness welcome and chuckled before pulling her into his arms and onto his lap. "I did not think you would."

He shifted into the position she had just occupied, his back against the pillows, legs outstretched with her straddling his thighs, the covers left behind in the move.

Marguerite blinked. "Oh, my."

Realizing she was naked, Darius groaned, then urged her mouth to his. Swept away by the intensity of his kiss, she leaned against him.

He held her closer, one hand stroking the tension from her back, the other tangled in the hair at the nape of her neck. The rough wool of his tunic scratched the delicate flesh of her breasts.

But his touch was such pure heaven, warming her with a teasing promise of desires fulfilled, that she cared not about the prickly fabric against her skin.

Need and desire long dormant burst forth. Marguerite rose on her knees, entwining her arms about his neck.

She smelled of lavender and tasted of cinnamon, cloves and wine, a combination more intoxicating to his senses than the drink he'd sought to avoid.

He trailed his fingertips down her spine, feeling her soft flesh shiver beneath his touch. The rounded swell of her hips gave way to the tightly clenched muscles of her thighs.

She shivered again when he stroked up the inward flare of her waist, lingering to cup the weight of her breast in his hand.

While the smoothness of her skin was familiar, the muscles beneath were softer than he remembered. Not a distasteful change—the fullness of her breast, the curve of her hips and slight roundness of her stomach made her look and feel more of a woman than the young girl in his memory.

But the girl he remembered had not given birth to his child. Marguerite had grown into a lovely woman—his only regret was not being permitted to witness the growth from girl to women.

Darius swallowed her impatient moan against his lips, breaking their mind-numbing kiss, then whispered, "We have the rest of our lives—there is no rush."

She found his neck with her teeth, nipping the length, her breath coming to rest hot against his ear. "There may be no rush for you, my lord, but I am afire with the wanting."

He laughed. "I would be happy to oblige you, my love, but it seems I am still fully clothed."

She tore at his tunic, pulling the hem from beneath him and lifting it along with his shirt over his head. "A matter easily remedied."

She tossed the garments to the floor and fumbled with the ties to his braies. Marguerite cursed as her fumbling fingers deftly mangled the ties into a knot.

Darius covered her hands with his own. He nearly choked on the laughter he fought to swallow. "Wait, let me help."

His fingers brushed the curls at the juncture of her legs and she froze on a gasp. He lifted his gaze and stared into her shimmering eyes.

A smile twitched at the corners of his mouth and he freed his hands to slide between damp curls and caress the quivering hotness beneath.

Marguerite closed her eyes, her face a play somewhere between agony and ecstasy.

It was the ecstasy he wished to see, and the rushing need of her body to claim it as he urged her into the swirling madness of desire.

He'd had no need to witness her longing before—he was young and his own need for release had been his main concern. Now, he wanted more than release. He wanted to watch passion deepen the blue of her eyes, to hear her ragged gasps, to feel her body tremble as she found fulfillment.

"Darius." She cried his name hoarsely, her slick sheath tightening around his teasing fingers, her fingernails digging into his shoulders.

He lowered his head and laved an already rigid nipple with his tongue, never ceasing the movements of his hand until she shuddered limp against him on another whispered cry.

Her heart pounded against his chest, his own an uneven rhythm straining to keep tempo with hers.

Marguerite released her breath, gave a long sigh and pushed herself upright. She narrowed her eyes and returned his smile. Raking her nails lightly down his chest, she laughed softly as he shivered beneath her touch.

This time, with more care, she unscrambled the knot securing his braies and slid them impatiently off his hips.

When Darius moved to tug them off, she pushed him back against the pillows. And in one fluid move she settled herself onto his hot, hard flesh.

He sucked in a deep breath as she flexed and relaxed her thighs, sliding up, then back down the length of him.

She leaned forward and suckled his flat nipples into small peaks. Darius grasped her thighs, guiding her movements faster as he thrust up to meet her.

Marguerite rocked against him, seeking her own release, and he obliged with the pad of his thumb.

She tipped her head back, and when she cried out his name again, his own rasping voice mingled with hers.

Chapter Ten

Marguerite awoke with a start. Disoriented by the unfamiliar surroundings in the pale light of dawn, it took a few moments to realize the arm holding her close and the warmth caressing her back were more solid than a dream.

The warm, steady breath gently lifting her hair from the back of her neck came from no apparition of the night. She held her breath, not wishing to awaken Darius this early in the morn.

More importantly, she had no wish to awaken him before she cleared the fog clouding her thoughts.

What had she done?

As the events of the previous day and night unfolded in her mind, Marguerite swallowed her groan of dismay. After vowing not to, she'd married him. Worse than simply marrying him, she had gone to his bed willingly.

What madness had bedeviled her, causing her to act with such haste?

A few more moments of quiet, a few more slowly

paced heartbeats and then perhaps she'd be ready to face the day. Perhaps...

As wonderful as it had been to be held and loved by a man last night, shame took seed in the shadowed corners of her soul.

It grew rapidly, rushing from the pit of her stomach up to her throat until she nearly choked on the feelings of guilt and betrayal. Henry had been dead only a few months. What sort of woman was she to go from one man's bed to another's with such ease?

"You are awake."

Her precious moments of quiet and calm lost, she could only nod and clasp his arm tighter about her.

Maybe if she hung on hard enough, or long enough, she could beat back the overwhelming remorse.

Darius rose up on one elbow and kissed her temple. "Did you sleep well?"

"Yes." Could he tell how she felt at this moment? Marguerite prayed he could not. If she had to continually worry that he truly could read her mind, she'd go utterly mad.

There were too many things she did not want him to know. At least, not until she had time to change matters at Thornson.

Darius pulled his arm free and brushed her hair from her face. "Where are you?"

She closed her eyes and swallowed hard before turning over onto her back and smiling at his disheveled hair and sleep-heavy eyes. "I am right here."

"You seemed to be far away. What plagues you this morn?"

"Plagues me?" Marguerite shrugged. "Nothing of any great importance."

"I doubt that. What?"

"I know Henry is dead." She looked across the room toward the recessed window opening, seeking words to explain the thoughts and feelings running rampant over logic. Sunlight had begun to stream into the chamber, making her concerns appear even more foolish. "Yet, I feel as if I have somehow betrayed him and all at Thornson."

Darius ran a fingertip down the length of her nose. "Do you suppose that perhaps this is something that will pass with time?"

"I can hope that is so," Marguerite sighed, uncertain that she would ever be able to forget her life with Henry. "But I do not see how."

Darius touched her cheek and turned her face to his. "Last night was needful to seal our vows, you know this. Otherwise, Marguerite, I never would have thought to rush you to my bed."

A blush fired her cheeks. "Oh, yes, *needful* explains my participation. I was, oh, so unwilling, was I not?" Her chest tightened—there it was again—the persistent pricking at her heart.

"Willing or no, if you cannot come into my arms without Henry looking over your shoulder, I would rather wait until he is gone."

Marguerite stared up at him in amazement. "You would do this for me?"

"Of course I would. I find I prefer two people in our bed. It feels slightly crowded with three. Marguerite, I know you will eventually put your memories of Henry to rest. I am content to wait."

"What if I can never release Henry from my mind or my heart?"

"It is not wrong to have cared deeply for the man you shared your life with, Marguerite. I do not ask you to forget him, only to set his memory aside far enough to let me in, too."

Let him in. She would like nothing more than to do just that—to let him be the one filling her mind and heart at all moments of the day and night. But could she? Would that shadowy dream ever come to pass? She stared up at him. "What if this process takes a lifetime?"

He traced a finger across her collarbone. His gentle touch rippled across her flesh. He stroked the valley between her breasts, sending a shiver down through her body. When she sucked in a sharp breath he chuckled softly before saying, "Fear not, it will not take a lifetime. Of that I am certain."

Darius rolled out of bed. "As delightful as it would be to spend the day teasing you, unfortunately there are tasks awaiting us both."

"Tasks? What tasks cannot wait?"

"It is time I get to know Marcus. Since the father he knew is gone, he needs to become familiar with the one he has left."

Marguerite agreed with this logic. "Be gone with you, then."

He leaned over and dropped a kiss on her forehead, before retrieving his clothes from the floor. He padded toward the alcove while pulling them on. "I will await you below stairs—with our son."

Another man might not have been as kind or understanding as Darius. Would he ever fail to amaze her? Marguerite shook her head. It was doubtful. She imagined that even at the end of her earthly days this odd man she had married would still find a new way to surprise her.

Had it not always been thus with Darius? Marguerite slowly drew in a long, deep breath and did something she'd denied herself for years—she let her mind wander back to her younger days. A time before vows and responsibilities weighed so heavily upon her shoulders. A time when escaping her maid's watchful eyes meant an afternoon spent with Darius.

It mattered not how their stolen day began—fishing, climbing trees, or just walking in the fields hand in hand; it always ended at the same place—the hunter's cottage. They'd sit close, sharing whatever food and drink they'd each swiped from the kitchens.

When they were full they'd move closer to each other, holding hands. Sometimes, Darius would steal a kiss or two. His fumbling attempts left her feeling as if she'd imbibed an entire jug of wine alone. Something that hadn't changed over the years.

Marguerite smiled as she remembered the last May Day festival at the village near their families' properties. She and Darius had argued over some comment made by another boy about the flowers in her hair; flowers that Darius had gathered and woven into a chain for her.

He'd been jealous that another had paid the slightest bit of attention to her. While she'd been angry with him for being so lack-witted, she'd been secretly amused, nay, pleased, that someone besides Darius had paid her a compliment.

He'd left in a huff and she'd stayed to enjoy the rare opportunity to laugh, dance and talk with others not from her father's keep. Before she knew it, the day had given way to night and the festivities had grown more bawdy.

It was soon apparent that the others her own age had either gone home, or had stolen away with their lovers, leaving her alone. The boys casting her admiring looks and turning her head with overblown praise were more men than boys.

One, bolder than the others, had declared her his own May Queen, and grasped her hand. She'd had no experience with this type of forwardness before and hadn't known what to say, or to do.

In the end it didn't matter. As the lout had started to tug her toward the edge of the surrounding forest, Darius came to her rescue. He'd pulled his sword, took her free hand and said, "This lady is mine." His tone had been so steely, so cold and determined that the other lad ran away.

It was the first time she'd looked at Darius as a man. He'd returned her to her father's keep without saying a word. And he left her alone for nearly a sennight before she could stand it no longer and tracked him down at their hunter's cottage.

She'd railed at him and he bore it silently until she'd spend herself. Then he'd taken her in his arms and kissed her until she forgot what she was supposed to be angry about.

As memories of the years spent with Darius floated gently across her mind, she was drawn to the clear realization that he would make a good and steadfast husband.

If he did not get himself killed in a battle, or die from a festering wound of some sort, they would grow old together. She mulled around the possibility in her mind and found that it rested easy on her heart.

Had she not known this once before? Why had she not fought her father harder? How many years had been wasted because of her cowardice?

Henry's laugh sounded in her ears. No, in all truth the years had not been wasted. What she faced now was another chance for happiness.

But, if matters at Thornson did not change, she feared that the beckoning happiness could easily be destroyed. While Darius would make a good and trustworthy husband, he could also make a deadly enemy. She swung her legs out of bed and rose.

Things would have to change. She would see to it herself. She was thankful that Darius had already taken care of one problem for her—Bainbridge. Perhaps with him out of the way, getting the smuggling base moved elsewhere would not be as difficult.

Neither King David nor Empress Matilda would be pleased with the decision. The barons already changed alliances with the shifting of the ocean tide, so did it really matter with whom Thornson sided?

Would swearing allegiance to one or the other make any difference in her day-to-day existence? No, she did not see how it would.

The course of her life so far had always been determined by her father or her husband, not by who wore the crown.

While her father and Henry had served Empress Matilda, Darius and his family did not. Like it or not, Henry was dead, and he was not coming back. Thankfully, her father was many leagues away and she had more to consider than just what crown to serve.

Her son's continued safety was of the utmost importance and she'd see to that above all else. Darius had already declared that Marcus, as Henry's son, was the rightful Lord of Thornson.

Without the king's blessing, it was little more than a pretty speech, spoken to appease her concerns. And for the most part it had succeeded.

Once Marcus and Darius had appeared in the courtyard together, Marguerite had heard the whispered comments passed between some of Thornson's men. If any thought to challenge Marcus's parentage, Darius's proclamation had put their thoughts to rest.

For that, she owed him more than the simple honor and loyalty required by her vows. She needed to set things right at Thornson. And to do so in a manner that would not involve Darius. She'd not risk his reputation or his name over something that was not of his doing.

After all he'd done for her, it was the least she could do.

Darius stared out across the practice field. A growing sense of satisfaction filled him. After many long, empty years, the wife he had never forgotten was finally his again. And he'd gained a son that made him proud. The more he grew to know Marcus, the more his heart swelled with joy.

To ensure they remained married and his family remained intact, he had sent a missive to Faucon explaining as much as he could. King Stephen could view Darius's actions in marrying Thornson's widow without permission as a blatant act of rebellion bordering on treason.

If that proved to be the case, Darius wanted Rhys's assistance in convincing the king of the benefits of this union.

He probably worried for naught. The king was so busy gathering his barons for war against Empress Matilda that in all likelihood little thought would be spared for the happenings at Thornson.

Which would be well and good as far as he was concerned. At the moment, Marguerite and Marcus's well-being concerned him more than receiving the king's blessing.

Darius knew that it would take time for Marguerite to forget all that had happened since they last were married, and he had not lied; he was more than content to wait for as long as it would take.

How could he not? She'd captured his heart years ago and had never set it free.

In the three days since they'd wed once again, he'd come to realize that he never wished to be freed. He would go to his grave loving Marguerite.

Although, he could not help but hope that she would soon look at him without Thornson standing guard over her shoulder. Even in this brief period of time it was becoming increasingly difficult to lie next to her at night sharing nothing more than a mattress.

Darius forced his attention back to the boisterous activity on the practice grounds. If he did not focus on something other than this physical need for his wife, he would lose his mind.

He studied the men waging mock battle on the uneven dirt ground and noted that most of them were from Faucon and King Stephen. A good number of Thornson's men were oddly missing.

Odd only in the sense that their absence was greatly noted. Before today they'd seemingly taken turns disappearing and reappearing a few at a time.

Today, however, it seemed that over a dozen of them were gone at the *same* time.

Darius caught Osbert's attention and motioned him over. He'd get to the bottom of this and soon—before any more *supplies* could find their way north to King David through Thornson.

"Osbert, take a few of our men and see if you can locate the rest of Thornson's troops."

Osbert glanced back at the field. "How many do you estimate are missing?"

"Ten and seven, by rough count."

"All are Thornson's men?"

"Nay." Darius raked his gaze across the field, re-counting quickly. "Only a dozen are Thornson's." Upon their arrival, he and Osbert had determined that thirty-five of the men belonged to Thornson Keep. The others could not be found on the rolls.

While the number of men remained constant, the faces changed on a regular basis. Not wishing to add to the growing suspicion Thornson's guards had toward those from Faucon, Darius refused to employ force while interrogating the men, so questioning them provided as little information as watching them did.

Just as Osbert turned to leave, Darius instructed, "Locate the men, discover what they are doing and nothing more."

"And if we catch them engaging in illegal activities?"

"Come to me immediately." Darius hoped that would be the case. More than that, he hoped he would find Bainbridge leading the activities. It would be the excuse he needed to hand the man over to King Stephen. He wanted this mission done and over with, so he could get on with his future. "I will be inside the keep."

He took another walk around the practice field. The safety of Thornson rested on his shoulders and the men needed to be prepared for battle at all times. After placing his squire in charge, Darius headed toward the keep.

Perhaps answers could be better gained by stoking the fires. The use of even a small amount of force might loosen a tongue or two. But first, Darius wanted to give Marguerite the chance to willingly provide the information he so desperately needed.

He needed to make her understand the importance of his mission here. He had no option. It was imperative for him to discover how these men were coming and going so freely.

How many entrances, tunnels and caverns existed below Thornson? If there were more than the three his men had already found, he wondered about the safety of the keep itself. Would they someday awaken to find that the buildings and land had fallen into a pit of their own making?

As he cleared the distance between the yard and the keep, Darius looked up at the imposing structure. Thornson was a fine keep and its impressive appearance bespoke of strength. What if the previous lord's penchant for hiding-holes had made that strength little more than a facade? It would be a shame to see such meticulous construction fall to ruin.

It would be *more* of a shame to see those living here die beneath the falling stone. Maybe it would be in his best interest to send Marguerite and Marcus south to Falcongate. At least then he'd not have their safety to

worry about. It appeared he already had enough to oc-
cupy his mind and time.

Unable to find Marguerite in the kitchens or Great
Hall, he sprinted up the steep winding stairs to their
chamber.

Silence and an empty room greeted him. Darius
paused, uncertain where to look next. Marguerite had
said nothing about leaving the keep for any reason this
day. If Bertha's sister had come to term, he assumed that
Marguerite would have gone into the village—but she'd
have sent him word first.

He briefly wondered if she'd again taken it into her
head to spirit Marcus north. No, she wouldn't. Not now
that they'd wed. And not after he'd kept his end of their
bargain.

What if she'd somehow come to harm? Would not a
servant or a guard have located him immediately?

His stomach twisting with doubts and unfamiliar
fears, Darius turned toward the door. The faint murmur
of voices slowed his exit.

Curious, since he'd seen nobody in the hallway upon
entering the chamber, he opened the door. As he stepped
through the doorway, Darius asked, "Have you seen
Lady…" His question trailed off. The hallway was
empty. Why, then, was he hearing voices?

His confusion increased when he walked back into
the chamber. No one was in the hallway, the chamber
or the alcove, yet still he could hear the faint sound of
people talking.

He followed the sound to the alcove. Darius stared
at the solid wall of the tiny side room before inspect-
ing the items inside. The cushioned benches, table and
candles bespoke of a small area for moments of quiet

contemplation, a spot off the main bedchamber where he and Marguerite could sit together and discuss whatever they wished in private.

Unfortunately, she was not here. A great pity. He would enjoy nothing more than a lively discussion about what concerned him most—an obviously well-used secret room between the lord's chamber and the one next door.

He leaned closer to the stone wall to better hear the muffled conversation. While he could not make out the words, he was able to discern the tone of both speakers and the identity of one.

Darius was not completely certain who Marguerite argued with, but he felt safe in assuming it was Sir Everett.

His earlier doubts and fears collided and built to anger, tightening his chest, pounding against his temples. He leaned away from the wall and ran his hands over the stone. Somewhere there was a door to this hidden room.

His determined search produced no obvious crack in the stone. No glimmer of light broke through the solid wall. He found nothing that would lead him to believe this was the secret entryway that would permit him to burst in on the unsuspecting duo arguing behind the stone.

Darius backed out of the alcove and turned toward the chamber door. If the entrance was not in his chamber, would it be in the adjacent one—the room that used to be Marguerite's?

Chapter Eleven

Marguerite squinted against the brightness of the torch's light gleaming in the darkness of this secret room.

In truth, the *room* was little more than a hidden corridor between the two main bedchambers. The entrance was in her old chamber, located on the back wall of the alcove.

Henry had cleverly designed the entryway. The wall was made of thick wooden planks, devised to look like an overlarge, ornate, metal-studded door, complete with leather hinges, locking bars and handle.

Anyone who had come into the chamber had at one time or another reached out and tried to open this *door*. To the amusement of all, they found nothing but a stone wall behind it.

What they didn't realize was that the wall itself was the true door. One had only to reach into the narrow space between the wood and the stone to find the handle that unlatched the real entrance to the hidden room.

The torch moved again, causing her to shield her eyes against the glare of light.

She had a sneaking suspicion that Sir Everett moved it around as he argued, knowing full well the light nigh on blinded her. Tired of his motions, she grasped his wrist with one hand and took the torch from him with her other.

"There we go." She stuck the torch in a nearby iron sconce. "Much better." The flickering light illuminated the room. She nearly laughed at the expression on Everett's face. Instead, she ignored his obvious pouting and asked, "You were saying?"

"Lady Marguerite, we cannot simply stop serving King David."

"And why not?" As far as she could tell, she could stop serving whomever she pleased, whenever she pleased. It was the penalty for doing so that worried her.

While waiting for Everett to think of what would surely be an unsuitable answer, Marguerite rubbed her arms, hoping the action would help warm her.

Unheated and unlit, the cold stale air seemed to flow right through her clothing and skin to seep into her very bones.

Finally, Everett sighed before saying, "My lady, we have been the main leg for supplies, arms and gold to Empress Matilda from the moment King Stephen stole the crown."

He spoke slowly, as if explaining something to a child. It was all Marguerite could do not to laugh in amusement at him—or snarl with impatience. Certain that he would soon get to his point, she remained silent. Although, she wished he'd hurry. She'd no desire to be gone long enough for anyone to miss her and come looking.

"To turn our backs now, without notice, would be

nothing more than an open invitation for King David to attack in retaliation for the slight against his niece."

"How can David or Matilda expect our continued support, knowing that Thornson is dead?" This was the first ploy she hoped would see them free of this mess. Why should she be held responsible for a dead man's vows?

Everett's eyes widened in apparent disbelief. "Have we not shown our intention to do that very thing? Even after Lord Thornson's death we have continued to keep the flow of goods active."

"Aye, but that was before I wed one of King Stephen's men."

An evil smirk briefly crossed Everett's lips. A sign that she knew would not bode well. He shrugged, then offered, "That is a problem easily solved."

Marguerite swallowed the flash of sudden fear. She held her ground and stared hard at Thornson's captain. "I never claimed it to be a problem, did I?"

"No, but—"

She cut him off with a wave of one hand. "There are no buts. You will do nothing to bring harm to Faucon." Marguerite narrowed her eyes. "Do you understand me?"

Everett returned her glare—another indication that it was well past time to see to his replacement. When she did not back down from his glare, he nodded.

"Yes, I understand."

"Good. I will warn you only this one time, Sir Everett. If any harm whatsoever comes to Faucon or his men, you will be the one to suffer the consequences."

"I will not be at fault if someone falls off the cliff."

She felt a chill of warning. "Pardon?"

He shook his head. "Nothing."

She'd heard his warning clearly and would see to it that Darius made certain he and his men were on guard against any threat, accidental or not.

Everett motioned behind him. "There is a shipment due to head north tomorrow night. What do you propose we do? The boats are already on their way. There is little I can do to prevent their arrival on our beach."

Marguerite wanted to tell him to dump everything into the sea, but she realized the cavern was full. She wished nothing more than to forget about the arrangement Thornson had with King David. But on that Everett was correct—such a drastic move would draw an unwanted army to her gate.

And the only way to stop the boats would be to darken the warning fires and let the wooden vessels crash and splinter upon the jagged rocks. That was something she could not do. She would not be responsible for bringing such a manner of death to the men on those boats.

As an idea formed in her mind, Everett opened his mouth and she quickly raised her hand to stop his words.

What if she had this last shipment go out as planned and sent along one of the men with a missive from her to King David? She could explain about her marriage and about the danger continued assistance would bring to her and her son.

Sooner or later, Darius would want to return to Faucon. She and Marcus would of course travel south with him. Once they were gone, the supply route could easily be reopened.

Satisfied with her idea, she addressed Everett. "Have the men continue getting this next shipment ready. It will be the last. I will have a message written to King David explaining the situation here. Choose one of the men to travel north with the shipment and let him know that he will be delivering my missive."

"This will not work, Lady Marguerite."

"Let me worry about that."

Everett snorted. "A fine lot of good that will do when the man I send north may face a sword through his heart."

"Do not be a fool." Sometimes she wondered how this man managed to captain a garrison. "Send one of David's men."

"And what if he still kills the man?"

"I do not think he will. But if he does, so be it." She disliked sounding so cold, but this would be out of her control.

"What about Lord Faucon? Do we simply load the boats under his watchful eyes?"

She'd already taken Darius into consideration. There were ways to keep a man occupied for a few hours during the night. It would take much convincing on her part to make him believe that Thornson did not still peer over her shoulder, but she'd find a way. "Let me deal with that."

"And his men?"

For that difficulty, she'd need Bertha's help. The maid had been with her since she'd first arrived at Thornson, and Marguerite felt certain she'd be able to enlist Bertha's assistance. "Do not concern yourself. I will see to the men, also."

"Very well." Whether in agreement or not, he sounded resigned to carrying out her wishes. While turning to leave, Everett added, "We can only pray you know what you are about, my lady."

She watched him disappear into the darkness of the corridor. When the echo of his footsteps no longer reached her ears, Marguerite opened the door that led back into her chamber.

The stone panel closed easily behind her with a soft *click*. The larger, false door was another matter. The oversize planks of wood had to be bullied back into place. She struggled with it for a few moments before putting her shoulder to the door.

A hand brushed in front of her nose before pushing against the wood. "Here, let me help you."

Marguerite's heart flip-flopped in her chest; her breath caught in her throat. She stumbled against the door as it was pushed closed.

Darius grasped her arm to keep her from falling, then leaned next to her. She hazarded a glance at his face. He didn't appear angry, or even surprised to see her coming through this entryway. She blinked. As a matter of fact, the slant of his brows, sparkle in his eyes and upward tilt at the corner of his lips made him appeared rather amused.

Certain she was mistaken and that his appearance of humor masked his real emotion, Marguerite tried to back away. But he still gripped her arm. His grasp, while not hurtful or overly tight, was secure enough to keep her in place.

The torch wavered in her hand. Darius easily took it from her suddenly lax fingers. He widened his smile and just stared down at her, ignoring her attempt to put some distance between them.

Heat raced up her neck and face at his silent perusal. Words weren't necessary. Marguerite could well imagine the accusations running through his mind.

She'd not the slightest doubt that each thought he eventually voiced would leave her without defense.

No matter what he would accuse her of doing, she

could not tell him the truth without involving him in Thornson's current problems, and that was the one thing she would not do. Right now it was still within her power to protect him, and she'd do just that for as long as she could.

Marguerite swallowed a groan. Why did he have to catch her leaving the secret room? He'd been out on the training field with the men, so she'd thought there would be more than enough time to talk to Sir Everett. What brought him off the field?

At the same moment she thought she could bear no more of his silent stare, Darius leaned forward and, in a near-breathless whisper against her ear, asked, "Did you and Sir Everett mend your differences?"

Differences? Dear Lord above, he had not heard through the wall, had he?

"We have no differences."

"Please, Marguerite, do not seek to play me for a fool. It was obvious by your tone that you were arguing and since Everett was absent from the practice field, I can only deduce he was with you."

Could she possibly become any more lack-witted? How had she not taken Everett's absence from the field into consideration?

Before answering him, she silently prayed for the strength and cunning needed to lie to his face. She would do anything, including surrender her soul, if she could keep him from discovering the truth of what she was about to do.

"I have not seen Sir Everett since earlier this morning. He was not with the other men?"

He made a sound that was something between a cough and a snort. Instead of arguing with her, he dropped his hand and reopened the wooden door. "Show me how this works."

There'd be no turning back from this discovery. Now that he knew there was a secret room and where the door was located, she'd have to show him how it worked and where the corridor led. Otherwise, he'd be exploring on his own—a move that would be unwise on her part and possibly dangerous for him.

Marguerite wrapped her fingers around his wrist and guided his hand into the space between the doors. "Feel the latch?" At his nod, she instructed, "Push it down until it clicks, then shove against the stone."

He did so, then stepped through the opening, holding the torch before him. When she didn't follow, he turned and offered his hand. "Coming?"

She entwined her fingers through his. "Of course. I would not want you getting lost."

"Or finding things I should not."

Marguerite missed a step and nearly fell against his back.

Darius acted as if nothing untoward had happened and simply continued to walk along the length of the corridor, with her following close behind.

"Did Thornson devise this?"

"Yes. While he was building the keep, he added this hallway into the plans."

He paused to lift the torch and peer around the tight space. "Where does it lead?"

"Just down to the Great Hall."

"Interesting."

"How so?"

"Is it not odd that Thornson incorporated a hidden entrance leading directly to his wife's chamber?"

Marguerite could not contain her burst of laughter. Darius's brief glare should have made her swallow the escaping mirth. "I apologize." She gently squeezed his hand. "It was the nearly the same question I voiced."

"And the answer?" He did not sound the least bit amused.

"For one thing, it is impossible to open the stone door without the latch being released. And the locking bars on the wooden door inside the alcove are always in place. So my virtue was never in danger."

"Your virtue? By the time you arrived here, your virtue had already been lost."

Marguerite cringed. Even knowing that his scathing comment, spoken out of anger, may have been deserved it did little to dull the pain inflicted by his words.

Darius stopped and turned around. The moment the words had left his mouth, he'd fruitlessly wished them back. The light from the torch sparkled in her hurt-filled gaze. Twin pinpoints of light glittered in her eyes, stabbing him as surely as any sword. This was not the way to gain her cooperation.

He released her hand and stroked the soft flesh of her cheek. "Now it is I who must apologize."

She shook her head. "Nay. You spoke only the truth."

"Make no excuses for my bad temper. Marguerite, we were wed. Your virtue was ever intact. I had no right to say such a thing to you, and I am sorry."

She placed her hand against his chest and leaned her cheek into his hand. "Thank you."

In that moment Darius was certain no ghosts crowded between them. A moment he would not let pass unchallenged. He slipped one arm around her and pulled her against his chest. Without coaxing, Marguerite turned her face up to his and met his kiss.

She was warm and pliant against him, and he wished he could toss the torch to the floor and hold her closer to his pounding heart.

He slid his hand up to thread his fingers through the loosely braided hair at the back of her head. She complied instantly to his unspoken request by tilting her head and parting her lips.

She traced the edge of his lips with the tip of her tongue, catching him by surprise. Emboldened by her touch, he slipped his tongue into the moist warmth of her mouth.

Marguerite curled her arms around his neck and rested the length of her body against his. He held her tighter, crushing the softness of her breasts against his hard chest, and groaned.

She stiffened slightly, and with that barely perceptible movement, Darius knew that Thornson had joined them once again.

His heart heavy with regret and his mind clouded with burning desire, he reluctantly eased her out of his embrace and took her shaking hand in his own.

"Darius—"

"No." He stopped her words with the shake of his head. "Say nothing to ruin the moment. I said I would wait and I will. Come, show me the rest of this hidden maze."

"Just ahead to the left are some rough-hewn steps." Her voice echoed ragged in the corridor. "Be careful."

"Why is there no entrance within the lord's chamber?" His question sounded as raspy as her words had.

"The larger chamber was reserved for guests."

"Ah." Which explained why it had been readied for his use upon his arrival. "Do you wish to move back to your old bedchamber?"

The space between them widened as she slowed her steps. "Alone?"

Darius stopped their descent, turned and looked at her. She frowned, staring into his eyes for a few moments, then asked, "Is that what you wish?"

"No. Do not mistake my question. If you are more comfortable in the smaller chamber, I will have *our* things moved there."

The loud release of her breath made him smile. If she'd been worried about his answer, then perhaps this excising of ghosts would be completed quicker than he'd first thought.

"There is no need to go to that amount of trouble. The chamber we now share is fine." She smiled sadly and added, "In fact, I prefer it."

He hadn't thought of it in that manner. It would most likely be easier for her not to sleep in the same chamber she'd shared with Thornson. He did not voice that thought. Instead, he said, "I am glad to hear that. No matter how secure, I would have to be ever on guard if we slept in a chamber with a hidden entrance."

She leaned closer and kissed his cheek. "Darius, promise me you will be careful. Safeguard yourself and your men."

"That goes without saying, my lady. But what do *you* fear?"

Marguerite stood upright. "Nothing. I simply worry as any wife would."

That had to be one of the biggest barefaced lies he'd yet heard come out of her mouth. Until he could convince her to open up to him, however, he would have to let it pass. In the meantime he would take heed of her fears and warn his men to be extra vigilant of their safety.

Darius resumed their downward journey. "Where are we in regards to the hall?"

"We are on the opposite side of the stairway. Once we reach the bottom, we will be facing the back wall of the Great Hall. The corridor will lead us across the back, to the far wall."

"Near the hallway to the kitchens, where the tables and benches are stacked?"

"Yes. To that very corner. The door is in the hallway."

Darius rolled his eyes. "Behind the linen chest."

She laughed softly. "Yes. To be more precise, the linen chest is the door."

The linen chest stood taller than he did. He glanced over his shoulder to see if she was making a jest. But the innocent look on her face said otherwise. "You are serious?"

"Oh, yes. The floor beneath has been smoothed and polished to perfection. The bottom of the wardrobe beneath its floor is hollow, leaving room for wheels. It rolls away from the wall quietly and with ease. You will see."

Darius cursed, then blew out a loud breath. "My lady, I hope you are enjoying this journey."

He heard her sigh before she said, "It will be my last, will it not?"

"Aye." He would immediately see to it that the entrance behind the chest was permanently sealed off.

They reached the bottom of the steps where the corridor widened, giving them ample room to walk side by side. Darius pulled her next to him, released her hand and draped his arm across her shoulders.

Marguerite rested her head against him. "My Lord Faucon, why are you not angry about this discovery?"

"Oh, I am. Very angry." He kissed the top of her head. "But I thought we would save the arguing for later in the day."

She poked a finger into his side. "You lie. You only thought to discover what you could, first."

"Of course." They reached the door and he put the torch in the wall sconce before turning her to look at him. With a hand on each side of her face, he caressed her cheeks with his thumbs and rested his forehead against hers. "Ah, Marguerite, you think I do not realize that you hold too many secrets close to your heart? You think I will cease pestering you before I ferret them all out?"

She closed her eyes, and he chuckled. "You give yourself away with little more than a glance."

"I hide nothing."

"You hide everything."

"I would never—"

He kissed her words into silence before saying, "Be warned, my love, I will not let your lies or your secrets become the death of us."

Before she could say anything, he released her and pushed the door open.

The shouts and yells of those scurrying about in the hall greeted them before Darius could fully open the door. After pulling Marguerite through the doorway and slamming the linen chest closed, he nabbed the first passing servant and demanded, "What is happening?"

The wide-eyed servant babbled something he could not decipher. Darius handed the man to Marguerite, who shouted, "Explain this!"

After taking in a huge gulp of air, the servant bobbed his head. "The earl, my lady. Earl William is arrived."

Darius clenched his jaw until he thought he'd shatter his teeth. *Of all the times for York to show up, he had to choose now? Now? For the love of God, why?*

Finally, he ordered Marguerite to return to their chamber, then jerked around toward the Great Hall, cursing.

He and the Earl of York held no great liking for each other. William considered him nothing but a young useless pup still in leading strings attached to Count Faucon's leash. He considered William little more than an overgrown, overbearing, loud-mouthed, arrogant lout, well deserving of the name *le Gros*.

In truth William was the Count of Albemarle, the Earl of York and the Lord of Holderness. The man reigned over more land than King Stephen. And he was not above making certain all knew that. Nor was he above ruling over his lands like a self-made king.

And Darius was nothing but the youngest Faucon with no title and no land other than what his brother placed in his care.

More curses left his mouth as he strode across the crowded bailey toward the gate. Obviously, William had not yet arrived within the walls. He hoped Osbert had enough sense not to keep the man standing there.

He could only pray the missive he had sent to his brother Rhys a few days ago arrived quickly, and that his brother saw fit to come to Thornson himself. There was little doubt in his mind that within a matter of days, or even hours, he would find himself locked up in a dank cell beneath the floors of Thornson or in a tower high above the keep.

Those options would be much better than having his head adorn a pike on the wall—something he would not put past the earl. In his mind's eye he could see William rubbing his fleshy hands together in glee right before swiping a broadsword across his neck. Rhys would not prove very helpful to a headless brother. Hopefully, he'd see fit to care for Marguerite and their son.

He climbed the ladder to the wallwalk and joined Osbert. "I understand we have company."

Osbert nodded toward the field. "Aye. And he brought his army along."

Darius stared out over the wall as he patted his side to make certain the pouch with King Stephen's orders was still at hand. He sucked in a deep breath, hoping to calm his racing heart. Osbert had been correct: the Earl of York was surrounded by at least fifty men.

Unwilling to pit Thornson's strength against the earl's power, he signaled the men in the gate towers to raise the portcullis and permit William entry.

It was doubtful that the man was here to bring harm to those at Thornson. It was more likely that somehow he'd discovered Darius's presence and had come only to alleviate his boredom by being a thorn in Darius's side.

Chapter Twelve

Marguerite tore the torch from the sconce and raced back up to the chamber using the corridor she and Darius had just descended. Any attempt to make her way through the throng of people frantically gathering in the Great Hall would have been of no use. It would be easier to gain their attention from the upper level.

After closing and locking both the stone door and the wooden door to the corridor, she paused to catch her breath. The Earl of York was no friend to Thornson. His brief visit upon her arrival years ago had made her aware of that fact. Instead of joining her and Henry in a festive celebration of their marriage vows, the earl had taken it upon himself to bring the party within a hairs-breadth of war—simply because Henry did not support the king.

Considering the sizable forces of both York and Thornson, it would have been a war that lasted years. Fortunately, Henry had swallowed his pride, backed down and sworn not to openly defy King Stephen.

Earl William had either missed the word *openly,* or

had realized that he'd never be able to stop Henry from supporting Empress Matilda. Either way, Henry had taken his support into the shadows and the earl had not returned to Thornson.

Until now.

Why, after all these years, had he decided to pay a visit? If he had wanted to take control of the keep, would he not have done so immediately following Henry's death?

It was not as if he did not know about the passing of Thornson's lord. Especially since rumor said Henry had taken the arrow on the outskirts of York. All had assumed the arrow had come from one of the earl's men.

Surely, being a lord in King Stephen's court, the earl knew Darius had been sent to hold Thornson. Is that why he'd come? To see to it that Darius performed his duty? As far as she knew, all of the Faucons were loyal servants to the king, so a taskmaster to oversee them would not be needed.

Why now of all times? How would they get the shipment out tomorrow night? Keeping Darius and his men diverted was going to be hard enough. How would she keep the earl from discovering what was afoot at Thornson, too?

Her heart lodged in her throat. Had he heard word about the shipments north? No. Dear Lord, let that not be so.

Marguerite slapped at the skirt of her gown and rose. She could sit here all day wondering and worrying for naught, or she could make herself useful.

She glanced at the ornate door and sighed. Like it or no, she would need to move back into this chamber. It would not do for the earl to discover one hidden room and go searching for more.

Darius would undoubtedly move into the chamber with her. But for the most part he would be occupied with the earl. And if by chance he did find the time to go snooping for other secreted rooms, she could more easily fabricate a tale for his ears than for Earl William's.

No sooner had she readied to leave the chamber than a knock sounded from behind the doors in the alcove. Marguerite paused. Darius would not have come back up through the corridor. It could only be Everett.

There was no time to deal with what would surely be the captain's fears. He would have to wait. For now she had enough of her own fear to quell, and more than enough frantic servants and guards to soothe before putting them to work.

She left the chamber and headed for the landing at the top of the stairs. The activity in the Great Hall below her had not lessened. If anything it had become more chaotic and louder.

"Silence!" Marguerite shouted over the din of voices. She waited until one by one those below calmed enough to stare up at her.

After taking a deep breath to gentle her own racing heart, she began a slow descent down the steep winding stairs while talking to those gathered. "There is no reason for this madness. Calm yourselves. It is not as if we have not had royalty in our midst before."

She stared at one of the older women. "Hawise, when Earl William was here before, were we not able to retain control of the party?"

The woman bobbed her head before answering. "Aye, my lady, but his lordship was alive then."

"True, but the new lord is also well able to control the visitors." Murmurs of agreement drifted from the back of the gathering, confirming her declaration.

She rounded one of the bends on the stairway and pointed down at another older woman. "Jessie, did we not entertain King David himself just this year past?" The woman's eyes widened before she nodded.

Marguerite picked out one of the men. "Stefan, did you not repair the saddle for Empress Matilda before she departed our company two summers ago?"

Stefan flashed a near-toothless grin before stating, "Aye, my lady, that I did."

Marguerite reached the bottom of the stairs and spread her arms out. "Well then, surely entertaining a lowly earl whom we have seen before should not cause you such concern."

"Lowly? My lady, he is one of King Stephen's strongest men. How can we be certain he does not mean us harm?"

She shrugged, trying to make them see that she was not worried in the least. "Lord Darius is Stephen's man, too. Has he brought us harm?"

"Not much—but then, he is not the Earl of York."

She didn't see who had spoken, so she addressed the throng. "Lord Darius is greeting the earl at the gate as we speak. He will assuredly permit the man entrance to our keep."

Marguerite raised her hand to silence the outburst from a few of the men. "Let us go about our business, treat the earl with the respect he deserves and leave all mention of politics or war to the two men. As long as we do not provoke Earl William, Lord Darius will not let any harm befall Thornson."

FREE BOOKS OFFER

To get you started, we'll send you
2 FREE books and a FREE gift

There's no catch, everything is **FREE**

Accepting your 2 **FREE** books and **FREE** mystery gift
places you under no obligation to buy anything.

Be part of the Mills & Boon® Book Club™ and receive your favourite
Series books up to 2 months before they are in the shops and delivered
straight to your door. Plus, enjoy a wide range of **EXCLUSIVE** benefits!

- Best new women's fiction – delivered right to your door with FREE P&P
- Avoid disappointment – get your books up to 2 months before they are in the shops
- No contract – no obligation to buy

2 **FREE** books
and a
FREE gift

We hope that after receiving your free books you'll
want to remain a member. But the choice is yours.
So why not give us a go? You'll be glad you did!

Visit **millsandboon.co.uk** to stay up to date
with offers and to sign-up for our newsletter

H0AIA

Mrs/Miss/Ms/Mr   Initials

BLOCK CAPITALS PLEASE

Surname

Address

Postcode

Email

MILLS & BOON®

MILLS & BOON®
Book Club

FREE BOOK OFFER
FREEPOST NAT 10298
RICHMOND
TW9 1BR

NO STAMP
NECESSARY
IF POSTED IN
THE U.K. OR N.I.

When none raised voice to disagree, she nodded. "Good. We have weathered worse together. This will be but a spring storm, that is all." Silently she prayed her words would prove to be the truth.

"Now, I need a few strong arms to move my possessions and Darius's back into the smaller chamber. And a few quick arms to make all of the chambers ready. Someone needs to run into the village and tell Bertha that I need her here with my son at my side."

After the people dispersed to do her bidding, she joined the cook to discuss meals for the next few days.

Sir Everett's legs shook beneath him as he scurried through the forest toward the hunting lodge. He'd not wanted to deliver this bit of information, but he knew it was too important to ignore.

He paused before the door gasping for breath to fill his straining lungs and enough courage to stiffen his spine.

Finally, when his heart slowed to a more normal, albeit unsteady pounding and his legs quaked a little less, he knocked on the door and called out, "My Lord?"

To his dismay, silence greeted him from behind the still closed door. He knocked again and called out with a little more force, "My lord?"

"Stop your caterwauling, Everett."

He cringed at the tone, but at least his efforts had been rewarded with some manner of response. "My lord, we have visitors."

Lord Bainbridge appeared at the unprotected window opening. After scanning the area outside the lodge, he frowned before asking, "Visitors?"

"Aye, my lord, at Thornson."

Bainbridge leaned his forearms on the window's ledge. "Were you planning to tell me who these visitors are?"

"Aye, sir." For his own safety, Everett took a step away from the lodge. If the news he wished to impart was not well received, perhaps he could save himself some injury by increasing the distance between him and the other man. "York. The Earl of York has arrived."

His decision to move away had been wise, judging from the obvious rage turning Bainbridge's face into a twisted mask of evil.

"What do you mean, the Earl of York has arrived?"

Everett wasn't certain how to make the news any clearer, so he took another step back and repeated, "Aye, the Earl of York is at Thornson."

To his utter dismay, instead of shouting his anger, Lord Bainbridge rested his head on his arm and laughed. The man's unexpected response left Everett speechless.

After a time, he began to wonder if the news had been too much. The urge to step forward, to see if perhaps Bainbridge needed aid of some sort was strong. But the desire to keep whole and hearty was stronger, so he remained where he was...out of reach.

Finally, when Bainbridge's laughter was spent, the man lifted his head and wiped the tears from his face. "Oh, bless you, Everett. Mayhap, I, too, will pay a visit to Thornson. This will be too rich not to witness first-hand."

"But, milord, Faucon said—"

"That I was not to step foot on Thornson's lands again. Do you think Faucon will risk having to explain my sudden death to the earl?"

"Nay. 'Tis doubtful Faucon would be that unwise."

"Of course, there is the minor consideration of my loyalties." Bainbridge appeared to be speaking to himself, so Everett remained silent. "Earl William might not welcome someone opposed to King Stephen. I will simply lie if the subject arises."

Bainbridge rubbed his chin a few moments, then smiled. "After the passing of the next two nights, I will be headed north. So, I need only hide the truth until then."

"Lord Bainbridge, how will we manage the shipment with the earl and his men wandering about?" What was normally a smooth operation would now be doubly hard. Not only would they need to thwart Faucon, but now Earl William, too. Everett shuddered at the thought of the task ahead of them.

Bainbridge's snicker floated off into the forest. "Would not tomorrow prove the perfect time to celebrate Lady Marguerite's new marriage?"

"My lord?"

"Think, my man, think. They call the earl *le Gros* for a reason. What do you think Earl William enjoys even more than battle?"

The question gave Everett pause for only a moment. "A celebration with much food and even more drink."

"Yes. I would wager that all we need do is pass around the word that Lady Marguerite never enjoyed a proper celebration of her vows to Faucon."

"Thus giving the earl an excuse to let the food and wine flow."

"Not that he needs an excuse, but yes."

Everett agreed that it would in all likelihood be an easily contrived plan—one that would not fail. However, he knew he needed to inform Bainbridge of Lady

Marguerite's plans about future shipments. He was positive this news would not be met with any form of glee.

Even though it appeared cowardly, Everett took yet another step away from the cottage.

Bainbridge leaned against the window frame, crossed his arms against his chest and said, "Obviously, you have more to tell me."

Everett swallowed, then explained. "Lady Marguerite insists that tomorrow night's shipment be the last. She wishes Thornson to have nothing more to do with helping the empress."

One of Bainbridge's eyebrows rose. He shook his head. "Oh, *she* wishes not? I will simply have to let the lady know how little her wishes matter in this."

"What about Faucon, milord?"

"By the time he figures out what is happening beneath his nose, he will be so embroiled in the goings-on at Thornson that he will have no choice but to accept his cloak as traitor to King Stephen."

Everett did not agree, but he was not about to argue. "It is all in your hands, Lord Bainbridge."

"Yes, it is. And you would do well not to forget that. For now, return to Thornson. I will slip in soon."

Not until Earl William and his entourage rode into the courtyard did Darius realize he and the men at Thornson all wore armor.

Since leaving Falcongate, it had become second nature to don chain mail on a daily basis. If he and the men were not honing their battle skills, they were scouring the area looking for the smugglers. Hopefully, the earl would realize that and not assume Thornson was prepared to do battle against York.

Darius prayed for any measure of luck the Saints could offer, and God's grace while waiting for William to dismount. It soon became apparent that Thornson's guards and servants were accustomed to high-ranking visitors.

To his relief, they all knew their tasks without being ordered. Men rushed to help the earl dismount; considering the man's size more than two able bodies were required. Others saw to his horse and then to his men.

Servants offered refreshment to quench his thirst. Darius glanced toward the keep, and for half a heartbeat wondered if the drink would be poisoned.

When William finally approached, Darius bit the inside of his mouth and briefly knelt in deference to the man.

"Ah, Faucon's pup. How fare you?"

Darius fought to ignore the heavily laden sarcasm in William's voice and rose. He grasped the man's forearms in welcome. "All is well, my lord. What brings you to Thornson Keep?"

William pinned him with his eyes. "No welcome greeting, just questions?"

From what Darius could remember, getting right to the crux of the matter had always been William's way. He arrived uninvited, unannounced, and wished to pass time with idle conversation? The odd desire to heighten the tension could only mean that something was behind this visit.

With the earl's stare still on him, Darius smiled before motioning toward the keep. "I beg your pardon, my lord. I forget my manners." As they crossed the courtyard toward the building, he asked, "How was your journey? Not overlong or taxing, I pray. When did you last sup? Do you desire nourishment? Do you find your-self tired? Would you care to rest for a spell?"

When Darius ran out of questions, the earl asked, "Are you finished?"

"Aye."

They strode the remainder of the way to the hall in silence. Once inside, William snapped his fingers at one of his men and held out his hand. "The missive."

Darius swallowed his groan. He would not be sur-prised if the earl had come with new orders from King Stephen.

William handed the scrolled document to Darius. "You might find this interesting. I did."

The instant Darius saw the broken seal he knew his life was in peril. It was the message he'd sent to his brother Rhys. He plucked it from the earl's fingers and slid it inside his tunic without making any pretense of reading the missive. "How came you by this?" Some-how, he needed to get word to Marguerite.

It would be better for all concerned if she used those secret tunnels of hers to take their son and leave Thorn-son immediately. If she could get to the village, he would find a way to have Osbert see her safely to Faucon.

William again motioned to his men. This time Wil-liam's men did not deliver a missive to him. Instead, they escorted one of Faucon's guards forward. Dar-ius's heart lurched up to his throat, making the task of swallowing his curses difficult.

Osbert entered the hall and came to such a sudden stop that he nearly lost his footing. After he took stock of what was transpiring before him, the blood drained from his face. Darius wondered if his own expression registered the same level of shock.

"You have nothing to say, Faucon?" The earl's mocking question brought the attention back to him.

Actually, Darius did indeed have much he wanted to say. Unfortunately, most of it would be of no use toward saving his hide.

Instead of spouting out what begged to leave his mouth, Darius calmed his tongue and took comfort in the knowledge that the earl seemed to have captured only one of the three men sent to look for Rhys. Hopefully, the other two had made it safely away.

Before William could wonder at his lengthy silence, Darius shook his head and asked, "What do you wish me to say, my lord? I can think of nothing that will tell you any more than what you already know."

"Do you not wonder how your man comes to be in my custody?"

Of course he wondered. But he would talk to his man later. Since he was certain the earl would gleefully answer his own question when he desired, Darius remained silent.

William waved his men away before beckoning Osbert forward. "Take your poor excuse for a guard and be gone from my sight." Not waiting for the hall to clear, the earl turned abruptly on his heel, crossed the room to the high-backed chair placed at the head of the table and took a seat.

York's steely glare was all the invitation Darius required. He wondered what would happen if he ignored the man and simply left the keep. A brief, albeit vivid image of his head swinging from the tower chased away any tempting thought of escape.

Cursing silently, Darius took a deep breath and joined the earl at the table.

A heavy silence fell between them, made more unnerving by William's unceasing glare. Darius resolved not to break. He would tell the man no more than necessary.

"Darius?"

Marguerite's call from behind him brought forth a new emotion—fear raced up from the pit of his stomach. Icy cold fingers seemed to swirl around his heart and close tightly.

Darius swallowed, then rose and turned to greet his wife. If the sound of her voice had not been enough to summon trembles to rush through him, the sight of the child at her side did.

At the earl's deep self-satisfied chuckle, Darius took a sharp breath. *Dear Lord, keep my son safe.* He glanced back at Marguerite and added her to his prayer for safety.

His own well-being mattered not. He was more than able to fend for himself. He no doubt deserved whatever fate awaited him.

But his wife and son did not deserve a fate meted out by the earl. Especially one that would not consist of happiness nor any measure of security.

While he was certain Marguerite had an active hand in the smuggling activities, he was also certain she did so only out of loyalty to Henry Thornson. The child was blameless; he could not be held accountable for anything that had occurred in his short life. Darius would protect both of them with his life if need be.

Earl William cleared his throat, prompting Darius to introduce his wife. Darius held out his hand, clasping Marguerite's cold fingers with his own. She clung to him like a drowning soul. He wished above anything else that he could promise all would be well. A useless wish that would not come true.

Since he would not voice a promise he might be unable to keep, Darius looked into her eyes and smiled. He hoped a show of bravery on his part would lend her strength to face what might lay ahead.

Marguerite briefly squeezed his fingers and returned his assuring smile. At the same time, she drew their son closer to her side.

Darius's heart swelled at the sight of the miniature Rhys. The boy looked so much like his uncle that it was breathtaking. Little Marcus came barely above his mother's waist, but he stood straight, with his shoulders back and head up. His inky eyebrows curved up like wings over his eyes. The light brown orbs shimmered with golden specks as the lad stared steadily at the earl in obvious question.

Darius was not certain whether he should laugh or gasp at the open arrogance evident on the boy's face. If the physical resemblance was not enough to declare this child a Faucon, the mannerisms would.

The boy would learn soon enough what his pride would cost him. Darius reached out and tipped the boy's chin down. While fatherly pride might find the arrogance in one so young amusing, he doubted the earl would view it in the same manner.

A rustle of fabric from the table reminded him of Earl William's impatience. Darius spared one last glance at Marguerite before turning around to face the earl. "My lord, may I present Lady Marguerite of Thornson...my wife."

Earl William's eyes barely flickered across Marguerite's face. He dismissed her with nothing more than a nod before swinging his gaze to the child.

Darius noted the wicked glint in the earl's eyes as he studied the boy. He could only guess at the evil thoughts racing about in his mind, but he'd not permit his child to be used as a pawn in any ruse the earl schemed.

"My lord earl." Marguerite released Darius's hand to stand behind her son. "May I present Henry Thornson's child, Marcus of Thornson."

The earl's wide-eyed gaze flew from the boy to Darius before coming to rest on her. His laughter rang loud in the nearly empty Great Hall. Finally, his mirth spent, he shook his head and declared, "And my horse has wings."

Chapter Thirteen

The Earl of York wiped tears of laughter from his eyes before slamming an overly fleshy fist down onto the oak table.

Marguerite's skin tingled with dread at the loud cracking sound. From the corner of her eye, she saw Darius move as if to step forward. She reached out and touched his arm, staying a confrontation that would surely end as an invitation to his death.

Her other hand still rested on her son's shoulder, and to her amazement, he, too, had tensed in readiness to…to what? Did he understand the insinuation the earl made? If so, what did he think to do?

Before she could begin to guess at his youthful motives, Marcus slipped from her grasp and stepped forward. He pointed a chubby finger at the earl. "You scared my mother."

His high-pitched voice bounced off the walls and filled Marguerite's heart with an overflowing love. *Good Lord above, he sought to defend her!*

"Marcus, mind your manners." Darius's sharp command sent the boy back to his mother's side. "I apologize for him, my—"

"Do not scare my mother again." When Marcus interrupted Darius's apology, Marguerite could not help but laugh at the surprised expressions on both men's faces.

Before their amazement could turn to anger at the child's audacity, Marguerite intervened. She slightly bent one knee in a quick half-bow before grasping Marcus's hand. "My pardon, my lords, I will return anon."

Still in shock at Marcus's disobedience, Darius silently watched Marguerite lead the normally well-behaved child up the stairs and out of harm's way. How had his own parents ever dealt with three headstrong sons?

"The child should be whipped."

Earl William's nearly snarled pronouncement pulled Darius's attention away from his wife and child. Ah, yes, now he remembered—whipping had been an oft-employed tactic by his sire. The long scar on his back burned at the memory. Darius jerked himself away from the past to answer, "That is his mother's decision, not mine."

"You are his sire. It is your responsibility to see to his upbringing."

This would not be easy, but Darius would rest in hell before giving the earl the truth. The man could suspect and insinuate all he wished, but he'd not be wholly positive until Darius confirmed his suspicions—and that was something Darius would never do.

Thankfully, he'd been wise enough to mention nothing about the boy in his missive to Rhys. He'd only written his brother about Thornson's death, the king's orders and his subsequent remarriage to Marguerite. He had informed Rhys that they needed to discuss another matter in person, but he'd not mentioned the topic.

So, for now and preferably for the rest of his life, the Earl of York *knew* nothing.

Darius shook his head and stepped closer to the table before asking, "Did you not hear Lady Marguerite's introduction? The boy is Henry Thornson's offspring."

The earl reared back. "Egads, do you think me blind and dumb?"

"Nay. Under a mistaken impression perhaps, but never blind nor dumb."

William narrowed his eyes. A weaker man might have been intimidated into giving the earl the information he sought. Darius, however, was not that man.

Instead, he took a seat on the bench to the left of the earl, and returned the look. Eventually, William unclenched his hands and broke the visual combat.

Darius relaxed slightly—only a fool would let his full guard down around the earl. He rested his forearms on the table, then asked, "So, why are you at Thornson?"

William smiled. A nasty, sly-looking grin that while curving up one corner of his mouth, never reached his eyes. "It will be best to wait for the Lady Marguerite to return."

Perhaps it was nothing, but Darius wondered at the use of Marguerite's name. Why had the earl not referred to her as Darius's wife, or Darius's lady? The hairs on the back of his neck rose in warning. Something, but he wasn't certain what, did not seem right.

All of his finely honed survival skills came alive, warning him of impending danger. The proverbial wolf was at his back with fangs bared, prepared to strike without notice. And yet, the beast sat across from him at the table.

Darius slowly rose. He crossed to the side table to retrieve a jug of wine and three goblets. Returning to his seat, he filled two of the goblets and pushed one toward William.

The earl hesitated not a second. He lifted the drinking vessel to his lips and drained the contents in one swallow before slamming the now empty goblet back onto the table. While Darius refilled the drinking vessel, Earl William leaned back into the chair.

"You do understand that these marriages of yours were never sanctioned by King Stephen nor officially, by the Church."

Even though he disagreed with the earl's conclusion, Darius refused to be drawn into a war of words. Since it was voiced as more of a statement than question, he remained silent. He raised his own goblet to his mouth, knowing the other man would eventually continue.

He was correct. Before Darius had a chance to swallow half a mouthful of wine, the earl leaned forward.

"Neither time did you request permission or even so much as voice your intentions."

Darius shrugged. "Our intentions were known to any who mattered—us. While the first ceremony may have been too lax according to current laws, this time promises were made, vows were exchanged before clergy and we—"

"Obviously."

The earl's interruption was an undisguised reference to Marguerite's son. A simple baiting tactic that Darius refused to take.

His silence only prompted Earl William to shake his head and sigh. "I hope your heart is not affected by this woman."

Affected? Nay. What his heart had known for some time rushed to the fore. He was not affected. She was everything he'd dreamed of for many long years—everything he'd ever desired. His heart was securely bound by the strongest of chains—love. But never *affected.* "Why?"

The expression on William's face did not bode well. The sly smile was closer to a smirk of intense satisfaction. "It will be best explained when Thornson's lady returns."

There it was again—not *your lady,* but Thornson's lady. Darius had learned long ago not to ignore his senses when they warned that something was afoot. And this something involved Marguerite, of that he was certain.

No sooner had the thought formed then Marguerite approached the table.

The earl rose and motioned to the bench at his right, placing Marguerite across from Darius. Once she was situated, the earl took his seat.

"Ah, Lady Marguerite, welcome back. We were just discussing you."

She flashed a questioning glance at Darius before asking, "Only good things, I trust?"

"Some might consider it so." The earl looked at Darius, the smirk again playing at the corners of his mouth as he continued, "Others might think otherwise."

The knot already forming in Darius's stomach tightened. The man was intentionally seeking to rattle his tightly reined composure, and it was starting to work.

"And what would some not find good, milord?" Marguerite fingered the swirling embroidered vines trimming the edge of her tunic's wide sleeves.

A small observance—one most people would have ignored. Darius knew better. Her composure suffered as much as his. He tried to send her a silent message of confidence, but she refused to meet his gaze. Instead, she concentrated on some imaginary speck of dust clinging to her sleeve.

A broad smile etched Earl William's face into a mask of pure merriment. A private joke was being played out at Marguerite and Darius's expense. A joke Darius wished would end quickly, before the torture became too much to bear.

Finally, after what seemed almost an eternity, the earl leaned toward Marguerite. He reached out and grasped her fidgeting hand with his larger one.

"My dearest lady, I am sadly lacking in manners. You have my deepest sympathy for your recent loss."

Marguerite accepted his condolences with a whispered, "Thank you."

"I know my last visit here was not the most conducive toward building a friendship between Thornson and York, but I did hold a great deal of respect for Henry."

Darius's eyebrows rose. So, this was not the first time the earl had descended upon Thornson. Obviously, his previous visit had not gone smoothly.

Marguerite remained silent, her steady gaze never leaving William's face. The earl clearly took that as a sign to continue. "Lady Marguerite, all are aware of the power a keep the size of Thornson controls. While I am certain Henry did his best to ensure you would be completely capable of ruling over this vast estate, I am afraid King Stephen wishes otherwise. And I find that I, too, must agree with his logic in this matter."

When she opened her mouth to respond, William lifted one hand to stay her words. "Wait until I finish. A man of experience and strength has been found to be your partner in Thornson Keep's future."

Darius gritted his teeth. He had known this was coming, so why did his heart and stomach both lurch in such a sickening manner? Why did his vision cloud with a red haze? Why did the breath in his chest come to a sudden halt?

"My lord earl, while I find your concern for the future of Thornson most touching, I am well able to choose my next husband and have already done so."

Even though she kept her voice soft and her words steady, Darius heard the steel beneath the statement. It was all he could do not to gasp aloud at what William would surely consider a declaration bordering on treason.

"You chose without sanction. Your marriage to Faucon is null and void. It will not be recognized by any— neither King Stephen nor the Church."

How many more times would Darius have to hear those words before he ran a sword through William's black heart?

If the earl saw Darius's hand twitch toward the hilt of his sword, he said nothing. Instead, he foolishly kept his attention fully focused on Marguerite.

"You should be thankful that I am not the sort to pass on tales. Otherwise, I would gladly spread the news of your unholy union far and wide."

Marguerite smiled. "And what would you gain by such action?"

She flinched at the earl's bark of laughter.

"Surely, you cannot be that naive. You would be branded a harlot. Willing or no, if you wish to remain at Thornson, you will go to the altar with the man of Stephen's choosing. How do you think this new husband would treat you, should he learn how you cheerfully opened your legs for another?"

The hiss of Darius's sword being pulled from its scabbard broke the heavy silence of the Great Hall. "You are speaking to my wife. If you wish to keep doing so you will keep a civil tongue."

Darius kept the point of his sword at the man's neck as the earl rose. It was not until that precise moment that Darius realized exactly how large a man the earl was. William towered over him by a full head. Darius had killed bigger men in his day, but never an earl of the realm.

Darius tightened his grip on the weapon. There was a first time for everything.

"Darius, please." Without him realizing how, Marguerite stood at his side. Her cool fingers rested lightly over his own. "Please, his idle threats cannot harm me. He is seeking only to force you into doing something without thinking."

She wasn't telling him something he'd not already guessed. Good Lord, now what? A single fluid jab would solve one set of difficulties.

But killing the Earl of York would place another, even larger set of difficulties at his feet and at those of his family. It would guarantee his premature death, while leaving Marguerite in the exact same situation she appeared to be in now.

And it would be a strike of dishonor his brothers would be forced to carry the rest of their lives.

What had he been thinking? A useless question—he hadn't been thinking. Instead, he had let his feelings overpower logic. A mistake that could cost him dearly.

"Drop your toy." William reached up and with one finger pushed the tip of the sword away from his neck. "If you were not King Stephen's man you would not have hesitated. There may be hope for you yet, pup."

Darius frowned. He'd seen men killed for doing less than putting a sword to the earl's throat.

"Lady Marguerite." William motioned toward her seat. "I apologize for my vulgar words. Make yourself comfortable and take your seat."

He looked at Darius. His eyes glittered and his jaw tightened with what had to be suppressed rage. "Out of respect for your brother, the comte, I will spare your life…this time. Do not be foolish enough to put yourself in this position again. Sit down."

Confused, Darius sheathed his sword. Aye, he'd been correct to listen to his senses, but what exactly had they sought to warn him about? Something *was* afoot. Danger *was* close. But was he looking in the wrong direction?

Marguerite sighed her relief as quietly as she could. If Darius sought to protect her, he could better do so by remaining levelheaded. His display of high emotions served no one. He'd be of no use to her or anyone if he ceased to live.

She smoothed down the skirt of her gown, regaining a measure of her own control. Though it was years old, the deep green linen was the best she had. The garment had been washed and dyed so many times that it was soft beneath her touch.

Just the act of stroking the fabric did its intended job.

Her heart slowed to a normal beat. She chanced a look at Darius. His anger had been replaced by what appeared to be utter confusion.

Marguerite couldn't begin to determine what had made him so uncertain. It was a mystery she would delve into later. For now, she had another mystery to solve.

After taking a long steady breath, she released it slowly, turned her attention to the earl and asked, "Who does King Stephen think to foist on me?"

"Foist?" The earl chuckled. "Not precisely an appropriate term to use in reference to your future betrothed, is it?"

Marguerite shrugged. "I know not what else to call it. Years ago, against my wishes, my father foisted Henry on me. While he proved to be a truly good and kind man, he was not my choice. And now the decision has been taken from me again."

William leaned back and raised his hands as if to ward off an attack. "Lady Marguerite, please." Laughter choked his words. "Your point is well made." He lowered his hands. "So be it. 'Foist' it is. The king is foisting Lord Marwood on you and Thornson."

A strangled groan escaped Darius's lips as he bolted to his feet. "Marwood? Surely not Lord Peter Marwood? That ancient battle horse can't possibly still be alive."

William rose, too—in a cursing hurry—and slammed both of his hands palm down on the table. "Cease!"

His actions knocked over one of the goblets. It hit the floor and bounced twice before rolling away.

Before Darius had a chance to move, the earl

warned, "If you so much as reach for your sword, I will have your head severed from your neck."

Warned but not bullied, Darius answered, "You cannot seriously expect me to stand by and watch my wife be handed over to some lecherous old gnome of an excuse for a man."

"Yes, I do. And more. I expect you to keep your mouth shut and do as you're told. Furthermore, I expect you to complete your tasks for King Stephen and then return to your brother's tender keeping."

Marguerite gasped at the heavy sarcasm of the earl's tone. Darius was too angry to realize William was intentionally taunting him.

"My brother's tender keeping?" Darius's tone was just as sarcasm laden. "Is that anything like the tender care Stephen showers on you?"

"Leave this hall, Faucon. Until you can learn to control your tongue, stay outside with the animals."

"Excellent suggestion." Darius reached an arm out toward Marguerite. "Come, we will leave the earl to play his game alone."

Before she could grasp his hand, the earl pushed Darius away. "No." He shouted for his guards, then stated, "She will return to her chamber and stay there until her betrothed arrives. And do not think to try anything untoward, Faucon. Her door will be guarded. The men will have orders to strike down any who approach without my permission."

When his guards arrived, he pointed at Darius. "Take him outside into the bailey. He and his men may bed down in the stables. Put my men in charge of this keep." He then took Marguerite's hand and placed it on his forearm. "I will escort the lady to her chamber. See that two men guard her door at all times."

There was nothing like the smell of horseflesh and dung to make a man take stock of his current situation. Darius leaned against a stall, his arms crossed against his chest, and scrubbed the toe of his boot through the straw at his feet.

If Earl William thought for one solitary moment that he could lock Marguerite up like a disobedient child he needed to think again. And if the earl believed he could banish Darius to the stables like a dog, and take control of Thornson himself he needed to find something else to believe in.

The overbearing, arrogant varlet could damn well go choke on his overblown image of himself.

Of course, at the moment it appeared as if the earl had won. Who was standing around seething in a dark, smelly, damp stable and who was eating, drinking and making merry in a well-lit, warm, dry Great Hall? And whose men patrolled the walls and guarded the gates?

"Darius? My Lord Faucon?"

"Over here, Osbert."

His captain followed the sound of his voice to the back of the stables. "Have you eaten?"

"I am not hungry."

"Do not choose now to act like an unthinking twit. You have not eaten since rising this morn and it is well beyond sunset."

Obviously, he had done no better than his brothers had at choosing a captain for his guard. For some reason known only to the Lord above, they had each hand-picked men who insisted on acting as a nursemaid at the most inopportune times.

"Osbert, I am not hungry. Do not seek to treat me like a child."

"As you wish, sir."

Osbert's dejected tone of voice made Darius want to shout. By the Saints above, he did not need this difficulty now. He shook his head, then reached out and touched the captain's shoulder. "No, in truth, I wish something to fill my belly before I grow more sour."

"Very good, milord." The man's tone lightened considerably as he placed a cloth-wrapped package in Darius's hand. "I scoured the kitchens and came up with some cheese, bread, fruit and a hunk of meat."

"That will be fine. More than enough, thank you." Darius tore off a chunk of the meat and while chewing asked, "Was Marguerite at the table for the evening meal?"

"No. A servant took food up to her, though."

"Is the earl basking well in his victory?"

Osbert paused for a few moments, then slowly, as if contemplating each word, answered, "No. He seemed rather distracted and surly."

"Good. Serves him right. In which chamber has he confined Marguerite?"

"Her old one, my Lord Faucon." The answer came from the maid. Both men jumped, swords drawn, at the sound of Bertha's voice coming from inside the stall next to them. They squinted as the light from the torch she carried crossed their line of vision.

Darius sheathed his weapon. "What in the name of the Saints are you doing?"

She shrugged. "I come at my lady's request to lead you to her."

"As if I can simply walk through the Great Hall to the linen chest entrance with none the wiser." He ended his statement on a half laugh.

"Please, milord." The words rolled off her tongue in an exaggerated drawl. "It would truly be a shame to have such a nice hidden passageway with only one entrance."

"How many…" He let the question trail off. She would not tell him how many entrances there were, so why waste his breath asking?

Osbert glanced over the gate to the stall behind Darius. "Go, milord. With a blanket or two, I can make a bed from straw and stand guard. If anyone wishes to check on you, it will appear as if you are asleep."

"We must hurry." Bertha tugged at Darius's arm. "I am charged with the care of the young lord. I left him in the kitchen with old Hawise and dare not be gone overlong."

He needed to speak to Marguerite and would welcome the opportunity to do so without distractions. Darius wrapped the cloth back around the food and slipped it inside his tunic. "Lead on."

The maid walked to the rear of the stall and pushed open what appeared to be nothing more than a small section of wall. Darius followed, helping her replace the section once they were outside in the night air.

"Stay here, milord." Bertha kept her voice low, torch held back as she peered around the side of the stable. Seemingly satisfied, she motioned for Darius to follow her to the small storage hut a few feet away.

His heart pounded while he crossed the narrow space

between buildings. If the earl's men caught him now, they would not rest until they discovered his reason for sneaking about in the night. Considering how many times the notion had crossed his own mind, it was easy to imagine Earl William dismantling Thornson stone by stone.

Once inside the hut, Bertha knelt and poked at the floor before sticking a finger into a hole and lifting a trap door. "After you, milord."

Darius paused. "This is not how you entered the stables."

"No." She tsked while shaking her head. "I have not much time, Lord Faucon."

Without further questioning, Darius climbed down a rope ladder and waited to assist the maid. Instead, she leaned over and handed the torch to him.

"This passage only goes one way, my lord. You will follow it beneath the bailey and then up inside the keep. Once you hear voices you can be assured you are by the Great Hall."

Darius took the torch. "And you?"

She laughed. "I will simply walk back into the keep through the main door." Bertha winked and added, "If anyone notices, I will safely claim that the rascally young Marcus led me on a merry chase. I will be certain he scampered off to the kitchens. And of course, I will be correct."

"Who devised this plan?"

"Your lady." She waved him away. "Now, be off with you."

Without further discussion, she closed the trap door. Then he heard her rearranging the straw to conceal the entrance.

As Darius made his way through the passage, he again marveled at the infinite number of tunnels and secret rooms built into Thornson. The areas were well planned, with stairs cut into the steeper ascents and descents and thick support beams shoring up certain sections.

Thornson had been born into the wrong profession. He should have spent his days designing and constructing buildings, instead of wasting his time as a warlord and traitor to his king.

Darius walked up another flight of stairs and around a corner. The din of voices filtered through the wall. Bertha had been correct—it was obvious he was in the passageway encircling the Great Hall.

One more flight of stairs at the end of this corridor, then a short jaunt along another stretch of hallway and his journey would end.

The sudden racing of his heart brought a smile to his lips. Until this moment his hands had been steady, but now the light from the torch quivered against the wall as tremors ran down his arm.

The mere thought of seeing Marguerite made him nearly drunk with mounting desire. But the current situation required calm, logical talk—not passionate embraces.

He needed to steady his nerves and strengthen his resolve not to share her bed again until she was free of Thornson. And he needed to do so before he took the final step that would put him at her door.

The soft *click* and nearly imperceptible *hiss* of the door sliding away from the frame surprised him. He stood frozen with his back against the wall and a hand on his sword.

Chapter Fourteen

"Darius?"

Marguerite's whisper reassured him that no one else lurked on the other side of the door waiting for him. He relaxed his stance and whispered back, "Aye." Then he stepped to the door.

The stone scraped as it slid open further, setting his teeth on edge. To him it seemed to scream with a promise of certain vengeance. Yet, he heard no shouts or pounding footsteps of approaching men, so perhaps the noise had echoed only in his own ears.

"Darius." Marguerite breathed his name on a sigh and drew him into the chamber.

She closed both doors between the room and the corridor while he turned to drop his bundle of food on a table and anchor the torch in an iron wall sconce.

He heard a rustle of fabric as it moved against her legs when she approached. Briefly, he imagined slipping the gown from her shoulders to pool at her feet.

His mind's eye lingered over the pale soft flesh of her neck and shoulders. The mental perusal continued, drinking the darker tipped breasts, the indent of her waist and gentle swell of her hips. Short burnished gold curls broke the vision of smooth flesh at the apex of long, shapely legs.

He mentally shook himself. Had he not just recently vowed to leave her be until Thornson's ghost departed? So much for spoken vows when they could not hold even as long as a sennight. If the Good Lord were well and truly kind, Darius would be struck dead for being such a fool.

Darius bit his upper lip, rested his forehead on his still-raised arm and willed his overactive lust to cool. When he was certain he had his mind and body under control, he turned to face her.

Darius could not prevent his suddenly dry mouth from falling open, or his heart from leaping to his throat. He could not stop the blood from racing hot and fast to his groin, engorging his manhood until it pulsed hard against his clothing.

He had not heard fabric rustling *against* her legs as she'd *approached*—it had rustled *down* her legs on the way to the floor.

Marguerite took a step closer, wearing nothing but the scent of lavender and the seductive smile of a huntress stalking her prey.

Marguerite knew she had shocked him. It was evident in his wide eyes and partially opened mouth. The notion thrilled her. Swiftly, before he could regain his senses, she removed his sword belt and placed it on top of a wooden chest.

Perhaps she had shocked him enough that he would forget his silly vow about not coming to her bed until she excised Thornson's ghost.

Memories of her years shared with Henry would never leave her completely. Everything she was today she owed to Henry Thornson. But with the earl's visit she now found herself more than ready to put Henry behind her and go forward with life. And this night seemed to her a good time to start living that life anew.

Darius had come up here to talk, to make plans for their precarious future. And they would talk…later. Much later.

She didn't know what tomorrow might bring. Their shared future together might very well be cut short by the Earl of York. She wanted…no, she *needed* this night. Needed a memory to hold on to in the days ahead.

Marguerite took another step forward, stood close enough to smell the lingering stench of the stables. She placed her palms on his chest and smiled up at him. His heart banged erratically against her palms. No matter what words would leave his lips, his body returned her desire.

Had that not always been the case? As young and inexperienced as she'd been, she'd known by the glimmer in his eyes, the sheen of perspiration on his face and the deepening of his voice that he had shared the same level of hunger as she.

Darius stared down at her and shook his head as if trying to clear his vision. With a groan that sounded to her ears suspiciously like surrender, he wrapped his arms around her and pulled her tight against his chest.

She loved the feel of his arms binding her to him. This is where she wanted to be, wanted to stay. It was hard to believe that when he'd first arrived at Thornson, she'd wished him gone. He'd been the last person she wanted inside her keep, inside her life…inside her heart or mind.

Yet now she could not envision a place more welcome than being enclosed within the warmth of his strong embrace. The beating of his heart pounded a steady rhythm against her breasts, promising a safe haven in which to rest.

Darius buried his face in her hair. "What sorcery do you weave around me, my love?"

His breath whispered warm against her neck, sending shivers of desire down her back that settled low in her belly.

Marguerite threaded her fingers through his inky black hair. The damp waves curled around her fingertips, binding her even more tightly to him. "No sorcery, no spirits of the dead. Just the two of us."

Darius lifted his head and searched her face. She stroked his stubble-covered cheek, knowing full well what he sought. "You will find nothing but me." She traced a path up one of his legs with her foot. The muscles tensed beneath her touch. "Just me and an insatiable desire to feel you atop me."

He inhaled sharply and she nipped at his chin, then soothed the spot with her tongue before whispering against his lips, "And a burning need to shiver beneath your touch."

Darius swept his hands down her back, kneading her rounded cheeks before drawing her up the length of his body. She wrapped her arms around his neck, and her legs about his waist.

He buried his face in her hair. "What if the earl, or the guards—"

She cut him off with a soft laugh. "This bedchamber's door is bolted from the inside, and thanks to my maids, the earl will sleep like a babe this night."

Darius lifted his head slightly. "He will not be harmed by any concoction you have fed him?"

"Heavens, no, do not think such a thing. I only wished him to rest peacefully after his long, arduous journey."

"Remind me to beware of what I eat and drink." A smile flitted at the corners of his mouth. "Although, I do appreciate the way your mind works."

Marguerite rested her cheek on his shoulder and whispered against his neck, "I am glad, my lord. It would be more difficult to have my way with you were you angry."

Have her way with him—years ago, she never would have entertained such a notion. This day, just the mere thought made her shiver in anticipation.

"Your way with me, is it?" Darius brushed her cheek with his own. "When you are finished—" he slid his hands along the curve of her bottom, fingertips trailing along the separating crease "—will it then be my turn?"

The throaty question and the insistent teasing between her legs took her breath away. "Aye." She laughed at the shakines of her own voice. "But you do not play fair, I have not yet begun, let alone finished."

He caught her mouth with his own, tongue slipping beyond parted lips to entwine with hers. Marguerite stretched up, to better meet his demanding mouth.

Darius fought a smile. With her legs wrapped tightly around his waist, her movement had only left her more open to his hands.

Before she could realize that he'd completely stolen her turn at seduction, he stroked and found the entrance he sought.

Marguerite stiffened for less than a heartbeat before

she moaned and tightened the hot, moist walls surrounding his finger. Darius groaned, cursing the clothing separating him from her flesh.

This they would have to try again later, when he was as naked as she. For now, however, he was determined to make this a night neither of them would forget.

With his free hand, he stroked the back of her thigh, adjusting his hold so he could easily reach between their bodies.

Darius brushed past the wet curls to gently circle the quivering flesh hiding beneath. He swallowed her gasp, turning their kiss more forceful when she began to move in rhythm against his hand.

As he longed to ride the crest of this storm with her, he rather enjoyed watching and hearing her take the journey alone.

If he were as lost in the throes of passion as she, would he as fully notice the hitch in her breath, or the trembling of her legs? Would he feel the fast and furious pounding of her heart against his chest, or the hot, rapid contractions around his finger?

She tore away from their kiss, digging her fingernails into his shoulders, and dropped her head back. A sheen of perspiration beaded her forehead and upper lip. Her pulse throbbed in her neck.

He lowered his head and slowly swirled his tongue around one passion-swollen nipple. Marguerite moaned, digging her nails harder through his clothing and into his shoulders. Her legs tensed around his waist.

"Darius—"

She was like a dead weight in his arms and he whispered, "Shh, my love, hush." Before the guards outside the door could hear her cry, he pulled her mouth back to his, walked the two steps to the bed and let her fall back onto the mattress.

She moved impatiently on the bed, picking frantically at his clothes, her breath ragged. Darius pushed away her hands and knelt on the floor at the edge of the bed.

Marguerite lifted her head and stared at him. "This was supposed to be my turn."

He shrugged at her breathless, panted complaint and pulled her legs over his shoulders. Alternating soft nips with kisses, he worked a trail up the inside of one thigh. When there was no more than a breath between his lips and her swollen, throbbing flesh, he met her eyes and said, "It is," before covering her with his mouth.

When he heard the moan start deep in her throat, he covered her lips with one hand and couldn't suppress his laugh against her wet, trembling flesh. If anyone saw them at this moment they would never believe this was a consensual act between a husband and a wife.

Marguerite half rose and grasped the covers at her sides for a moment before falling back limp on the bed. He took his hand away from her mouth and slid up over her, resting on his elbows.

Darius stared down at her in amazement, then kissed away the single tear running down the side of her face. "What is this?"

She turned her head away. He cupped her cheek and brought her back to face him. "Do not hide from me. Answer me."

Marguerite wrapped her arms around him tightly, as if she'd never let go. "Now that we have come together again, I cannot imagine not having you here with me."

"Ah, love." His heart constricted as he held her to him. "Can we put tomorrow aside for this night?"

"Tomorrow will still come. We cannot escape the earl's plans any more than we could escape my father's."

"True, we cannot. The world will always dictate our future—it is the way of life. But can we not live for this moment now and let the next day take care of itself?"

She drew a shuddered breath beneath him. "We can try."

"And we will succeed." He rolled off her. "Are you hungry?"

"Food?" She laughed. "A chance for a night of love-making and you think of food?"

Darius rose from the bed, lifted one eyebrow in what he hoped was a haughty manner, stared down at her and said, "It seems to me that I might need my strength to finish this night."

A pale rose hue colored Marguerite's face, but she returned his look easily. "You do realize that it was supposed to have been my turn first, do you not?"

He nodded.

"Well then, since you so slyly took my turn, I get the next two."

What man in his right mind would deny his lady that opportunity? Darius shrugged. Not him. He reached out to help her up from the bed. "I apologize. Please, feel free to have your way with me, at your will."

Marguerite laughed softly as she came up against his chest. "It has in likelihood cooled by now, but there is a waiting bath for you."

A bath, warm or cold, sounded like heaven to him. "Are you saying I stink?"

She nodded. "Aye, milord, like the beasts in the stables."

"Beasts?"

"Yes. Beasts." She leaned closer and kissed him on the chin. "Although, I do rather enjoy this beast."

Darius felt the heat of his own blush race up his neck to cover his face. "You are a brazen wench tonight." He lifted her in his arms and headed toward the wooden bathing tub. "For that boldness you can act as my maid."

She rested her head on his shoulder. "That has been my plan all along."

When he stopped at the edge of the tub he held her over the water. Marguerite wrapped her arms about his neck. "Do not even think of such a foolish trick."

Darius lowered her slowly toward the water. She clung even tighter. "I will scream if you do."

He turned slightly and let her feet touch the floor. "Consider yourself saved this time."

Marguerite dipped a hand in the water. Satisfied that it had not cooled over much, she helped Darius shed his clothing. After struggling to take off his boots, she slowly removed one article at a time, letting her fingertips or knuckles graze his skin. She savored the act, knowing full well the opportunity might not come again.

Not many days ago, she'd called him a childhood friend. Much had passed between them in that short time. He'd beckoned her memories to awaken and he'd assured her heart that his love was still there for the claiming.

Henry Thornson had shown her the ways of the

world, the ways of men and women. In the end, he'd granted her the opportunity to grow into a woman bold enough to take what she wanted. And what she wanted, was all Darius offered—passion, desire, safety and his undying love. Everything he had always offered. Everything they stood the chance of losing again.

He bid her to live for this moment, to let tomorrow take care of itself. It would rip the heart from her body to lose him now. Instead of dwelling on nightmares that might be, she would savor the reality of this night.

When Darius stood naked before her, she could not stop herself from stroking the flesh covering the muscles of his chest. She leaned forward and placed a soft kiss over his beating heart, before leaning against him.

His pulse quickened at the contact of flesh against flesh and he drew her into his embrace. Strong muscles cradled her soft yielding breasts. Marguerite arched into him, rotating her hips against the rapidly growing hardness between them.

"Your first turn will not last long at this pace." His ragged voice, deep and husky, brushed against her ear, spreading the already growing fire racing through her limbs.

"Perhaps." She traced a scar running the length of his back, wondering briefly what had caused so grievous an injury. Marguerite lowered her arm, kneading the muscles on the side of his hip before turning her hand to stroke his shaft. "But then the second turn will only last longer."

She felt his shudder of anticipation against her hand. She sank to her knees, easily shrugging away from his grasp as he tried to hold her against him.

"Marguerite—"

A light feathery kiss against the soft flesh stopped his words. She smiled at his sudden intake of breath. "It is my turn, milord. You need do nothing but surrender."

He sank his fingers through her hair, stroking her scalp. "I am your slave."

She laughed softly before testing his words. There was no doubt in her mind that he would only play slave to her ministrations for so long—giving up control had never been an act he enjoyed. She had every intention of taking advantage of that time, no matter how short it might be.

He was hot and hard against her lips. His flesh twitched and she let the beat of his heart race against the length of her tongue. With quivering hands he rubbed her neck and traced the shells of her ears before sliding his fingers back into her hair.

To her amazement, he let her set the pace, tightening and relaxing his grip on her hair until he gasped and pulled her to her feet. "No. I want—"

He wanted the same thing she did, to be inside her, but the bed seemed a league away. Marguerite took one look into his glazed eyes and knew he was as close to the edge as she.

She pushed him down onto the bench next to the tub and straddled his lap, coming down onto his rigid manhood in one fluid motion. Darius gathered her close in a hard, possessive embrace before thrusting up on a groan.

They fit together perfectly, melding into one. Their hearts pounded in unison, gasping breaths inhaled and exhaled at the same moment. Dear Lord forgive her, but no other man could make her feel this complete.

She bit his shoulder, tasting the sweat of his labors. He nudged her head with his own, silently seeking contact with her lips. Marguerite returned his hungry kiss with one equally demanding.

It truly seemed as if a storm raged around them. Furious and full of danger it threatened to consume them. But she felt no fear, only an insatiable craving for his touch.

She hungered for him, for the safety and the love he so freely offered. After all she had put him through, he came to her and accepted the fact his eldest child bore another's name. He did not begrudge her having shared another man's bed.

Instead, he offered her his hand and his name as a guarantee of safety for her and their son. In the end, whether he admitted it or not, he had given her his heart. She felt it in his touch, in his kiss, and it filled her soul with such gratitude and love that she could not hold back her tears.

When the storm broke around them, Darius shuddered against her, swallowing her sob. He threaded the fingers of one hand through her hair and cradled her head against his shoulder. Slowly rocking on the bench, he stroked her back with his other hand. Once his heart ceased its wild pounding, he felt the wet heat of tears against his chest.

"Do not, Marguerite, not again. Do not fear what may never happen."

She shook her head. "How can you be so gentle, so giving…after what I've done to you?"

"You cry for the past?" He pulled her away from him and wiped the tears from her face. "You waste tears for things we cannot change."

"I do not deserve this."

He smiled. "You are right, you deserve more than I could ever offer."

She blinked through the moisture blurring her vision. "Do not tease me."

"I am not teasing you. We cannot change the fact that your sire took you away from our marriage bed and gave you to another. We will never be able to change the fact that my sire beat and then disowned me. It is a waste of time to even try. But we have today. We have the future. It will be enough for me. Will it be enough for you?"

"Aye." She bit her lower lip. Now she had a good inkling of how he had received the scar on his back. Her heart constricted with the knowledge that he had gained it because of her.

He brushed the wayward locks of hair from her face. "Marguerite, hear me well." He waited until she gazed into his eyes. "You are everything I ever dreamed of, everything I have ever desired. I will let nothing happen to you. Nobody, nothing will come between us again. Do you understand me?"

When she nodded, he continued. "Your marriage to Thornson happened. That is a fact and cannot be denied. He came into your life through no wish of your own, no wish of mine. But he cared for you. He cared for my son. He kept the both of you safe so that this moment could happen. I thank him for that, my love. But no man will ever again hold what is mine in his arms."

Her heart swelled until she thought it would burst inside her chest. The tears she'd fought so hard to stop, flowed anew. She leaned against his chest, unable to find words to describe what she felt.

He patted her shoulder before pulling her hard against him. "If you dissolve into a watering pot every time I declare my love for you, I will cease to do so."

"I cannot help it."

He sighed and she fought to swallow against the lump in her throat. Finally, hoping she would be able to contain her tears, she sat up and laid a hand against his cheek. "I do love you so, Darius, and I would rather die than be given away to another."

He placed a kiss on her palm before resting his forehead against hers. "Then we need find a way to ensure your long life."

"Tomorrow." She repeated his words. "We can dwell on it tomorrow."

"And how will we ever entertain ourselves the rest of this night?" His chuckle rumbled in his chest.

She nodded toward the tub, wrinkling her nose. "Well, there is still the matter of your bath."

"Ah, yes, I so look forward to a nice cold bath."

Marguerite lifted her eyebrows as she leaned away from him. "I will warm you, milord."

Marguerite watched the night sky lighten. Soon Bertha would arrive, heralding the start of another day.

She turned her back on the rising of the sun and snuggled against Darius's side. Heavens, what a night it had been. If any dire harm befell her this day and sent her to her grave, she would surely go there with a smile on her lips.

She rubbed a hand down his chest and knew from the unsteady beating of his heart that he was awake. "Did you sleep well?"

"Sleep?" He turned to face her. "When did we sleep?"

She lowered her hand toward his groin and he grabbed her wrist. Darius groaned. "Oh, love, no. There is not one muscle in my body that does not ache."

She leaned over him and dropped a kiss between his eyes. "It is a terrible thing to grow old, is it not?"

"Old?" Darius threaded his fingers through her hair, drawing her closer. "Watch you tongue, milady."

Marguerite laughed, then flicked the tip of her tongue across his lips. "That sounded almost like a threat."

He stopped the banter with a kiss that stole her breath. The moment her fingers curled tightly around the bedcovers, a knock sounded on the chamber door. She bit her lips to keep her cry of frustration quiet. Darius cursed softly.

"Lady Thornson." The earl's shout floated through the thick wooden door. "Open the door."

Marguerite rose on legs that threatened to fold beneath her. She wiped the perspiration from her face and wondered if the earl would see the lingering passion in her eyes.

At least he would not see Darius. Marguerite silently gave thanks that they'd thought to hide Darius's clothing and sword beneath the bed. Darius rolled to the far side of the bed, then scrambled off and beneath.

Her heart pounded wildly from the combination of unfulfilled desire and fear as she shrugged quickly into a gown. "I am hurrying as fast as I can." She heard Darius's snort from beneath the bed and resisted the urge to throttle him.

She removed the locking bar from the door and opened it. "My lord earl, what brings you to my chamber so early?"

Earl William stepped into the room and slowly inspected every inch before facing her. "I am off for a day of hunting and wanted to tell you that while you have leave to go about the keep and inner bailey at will, you are not under any circumstances to go beyond the walls of Thornson."

It set her teeth on edge to have anyone command her inside her own keep. With a tight rein on her temper, she nodded. "As you wish."

"Good." He turned to leave and then halted at the door. "Oh, Faucon, you are not to leave the keep, either."

Marguerite's breath caught in her chest. Surely he had to be guessing.

Earl William laughed before he touched his nose. "The smells. Horseflesh and sex." He walked out the door adding, "Faucon, we will speak about this matter later."

Chapter Fifteen

With a smothered curse, Darius scooted out from under the bed, dragging his clothes with him. Some of his suspicions about the earl had been answered. York was up to something, and Darius doubted it had anything to do with him or Marguerite.

Quickly dressing, he urged, "Go about your day as if nothing were amiss."

She'd removed her hastily donned gown and slid back under the bedcovers. "You are leaving?"

"Aye." Darius grabbed his boots and sat on the bench to tug them on. "Earl William is up to something that does not bode well. I need to discover what he is about."

Marguerite picked at the edge of the covers. "If I remember correctly, it has something to do with a Lord Marwood."

He heard the slight tremor in her voice and crossed the short distance to the bed. "Stop that." He grasped her hands to quiet the fidgeting.

"Marguerite, I do not believe Lord Marwood exists. At least, not in the sense we were led to believe."

"How can you say that? What reason has the earl to lie?"

"I know the day is early, and our night was long, but try to think clearly." He ignored her glare and continued. "If this Marwood were truly your future betrothed, do you believe the earl would have dismissed my presence in your chamber so lightly?"

She shook her head, obviously not in agreement. "He was not positive you were here—he only guessed."

"Horseflesh and sex?" Darius still marveled at the man's ability. "He was as certain of my presence as I am that the sun will soon rise."

"If what you say is true, what do you think he actually plans? Why is he hiding his deviousness behind a lie?"

Darius had already gone over the conversations with the earl in his mind, repeatedly. Yet, he could not completely separate the fact from the fallacy. "Perhaps it has something to do with Thornson, not us."

"What?"

Marguerite's sudden gasp drew his attention fully to her. The fingers beneath his hands worked the covers' edge. He stared at her face, oddly pale and tense. She looked everywhere but at him.

Darius's chest tightened. "What have you done?" He grasped her chin, forcing her to meet his gaze. "What is afoot here?"

"Nothing." She pulled out of his grasp. "I have done nothing."

The earl was not hunting for game. He was hunting for the very same thing Darius had sought since the day he'd arrived at Thornson. The smugglers. "Your tunnels and caves will seal our deaths if the earl finds them first."

Marguerite slid lower in the bed. She would not escape that easily. He leaned forward and pulled her roughly to him.

"We have a son to raise, Marguerite. Do not let some misplaced sense of duty destroy all that is before us."

"No." She burrowed into his chest. "Nothing will be destroyed. It is over."

"Over? What is over?"

"The smuggling is over. With Bainbridge's death, there is no one left to give orders but me. And I have already told them to cease."

Darius swallowed hard, fighting the bile that had risen to his throat. "Bainbridge's death?"

She pulled out of his hold and looked at him, a question creasing her forehead. "Yes. How can you not remember killing him?"

"Holy mother of God." Darius bolted from the bed, strapped on his sword belt and ran a hand through his hair. "What ever made you think I killed him?"

Marguerite lifted trembling fingers to her throat. "You said you dealt with him. I thought…"

"You thought wrong. I had no reason to kill the man—it would have been murder. I only ordered him from Thornson's lands." Darius needed to capture Bainbridge in the act of smuggling. Had Marguerite done something to thwart his plans?

She scrambled from the bed, groping for her gown. "I must go. I have to stop them."

With a shout of frustration, Darius grabbed both of her arms, stopping her frantic motions. "You will do nothing of the sort."

When she tried to pull away, he tightened his grasp

until she flinched. "Stop it this instant." Certain she would cease her struggles, he relaxed his hold but did not release her. "I am the lord here now. I will deal with the trouble, not you."

"It is *my* duty." She tried to step away.

"Woman." He shook her. "Listen to me. It is *my* duty and mine alone. Your duty is to your son. Do you hear me?"

"Marcus." His name was but a whisper falling from her trembling lips.

"Yes. Marcus. Find him and hold him close to you this day. Marguerite, do nothing rash."

"But the men, the caves—"

"If you would but tell me where they are, I will see to them myself. It is a responsibility I willingly accept."

"I cannot." She shook her head. "Nay. Darius, do not do this. I cannot send you to certain death."

He glanced out the narrow window at the rising sun. Time was not on his side. He could not stand here and argue with her all day.

Not knowing what else to do, he jerked her hard against his chest and lowered his mouth to hers. When she clamped her teeth tightly against his tongue, he twisted his fingers in her hair and tugged until she opened to him.

Only when her knees buckled and she rested heavily in his arms did he gentle his assault. "Where?" he whispered against her kiss-swollen lips. "Tell me where, my love."

He ignored her half cry of surrender, the tears forming in her eyes, and claimed her mouth again. Darius knew that eventually she would make him suffer for this heavy-handed treatment, but right now he would do anything to obtain the information he needed.

Her breath caught on a sob and she pushed at his shoulders. He lifted his head, but did not release his hold on her hair. "Where?"

Marguerite closed her eyes. "The maps are in the chest by the bed."

Darius loosened his hold and brought her gently into his embrace. "Thank you, Marguerite."

"I hate you, Faucon." Her statement carried little conviction, especially when they were punctuated by a shuddering hug.

He laughed softly and kissed the top of her head. "I am sure you do."

"You will pay dearly for such high-handedness."

"I promise, I will hold you to that threat."

He tightened his arms around her briefly, then stepped away.

She crossed to the chest and handed him a rolled set of maps. "What will happen if the earl discovers you in the smugglers' company?"

Darius reached out and stroked her cheek. To never look again on her face would cause him great distress. But he had to answer her truthfully. "I will die a traitor's death."

She gasped and made a move to pull the maps out of his reach.

Quicker than her, he easily retrieved the bundle. He looked at the door to tunnel, then back at her. "Marguerite, as my wife and as my son's mother, I beg you promise to follow my orders."

She bit her lower lip and nodded.

"Keep Marcus safe today. Keep yourself out of danger's way. If anything should go wrong, if anything should bring about my demise, go to Faucon. Go to Rhys." He reached inside his tunic, pulled a heavy ring from the pouch strapped to his side and handed it to her. "Take this to him and he will see that you and Marcus spend the rest of your lives in safety."

She turned the ring over in her hand, tracing the worn etching of a falcon. "This was your father's."

"Yes. It was the only thing he did not take from me before sending me away."

She flinched before placing her palms against his chest. "I am so sorry, Darius."

He gently grasped her hands. "There is no time to worry about that now." He lifted her hands to his lips and kissed her fingertips. "My love, we must fight for our tomorrows. Promise you will do as I ask."

She nodded.

"No. Marguerite, I need to hear your promise."

She leaned against his chest and stared up at him. "Darius, I vow to keep Marcus safe while we await your return. I will go to Rhys only if need be."

"Osbert will see you safely there." He released her hands and placed a soft kiss on her lips before moving away toward the tunnel entrance.

Without looking back, Darius worked the locks on the doors, stepped through and closed them behind him. Then, when he was certain he could no longer see her, he rested his forehead briefly against the coolness of the door.

A shudder seized him. Dread of what this day might hold and anticipation of a battle soured his mouth.

The sensations were familiar. Every fighting man felt them in the moments before going into action. The odd thrill of a coming war racing hot and liquid through his veins lent him strength to complete his mission. The scent and the taste of bloodlust prepared him for the sounds and acts to come. The warning dread heightened his awareness of pending doom. All of it served to finely hone his practiced skills for what lay ahead.

He lightly tapped the door once with the back of his fist, whispering, "Be safe, Marguerite." Then he headed back toward the stables.

Marguerite leaned against the door. She heard his light tap and felt his love and concern as it seemed to pour through the stone and wood to swirl around her.

How could she sit here and do nothing to help him? She could not—she *would* not—simply stand by idly while Darius put his life in jeopardy for those at Thornson.

And how could she not warn the men who had so faithfully served Lord Henry Thornson? While others might consider them traitors, these men had honorably followed their liege lord's orders. She could not let them suffer for doing no less than their duty.

Bertha entered the chamber. "Lady Marguerite, are you awake?"

"Aye." Marguerite briefly touched the entrance to the tunnel. *Take good care, my love.* Sure of her ability and more certain of her need to stop Thornson's men before anyone, including her husband, found them, she left the alcove. "Help me dress, Bertha."

The serving woman looked around the chamber. "Did Lord Darius find his way here?"

"Yes, he did, thank you."

"And did the two of you have a…pleasant evening?"

While she ignored the question, she could do nothing about the flush heating her cheeks. Instead of answering, she asked, "Are any of Henry's tunics still here?" She bent and opened the chest that had been his.

Bertha joined her. "What for, milady?"

Marguerite pulled out an old brownish woolen tunic and held it up. "This will suit my needs. Find me a shirt, braies and some stockings."

"Are you thinking to disguise yourself as a man?" The maid inhaled sharply. "No, not again. My lady, you cannot be serious. Tell me that you would not be thinking to join the men."

"I have no choice, Bertha. The earl and Darius are fast on their trail and I need warn them away from the caves."

Bertha grasped her arm. "No. Let it go. You will gain nothing except Lord Darius's anger."

Marguerite's heart skipped a beat. "I know this. But in time his anger will fade." She pleaded for understanding, "Do you not see? I can live with his anger, for as surely as I know my own name, I know he will eventually forgive me. But I cannot live with the guilt should Thornson's men die while I did nothing to try to save them."

"Oh, my lady, he will punish us both." The maid shivered, but she rooted through the chest looking for the other garments.

Once dressed, Marguerite held Bertha's hands. "Thank you. Now, I need one more favor from you."

"Anything."

"Take my son to the village. Stay there with him until I return."

Bertha frowned. "Lady Marguerite, what you seek

to do holds much danger. What if you are caught? What if the men refuse to listen to reason?"

Marguerite crossed to the alcove, picked up the Faucon family ring, returned and placed it in Bertha's hand. "Take this with you. If anything untoward should happen to both me and Darius, find one of Faucon's men, give this to them and show them Marcus. They will take him safely to Faucon."

"I do not understand. How will they know I did not steal the ring?"

A battle raged in her mind and heart. Finally, Marguerite put her son's safety above all else. "Bertha, anyone from Faucon who sees Marcus will know he is of their blood."

A half smile lifted the maid's lips. "I thought he looked a little too much like Lord Darius."

Marguerite laughed. "Like Darius? Heavens, you have no way of knowing it, but my son looks exactly like his uncle, the comte."

Bertha closed her fingers around the ring. "That is even better. As you wish, my lady. But I would much prefer if you and your lord returned hale and hearty."

"I would also." She pushed Bertha toward the door. "I must go quickly. Be off with you."

Once the maid left the chamber, Marguerite slipped through the entrance to the tunnel with a prayer on her lips. *Dear Lord, may he forgive me for what I am about to do.*

Bainbridge leaned on the tower wall and smiled. Life was good. He held back a satisfied laugh. In truth, life was much better than simply good.

Thanks to Marguerite's imbecile serving wench, his plans had fallen neatly into place.

Last night he had watched as the maid left the young master in the kitchens before she made her way across the bailey. He'd followed her to the stables and heard her conversation with Faucon. While Darius and Marguerite had in all likelihood rutted the night away, he had set his plans in motion.

As a loyal servant to the Crown, although he'd not say which crown, he'd felt it his duty to share his concerns with the Earl of York. With Falcon's men banished from the keep, getting to Earl William proved easy. By staying in the shadows, he'd crossed the inner bailey without notice. Since the walls and entrances were guarded by the earl's men, access to the Great Hall had also been uneventful. He had to give Marguerite her due: he had almost fallen prey to the sleeping draught she'd slipped into the wine.

But the far-too-tired yawns of the men gathered in the Great Hall spoke volumes. As a few of them drifted off to an early sleep, he had replaced the earl's tainted wine with fresh. The improved beverage had allowed the two of them to talk of traitors and smugglers far into the night.

He'd been careful. The earl was nobody's fool, so he'd only hinted at things that he'd heard. And he'd lamented the disturbing fact that Lord Faucon, King Stephen's own man, was unable to discover the truth.

Bainbridge chuckled at the memory of Earl William's look of shock and dismay. He'd known full well that the earl would take it upon himself to spy on the happenings at Thornson.

As he watched the earl leave the keep he knew he'd been correct.

He'd also guessed right about the level of pride in

both the Earl of York and Lord Darius. It did not require a great deal of thought to realize they would each be driven to find the smugglers first. And considering Marguerite's tender concern for Darius, he'd come to the conclusion that she'd eventually hand over the maps.

His spies had already informed him that Darius did indeed have them. Excellent news. With that information in hand, Faucon would be in the midst of the smugglers by the time Earl William found the caves.

Faucon would soon be gone. Bainbridge would make haste to offer his services to York in regard to Thornson. After all, a keep this grand needed a loyal and trustworthy servant in charge.

Along with Thornson, he would also gain possession of Lady Marguerite. Bainbridge's blood ran hot and fast to his groin. Whether he would marry her or not was something that could be determined later. For now it was enough to know that the conniving harlot would warm his bed, or anything else he so ordered.

"My lord Bainbridge."

He jerked around at Sir Everett's interruption. "What do you want?" The man was to simply guard the door to the tower, not speak.

Everett pointed out toward the cliffs, then swung his finger in the other direction. "The lady is headed for the caves. Her maid takes the boy to the village."

Bainbridge cursed. It was about time someone taught that woman how to obey orders. Since it was apparent that neither Faucon nor York was capable of the task, he would see to it himself.

He slammed a fist into the wall, then smiled at the realization of what joy the task would bring. "Gather three of the men. We need overtake her, quickly."

* * *

Darius spread the maps out on the floor of the stable. Osbert and the men from Faucon flanked him. "We must find the quickest route to the cave on the beach."

"My lord?"

While studying the larger map, he explained, "I am certain the smugglers will be active tonight when the tide goes out. Earl William is already hunting for them. If we wish to save our necks, we need find them first. Otherwise it will appear that I have failed in my mission for King Stephen."

Everyone moved in closer and intently studied the maps. Each knew what failure would mean for Faucon and ultimately for himself.

One of the men pointed to a tunnel. "This one, my lord."

At the same time another man asked, "What about this one?"

Darius took both maps and placed them in the center of the circle of men. The first one appeared to be a tunnel that led out toward the forest, then veered off toward the cliffs. He touched the markings at the water's edge. "What do you think this represents?"

Osbert shrugged. "The location of the cave's mouth perhaps?"

"Do you suppose Thornson's men scale the cliff down to the cave?" His own family raised and trained falcons. At times it had been necessary to take the young raptors from their nests perched high on rocky ledges. An ascent, or descent of a rock cliff did not bother him overmuch, but he was not certain the other men would have the same type of practice.

"Aye." Osbert paused. "Maybe that is not the best idea."

"Agreed." Darius set that map aside and spread the other one out. He looked at the man who had chosen this map. "What did you see here?"

The man ran his finger along a line. "Here, my lord. It appears to be a path running from the back of the kitchens along the bailey to the inner wall, and then it just stops."

Something he'd seen earlier tapped at his mind. Darius flipped through the rest of the maps, grabbed the smallest one.

He held the smaller one next to the spot on the larger map where the path seemed to disappear. Osbert nodded. "The tunnel heads across the bailey and then drops down at the edge of the wall."

Darius rolled the two maps together and slid them inside his tunic while rising. "Take the others along just in case. But we try these first."

Osbert looked from him to the door of the stable. "How are we going to get to the tunnel?"

Darius shrugged. "Walk."

"What about Earl William?"

"He is already gone from here and his men are with him." Darius ran a cloth along the edge of his sword before sheathing the weapon in the scabbard strapped at his side. "There are nine of us. If anyone stops us, draw your weapons."

The men laughed. Osbert shook his head. "That might not be wise."

He placed a hand on his captain's shoulder. "Good heavens, my man, if I started making wise decisions now you would complain that I was not enough of a Faucon to suit you." Darius relented in his teasing of the man. "Come, Osbert, we go to do battle."

Just as Darius knew they would, the captain's eyes lit with a familiar yet unholy light and smiled in anticipation. "Excellent, my lord."

Marguerite paused on the rope ladder, wrapping one arm around the side, and used her free hand to tuck her braid back down inside the tunic. Never had she been so grateful for the use of Henry's clothing. She would have ruined one of her gowns had she worn it to make this descent to the mouth of the upper cave.

As it was, she'd already torn one sleeve of the tunic while fighting with the heavy ladder. One of the men had always secured it to the trunk of the tree and dropped it over the edge of cliff for her. She'd never had to do it alone before.

Henry's hard lessons had served her well. The knots she'd tied held the ladder securely. But without a man to hold it steady from below, the whipping wind slammed her back and forth across the rocky cliff face. Her efforts would be of no use if she were to fall before reaching her goal.

She looked down, trying to determine how much farther she needed to climb, and was relieved that only a few rungs remained. She closed her eyes and prayed that the strength in her arms would not give out before she reached the entrance.

Marguerite took a deep breath and began the final descent. The wind picked up force and she flinched as the ladder whipped against the rocks cutting into her knuckles and scraping the side of her face.

She hung on tightly and waited for the wind to pause, before reaching out to grab a nearly unseen handhold next to the cave's mouth.

"Blast." She gritted her teeth as she missed on her first attempt. She filled her lungs with air and reached out again.

"Here, Lady Marguerite, let me help you."

Marguerite nearly lost her hold on the ladder as Bainbridge grasped her wrist.

Chapter Sixteen

Marguerite waited until she gained a firm foothold inside the mouth of the cave before trying to jerk her arm away from Bainbridge.

He only laughed at her and tightened his hold, shouting for Everett. "Bring that torch over here and lead the way."

She glared at Everett. "Consider yourself relieved of duty."

The captain ignored her; obviously he already took his orders from Bainbridge. She wondered how long that had been happening.

Once the captain was in place, they headed deeper into the cave. Their pace was quick. Bainbridge tugged on her arm, nearly dragging her behind him. "You can either keep up with me, or I will pull you along on the floor. The choice is yours to make."

Marguerite stumbled in surprise at the evil tone of his voice. Immediately regaining her balance, she quickened her pace. "What are you doing here, Bainbridge? I thought Darius told you to stay off of Thornsons' lands."

He again laughed. "That will soon be an order I need not worry about. By this time tomorrow, or at the latest perhaps the day after, Thornson will be mine." He glanced over his shoulder and smiled. "And so will you."

"Over Darius's dead body."

His head bobbed up and down. "That is the plan, yes."

Her heart slammed against her ribs. "What are you talking about?"

Bainbridge came to a halt, turned and hauled her against his chest. "Sweetness, the first lesson you need to learn is when to keep your mouth closed. Now would be a good time for you to begin."

"Go to—"

He cut off her curse by slapping his free hand over her mouth and nose. Not only did it stop the words from leaving her mouth, but it stopped the air from entering her lungs.

Marguerite struggled uselessly against him. The more she tried to break free, the harder he pressed his hand into her face. The rocks beneath her feet started to sway; the walls closed in on her. She ceased her fight for freedom and hung her head.

Bainbridge removed his hand. "See, that was not so hard, was it?"

Certain that he would think nothing of killing her, Marguerite kept her mouth closed and shook her head.

He turned away from her and resumed his fast-paced trek through the tunnel.

She followed along, one foot following the other. She doubted not that he would gladly drag her on the floor of the cave if she fell.

What had she done? How was she to warn the men of impending danger? Another thought, a more frightening one, entered her mind. Would she come through this alive? Would she get the chance to hold her son again? Or to embrace her husband?

"Here we go." Bainbridge swung her into a smaller room deep inside the cavern. He released her and she tripped, falling on her knees to the hard floor. "That appears to be a good position for you. On your knees."

She heard the rattle of a chain and scrambled for the rear of the room.

"Oh, fear not. I will not use these unless you make it necessary." Bainbridge whispered something to Everett that she could not hear before he came to stand over her.

He reached down and stroked the side of her face. "My lovely Marguerite, you are not quite in command at the moment, are you." He tugged at her braid. "Get used to it, my sweetness."

She resisted the urge to spit at him. Instead, she bit the inside of her mouth to keep her tongue in check.

"You stay right here. Everett will keep you safe." Bainbridge ran a finger along her jawline. "I promise that when all is done, I shall escort you back to Thornson and our waiting bed."

She shuddered in revulsion at the mere thought of sharing a bed with him. He stared down at her, his face distorted by a questioning frown that marred his forehead, and a smirk of satisfaction curling his lips.

Finally, when she was near to screaming in frustration, he spoke. "You have no response to my promise?"

It took a great effort of will to silently shake her head.

His eyes widened with surprise. He mused, "Considering how much you appear to loathe me, I am forced to wonder if perhaps you detest Faucon more? Is that why the thought of sharing my bed leaves you speechless?"

"You are mad to even think that might be so." No effort of will could have kept her silent at his mistaken assumption. "I would rather die than so much as step near your bed."

He laughed. The vile guffaws bounced off the rock walls of the small cave. "That is more like the response I expected of you."

Marguerite wished she could take back her outburst. It'd been a mistake to give him verbal proof of her outrage.

Bainbridge reached inside his tunic, then leaned toward her. "Who would you pine for more, my lady? Faucon, or your son?"

Darius could fend for himself and thankfully her son was safe. So instead of answering his question, she posed one of her own. "Why do you ask such a thing?"

He motioned Everett to bring the torch closer and held out one hand. Light glinted off the object resting on his palm. "My generosity should please you—I let your maid live."

Terrified but curious, she stretched up to see what he held. The sight of the sparkling ring sent cold tendrils of fear racing toward her heart. She reached for the Faucon family crest, only to have Bainbridge close his fingers around the engraved gold.

"No, this will remain in my possession until you see fit to fulfill your sworn vow to Thornson."

Marguerite choked down the fear threatening to

close her throat and cloud her mind. Was she being offered the chance to keep her son safe? What would it
cost her? "What vow?"

"The one you made right after Henry's death."

She'd been angry, hurt, lost and in mourning—what
had she vowed? The memories slowly flooded back.

Before she could put voice to them, Bainbridge supplied the answer. "To keep the shipments to King David
flowing."

"No." She'd made more recent promises...to Darius.
"I cannot."

"So be it." Bainbridge stood upright. "Just remember when you bury your son and new husband that you
had denied them the chance to live."

She lunged after his retreating form and grasped the
hem of his tunic. "Wait. Please, wait. What must I do?"

His cold, smug look of satisfaction made her shiver.
Marguerite realized that she had just sold her soul to
Satan's helper and there was little she could do to regain it. She was on her knees before the man she hated
and feared more than any other.

Marguerite bowed her head in defeat and asked,
"What must I do?"

"It is simple, really. You will remain here, under Everett's guard, until I send word. Then, you will be released to make your way to the main cavern and ensure
neither Faucon nor his men leave there before I arrive
with the Earl of York."

"You would brand my husband a traitor?"

"Yes. Gladly."

Her heart throbbed heavy in her chest, the pain of it
bringing a cry of loss to her lips. "He will be put to
death."

"And I will dance on his grave."

"My son?"

"After Faucon is confined to a tower cell, I will give you this ring and your son. You will be free to leave Thornson and not return. I will not even force you to watch Faucon's death. How much more giving could I be?"

Where would she go? Not to Rhys. Comte Faucon would slit her throat in retaliation for her trickery. She would have no choice but to return to her father's keep. The thought of living under her sire's roof was abhorrent, but living without her son would be impossible.

"What did Darius ever do to you to deserve such treatment?"

"He is King Stephen's man. He thought to take not only the Lady of Thornson from me, but the keep itself."

"The lady was never yours for the taking."

He sighed. "You would have been. Once you saw the danger that thwarting me could bring, you eventually would have come begging me to take you for my own."

Not in a dozen lifetimes would she have begged him for anything. She'd have killed him first. But it was now too late to do anything except what he ordered.

"You will comply with my wishes?"

Marguerite hesitated, trying desperately to think of a way around what he planned. Unable to devise a plan, she nodded. "I will."

"Your simple word is not enough." He hauled her to her feet. "Seal your vow."

Dear mother of God, what did he want from her now?

He pulled her close, until his lips moved against hers

as he spoke. "Fear not, my sweeting, this will not hurt overmuch."

She closed her eyes, seeking to block out what he was about to do. Before she could make sense of his actions, he stepped away, grabbed her wrist and slid something sharp across her palm.

Marguerite yelped with pain and pulled her bleeding hand away from his grasp. She stared in shock at her hand. "You cut me!"

He swiped the dagger slowly down the sleeve of her tunic, wiping the blood from the blade, before jabbing the weapon back into a loop of his belt. "It is nothing compared to what I will do if you fail me."

His tone of voice set her limbs to quaver. He only patted her cheek, laughing before he turned and left her alone in the dark.

She fell heavily back onto her knees. She was lost. *All* was lost. There would be no future for her and Darius. No future in which they would raise their son together. There would be nothing, except many long, cold years filled with guilt and regret.

She could not live the life Bainbridge thought to hand her. She would rather die with Darius than live without him. But she had more to consider than just her wants or wishes. If she left this earthly plane, Marcus would be alone.

Marguerite pounded the floor of the cave with her fist. *Think, you fool, think.* There had to be a way around this. A way to save both Darius and Marcus.

She slapped a hand over her mouth, hoping to cut off the threatening sobs. She could not think of a workable plan. Bainbridge would easily discover anything she tried before he arrived in the cavern with the earl. Even were she to escape Everett's watchful eye and make it to Darius in time to convince him to take his man back to the keep, Bainbridge would know.

What would he do to Marcus? She could not risk her son's life in that manner.

Her heart jumped. If she could do nothing beforehand, what about afterward? Once Marcus was safely in her arms again, what was to stop her from going to the earl herself and explaining all?

Bainbridge? Nay. It would be his word against hers, and who would the Earl of York believe?

Marguerite frowned. Would he believe her? Was that a risk she wished to take?

But what if she could quickly find Comte Faucon? Would he not be able to convince York of the truth of her words? Rhys would never believe his brother capable of traitorous activities and he would fight for Darius's freedom.

That could work. She would have to find a way to get the earl to hold off executing Darius. Surely, at the very least he would grant the Lady of Thornson a little time.

First she had to find a way to lie to Darius's face. The thought of what he would do when he discovered her treachery caused her breath to catch. He would be angry. More than angry. He would quite likely never trust her again.

Not that she would blame him. But she would spend the rest of her days proving her love to him. At least he would be alive for her to do so. And that was what mattered.

"I am sorry, my love. So very sorry." Her whispered apology fell on the damp rocks beneath her. Her soft laugh followed. She was back where she'd started before she and Darius had shared their night of passion.

She'd told Everett that she'd see this shipment through...that she'd deal with Darius and his men. But after the shared night with her husband, she'd changed her mind and agreed to let Darius take charge.

Unfortunately, neither of them had counted on Bainbridge's interference. Now she wished she'd never given Darius the maps to the tunnels. If he'd not had those in his hands, when night fell he might still have been searching for the caves.

No, she could not change the past; no amount of wishing would make it so. The only thing she could do now was to wait for Everett to release her. Wait and pray that this hastily devised plan of hers would find success.

Darius stood at the door to the kitchens and took a steadying breath before motioning his men to follow him into the cookhouse.

"What the..." The cook's shocked question faded as soon as she looked at Darius's face. With little more than a nod toward the storage room, she ordered her helpers to resume their work and turned back to her own tasks.

He followed the direction of her nod and looked around the storage area, seeking anything that might be an entrance to the tunnels. Osbert tapped on the walls with the pommel of his sword.

"Here, my lord."

The hollow tone of Osbert's tapping told Darius that his captain was correct. With the memory of the false cupboard door inside the Great Hall fresh in his mind, he tugged at the shelving.

The wooden structure moved away from the wall, creaking on concealed leather hinges as it swung open, scraping across the hard-packed dirt floor. He and his men wasted no time filing through the opening. The last man through pulled the shelving unit closed behind them.

With the torch held aloft, Darius led his men in the direction of the sea. The tunnel was only wide enough for them to walk single file.

Battle in this confined space would be nearly impossible. Without enough room to swing a blade, they would be reduced to hand-to-hand combat with nothing more than their wits and daggers.

Even though his bloodlust had strengthened with the passing of hours, he would prefer to employ his sword. The length of the blade somehow made killing another seem less personal.

When the tunnel widened and branched off in three directions, Darius paused to unroll and study the map. Osbert peered over his shoulder. Between the two of them, they decided not to take the path in front of them. By the map's description, that would end too far before the cliffs.

The tunnel to the right appeared to lead to the forest and the village beyond.

Instead, they chose the corridor that veered off to the left. Darius kept his voice low as he ordered, "This way. We can only hope the designer of these maps has not purposely set us off on a false trail."

The men followed him single file. As he turned a corner, a slight breeze rushed across his face. The smell of the ocean broke the staleness of the dead air and he knew they were on the correct path.

This tunnel steadily widened until Darius could see the opening to a chamber before them in the distance. He lifted his arm, bringing his men to a silent halt.

Osbert stepped up beside of him and motioned toward the doorway. Darius nodded, giving his man the signal to investigate. The last move he needed to make at this moment was one that would lead him and his men into a trap.

His captain stayed close to the wall and moved as silently as a spirit toward the opening. He peered inside for a moment before waving the others forward.

Darius and the remaining men entered the large cavern and paused. Crates and bags loaded with what he could only assume would be weapons and gold littered the floor. Only a small path wended its way through the stored goods, leading to yet another tunnel.

Darius approached that pathway cautiously. He heard the lapping of water nearby and knew that once the tide went out this would be the exit to the beach. His heart raced at their accomplishment.

He turned and ordered, "Move these crates to the sides."

"Leave enough room behind them to use as cover," Osbert added.

While the men bent to their task, Darius inspected the contents of some of the wooden crates. He'd been correct—they were loaded with swords, daggers, jewels and enough gold items to fund a war.

And he had little doubt that these riches would soon be on their way to the Empress Matilda via her uncle, King David of Scotland.

Not if he could help it. He let a lid fall closed. King Stephen had often run short of gold, and this would go far to replenish his coffers.

The men labored together, making short work of re-arranging the bags and crates. They would be able to hide behind them, keeping their presence a secret until Thornson's men arrived to carry out their smuggling duty. Osbert had made certain that they'd left enough of the items strewn about the entrance so that anyone approaching would not be suspicious until they were within reach.

Darius leaned against the opening of the corridor that led back to the keep. If luck was on his side this day, all would be accomplished well before Earl William discovered this cave.

A noise broke into his thoughts. He moved away from the door, waving at his men to take their hiding positions, and waited.

There, he heard it again. Soft footsteps heralded the approach of what he deduced was a single person. Maybe someone had been sent here early to check on the readiness of the shipment.

He would be in for quite a surprise.

The approaching torchlight wavered along the wall of the tunnel. Darius gently drew his sword, holding it against his leg, and curled his fingers tightly around the leather-wrapped grip.

The footsteps came nearer. His heart thudded inside his chest. He glanced at Osbert, noting that he too had drawn his sword.

The light from the nearing torch flickered brighter. Darius planted one foot hard on the floor of the cave to better balance himself to lunge.

Osbert slowly, silently crept to the opposite side of the opening. Experience and instinct wordlessly formed their plan of attack. The captain would grasp the intruder, at the same time swinging him around. Darius would instantly plant his sword at the center of the man's neck. This foolish intruder would be defeated before he knew what had happened.

When the footsteps were an arm's length away, Darius mouthed, *Now*. Osbert immediately reached out like a bird of prey attacking its food and grabbed the man's arm, quickly drew him around to face Darius's ready sword.

A gasp, issued in unison from his men, held his hand steady. Darius's gaze followed the length of his sword to the point where it pressed against Marguerite's neck.

He clenched his jaw until he thought his teeth would shatter. The tic in his cheek traveled up to his eye. "We both might be better served if I follow through on this thrust."

She said nothing, only blinked at him, her wide eyes shimmering in the light of the torch she still held.

He angrily jammed his sword back into the scabbard and tore the torch from her seemingly frozen grasp.

"Our son is well?"

After a brief hesitation, she nodded.

"And our bedchamber, it is occupied by my wife and her child?"

She shook her head and shrugged.

When she opened her mouth, he quickly placed two fingers over her lips. "The last thing I want to hear is your voice."

Osbert cleared his throat. "My lord, perhaps I should ensure her safety?"

Darius did not even pretend to misinterpret his captain's meaning. "It is not as if I will kill her." Although at first, the thought had been strong in his mind. Only the wild lurching of his heart had stayed his thrust.

A heavy silence fell over the cavern. Nobody moved. Nobody spoke. It was as if all held a collective breath. When the pall became unbearable, Darius pushed the torch toward Osbert and pulled Marguerite to his side.

"Perhaps we should talk," he said, nearly growling the statement of the obvious through still clenched teeth.

She did not disagree. Instead, she nodded toward the exit at the other side of the cavern.

Darius draped one arm around her shoulders and held her tightly to his side. He pressed his fingertips hard into her upper arm, conveying his anger. The slight stiffening of her body gave him proof that she understood.

He kept his eyes focused in front of him as they crossed the cave silently. He knew the men watched and waited for what they would consider little more than entertainment at his expense. He would be damned if he'd supply them with the much-anticipated enjoyment.

When they were at the edge of the receding water, Darius swung Marguerite around, putting her back against the damp wall.

He took a deep breath. "What in the name of heaven were you thinking? Do you not comprehend the danger in which you have put yourself? Do you not care about the safety or the future of our son?"

Without being told to, she remained silent while he drew breath to renew his tirade. "Did you not hear my words this morning? Did you not swear to keep yourself and Marcus safe? Did you not take my need to focus solely on this task into consideration? How am I to concentrate on a coming battle while worrying about protecting you at the same time?"

Marguerite chewed on the inside of her lip. Her pounding heart had slowed enough that she clearly heard his last question.

His obvious concern gave her the faith in his love that she needed. Oh, aye, he was angry. That much was evident in the hard way he'd escorted her to this place. But his anger this moment was nothing compared to the rage he would soon experience.

She could not allow herself to panic. She needed to see this treacherous scene through one heartbreaking step at a time. The first thing she needed to do was to convince Darius that she'd come to help.

She lifted her hands and grabbed the front of his tunic, tugging at him. "And how was I to remain safely idle in our chamber while sick with worry for you and my men?" That was an honest enough question.

Emboldened by the ease of the first lie, she rattled off a myriad of her own questions in the same manner he had employed. "This is my keep. Mine. Is it not my duty to see to the safety of all those at Thornson? Did you expect me to stand on the wall wringing my hands while waiting to see what fate would deliver? Do you not know me at all? Do you think that because I am a woman I have less pride? Less strength of conviction? Less honor?"

Honor. What eternal damnation would she suffer for claiming to have honor? She drew back her shoulders and stared into his eyes, raised her voice a notch. "Was I not a Faucon before taking Thornson's name?" The words nearly stuck in her throat.

The tic in his cheek disappeared, to be replaced by an indent foretelling the coming smile. Darius pulled her into his arms. "What am I going to do with you?"

"You could help me save my men." That, too, was true enough—he would in the end be helping to save all of Thornson. She prayed to God that she'd be able to save him at the last.

He nodded, his chin bouncing into the top of her head. "Aye, my liege. But I will promise you one thing. If you get yourself killed, I will beat the living daylights out of you."

Marguerite laughed at the absurdity of his promise. She rubbed her cheek against his chest, ignoring the hard bite of the chain mail beneath the fabric of his tunic. It would be small, seemingly insignificant moments like this that she would cherish in the days ahead. "I would like to see you try, my lord."

He pulled her tighter against him for a moment before releasing her. "Enough of this. We have work to do."

She ran one hand down his mail-covered chest, hoping to perhaps change the direction of his thoughts. "There is never enough of this."

Darius snatched her wrist and pulled her around to his side. "Later, love—" He stared down at her blood-covered palm. "What is this?"

"Nothing." Marguerite's nervous laugh sounded forced even to herself, but she added yet another falsehood to the ever-growing pile. "It is nothing. I cut myself coming down the rope ladder to the upper cave's entrance."

"Upper cave?" Darius's eyes narrowed. "You used the cliff entrance?"

She laughed nervously. "Come, come—how many times did we scramble up and down Faucon's cliffs for your sire?"

"True, but explain to me how a rope can leave a wound such as this."

"Yes, well…I used the rope ladder to descend the side of the cliff."

He nodded. "You have already said that."

Marguerite needed to think fast—before he began to question her more closely. "I slid. It was so windy that the ladder beat against the cliffs, and when I started to slide, I reached out to grab the wall and cut my hand."

"On the rope."

She could tell by the slight hint of sarcasm that he was already beginning to doubt her words. Marguerite rolled her shoulders and her eyes at him. "No, heavens no, I cut my hand on a jagged rock."

Darius released her hand and crossed his arms over his chest. The tic had returned. "Did you suffer any further harm?"

"No. A few bumps and bruises, but that is all."

"That hand needs tending so it does not fester." His gaze slowly drifted over her body. "But other than a few scrapes, you do not appear to be harmed."

"Truly, Darius, I am not."

"Good. And you met no one else on your way to this cavern?"

Her heart paused before slamming against her chest. "No. Are others here besides you and your men?"

"Not as far as I know. But I am convinced Bainbridge has made himself known to the earl."

"Wh—what makes you think that?"

Darius's eyes narrowed again. Marguerite knew she

was walking on not so solid ground. Finally, he answered, "The earl left in far too much of a hurry this morn for it to be a simple coincidence."

"Do you think Bainbridge filled his ears with information?"

"Information and lies. I wonder what he hopes to gain."

"Thornson, perhaps." Marguerite fruitlessly wished the words back into her mouth.

"What makes you say that?"

Even without meeting his gaze, she felt his stare. Why had she thought for one instant that she would be able to pull this off? But she was too far in now to pull back. "He has sought to claim Thornson ever since Henry died. He would stop at nothing to gain what he considers his greatest prize."

"Then, I guess we will have to ensure he loses."

If God was truly merciful that would happen soon.

"One more thing before we join my men. Since you are here and in apparent good health, how and where is our son?" His tone was accusing.

"Oh, yes, I am sorry." It wasn't exactly that she had forgotten Marcus, it was more that she wished not to dwell on his safety for fear she would lose her mind. Instead of lying outright, she would give Darius as much of the truth as she dared. "I sent him to the village with Bertha. He will be well cared-for there." He'd best be cared for, because if one hair on his head was harmed, she would make Bainbridge pray for death.

Darius's brows winged over his eyes briefly before he asked, "And should anything happen to prevent our return…?"

Marguerite looked at the ceiling. *Steady. Keep your*

voice steady. "I gave Bertha your ring—" she lowered her gaze to his "—with orders to find Comte Faucon should anything happen to us."

"Rhys will be thrilled, I am certain."

A doubt niggled. "But he will care for Marcus, will he not?" *Ah, but would he care for Marcus if she failed to save Darius?*

"Of course he will." Darius took Marguerite's hand in his. "I would prefer the task be left to us, though."

He placed her hand in the crook of his bent arm and reentered the large cavern, where he called to the men. "Osbert, bring the maps. All of you gather around—we have much to discuss."

Chapter Seventeen

Darius paused at the opening to the cavern and looked at his men. His lips twitched with amusement. Marguerite glanced at the men and noticed their crestfallen faces. They'd expected to witness a boisterous row from the lord and lady and were obviously disappointed.

He released her hand and took the maps from Osbert. The top of a crate served as a table where he spread out the maps of Thornson. "Where will the men from Thornson enter this cavern?"

She wished that she could tell him that the men would not be coming. Instead, she pointed to an area not far from where they were currently gathered. "Here." *Here is where the earl and Bainbridge will come, seeking to seal your fate.*

"When can we expect the boats and Thornson's men?"

"Very soon." Everett had held her in the smaller cave until shortly before sunset. With the passing of the time between then and now, the tide would quickly be out, if it was not already. "The boats sit anchored just beyond the outcrop farther down the beach. They will remain there until Everett lights a fire on the farthest point of land at sundown. That is when the tide recedes enough to uncover the beach directly below the exit of this cave. Only then will they approach."

"Good. Then our wait will not be long." Darius nodded toward one of the men. "We have ten men waiting for orders in the forest. Go, send one to act as lookout from the outcrop. Have another two ready to relay messages. When you are done, return here and bring four of the strongest with you."

"Darius, that will leave only three men out there." Marguerite did not understand his logic. If he was seeking advance warning of the boats, he might already be too late. And in the process he was bringing more men to the caves for the earl to capture. But she could not warn him of that folly without giving away all.

"It will leave only three of Faucon's men for the earl to capture. Three loyal men who know little of what we are about."

"It is but a tactic to stall the earl should he discover the men," said Osbert.

"Oh." Since neither Darius nor Osbert realized that the earl was headed in this direction and not to the beach, what they were doing was logical. She could not help but feel sorry for the three being left as decoy. What if Earl William, in his anger and impatience, did come upon them first and decided to kill them where they stood?

"But, my lord, why would they willingly give their lives for this?"

Darius stared at her. "They will do whatever they are told." When she gasped softly at the coldness of his statement, he explained further, "Fear not. Earl William and I hold no great love for each other, but William and Rhys are fast friends. Contrary to what you have seen here, York and Faucon are allies. My men will be doing nothing that could brand them traitors. William will not harm them. He will simply ask them questions, and I have ensured they will have no reason to provide lies. They will truthfully not have any answers to provide."

"Oh," she repeated, unable to find words to voice what she truly thought. York was no ally to Faucon, at least not to Darius of Faucon.

"What about Thornson's men?" Darius prodded. "How many will there be? Will they be armed? Are they trained to use weapons?"

"About twenty men will arrive. Most are villagers and will be armed with little more than pitchforks and axes. Five or six of them are Thornson's guards."

"Who will lead them?"

"That used to be up to Henry." She shook her head. "But with his death, I truly do not know. Everett is no leader, so that was never his task. You killed Matthew upon your arrival, so they are unable to look to him. It will most likely be Bainbridge."

She could mix truth in with the lies, but it did nothing to lessen the cost to her soul. Each lie, each half truth cut into her heart like a searing knife.

Darius asked, "Who led them the last time? The time we foiled their shipment?"

Marguerite slowly looked at each face surrounding her. "I did." Her voice was but a whisper. She squared her shoulders and met Darius's eyes. "I did." This time her answer contained the strength he expected of her.

The laughter from the men around her surprised her,

but she was more shocked when they voiced their approval.

"Do not be so surprised." Darius touched her shoulder. "Never forget, we are all Faucons here. Our women are not known for backing down from a fight."

"It was not as if I was successful in that task, was it." However, she would be this time and it would place him in much danger.

"Fear not. This time will be different," Osbert reassured her.

She slapped her hand down on the crate. "I cannot fail this time."

Darius covered her hand with his own. "You will not fail. We will not permit it to happen."

The others murmured their agreement. Marguerite shuddered. They did not understand her statement, nor would they understand the action she was about to take. They would later, but would that moment come far too late to save her love?

Darius watched her closely. Something bothered her, something she'd not shared. He had no choice at the moment but to trust her. While the outcome of this mission rested in his hands, she would be a factor in his success. She would be better able than he to stop her men from doing anything foolish. And Darius wished not to take any man's life unnecessarily.

Ack, he worried for naught. He'd chosen her as his life's mate long ago. Even though years had separated them, he was as certain of her now as he had been the first time they'd exchanged vows. She had no cause for concern, no cause to doubt the support of the men in this room, or of any from Faucon. He wanted her to understand that simple fact.

Darius dropped to one knee and brought her hand to his chest. "Marguerite of Faucon, my men and I are at your service. Nothing will sway us from our successful completion of this battle to save Thornson and its men from harm."

Osbert and the others followed suit, adding their "ayes" to his vow.

When Darius rose, he pulled her against him and whispered into her ear, "You can reward me later."

She stepped away, her face a shining flame of red. The color conveyed not the words, but the meaning of his whisper to his now-whooping men.

Her flush deepened. She placed a hand over her heart. "I thank you, but I...I am not worthy of such a gift."

Darius heard the tremor in her voice and rolled his eyes briefly to the ceiling. Let her not act the weakling now. He was rewarded by the sound of her long, steady intake of breath.

He clapped his hands together once to get the men's attention. "We need get to work. Bainbridge and the others will be here within moments."

"Do you think he will bring the earl?" Osbert asked.

"He might." Darius stared pointedly at his men. "If that is the case, do nothing to harm William. Escort him out of harm's way immediately."

Marguerite asked, "Could we not just toss this shipment into the water, return to the keep and be done with it?"

"Yes, we could. But we would be depriving Stephen of much-needed gold, and I will not do that."

"So either way, these items will be used to fund the ongoing war?"

The men stared at her in shock. Darius stepped forward. "Marguerite, do not seek to come between us and our king."

"I meant no disrespect." She took a step back and raised her hands. "I have voiced the same thing about King David and Empress Matilda. Sometimes it is hard to quell a mother's fears for the future."

He hid his smile. Thankfully, she had the ability to think quickly. His gaze dropped to the side of her tunic. Her fingers furiously worked at the seam.

Darius took her hands between his, lifted them to his lips, then pressed a kiss to her fingertips. "You worry for naught. You will be safe. This will all be over soon."

Marguerite closed her eyes. This would all be over sooner than he thought. Her stomach knotted. She could not do this, not to him, and not to the men who had just sworn an oath of loyalty to her.

When he released her hands and made to turn away, a fear greater than any she'd ever known twisted her stomach and tore at her heart.

Marguerite could not continue the lies. "Darius—" Terror and regret overwhelmed her, and the floor seemed to buckle beneath her feet. She fell against him, grasping at his arm, grasping for a way to hold him safe. "Darius, I am sorry, forgive me."

Footsteps echoed from the corridor. He stared down at her, confusion in his eyes. She watched as he took in the sound of the approaching men, swords clanging at their side, spurs clinking on the rock floor. He closed his eyes, then opened them. His hands shook as he set her forcibly aside.

"What have you done?"

Not waiting for her answer, Darius turned to his men. He laid his sword and dagger on top of the crate, then removed his battle gloves and helmet. "Disarm, now. Do not fight." At their outspoken disagreement, he slammed his fist on the crate, splintering the wooden top. "Drop your weapons. Do as I order."

Osbert stepped forward. Marguerite flinched at the glare he directed toward her before placing his weapons atop Darius's.

The other men followed suit. Moments ago they had knelt and sworn an oath to protect and serve her; now they walked by her with varying degrees of anger and hatred etched on their faces.

Once all of those gathered had given up their swords and daggers, Darius drew in a long, shaking breath, lifted his chin and stared down at her. "Have you forfeited only my life, or those of my men, too?"

Unable to meet his pain-filled gaze, she kept her eyes trained on the floor. She choked on a sob as she answered, "The men were never mentioned."

"Save your tears for later, when I will not have to look upon them and know what lies they concealed." His harsh laugh raked across her ears. "I do thank you for the lives of my men."

She could not let think she did this willingly. "Darius, I—"

"Cease. Close your lips and save it for another more willing to hear your voice." He turned away from her, but stopped abruptly, his back to her. "Has your hatred for me always been this strong?"

She had expected his anger, rage and pain. She had thought she'd prepared herself to bear the weight of her deceit. By telling herself it was needful before they could have their future free from Bainbridge, free from the threat of treachery, she had thought she would be able to bear it all.

She'd been wrong. Nothing could have prepared her for the crushing agony pressing against her chest, or the shards of glass cutting at her throat, or the burn of her tears flowing like fire from her eyes.

She could not bear it, not alone, not without him knowing why. "Darius, please, I—"

"No!" He held up his hand. "No more." He resumed his walk toward the corridor. "I would rather go to my death without the sound of your betrayal ringing in my ears."

He paused at the entrance to the corridor and looked back at Osbert. "Do what you must to get the men home to Faucon." At Osbert's nod, Darius added, "And take my son to his uncle."

"No." Marguerite stepped forward, but Darius ignored her and left the cavern, heading toward the approaching danger.

She turned to Osbert. "No, I will not let you."

Sir Osbert grabbed her arm. "Have you not done enough harm already? How can you believe any of us here would allow you to have the same power over another Faucon—even one as young as Marcus?"

"I am trying to save my son, and his father."

"By making him appear a traitor to his king?" The captain snorted in disbelief. "Tell your lies to someone who will listen."

"Osbert, for the love you bear your lord, Bainbridge is holding my son—Darius's son—hostage under the threat of death if I do not help him capture Darius."

The captain's curses burned her ears. He looked back at the men, then brought his attention back to her. "You seek to trick me."

"Nay. Upon my son's life I tell you the truth." Marguerite broke free of his hard grasp, lunged toward the wooden box and grabbed a dagger from the pile of weapons.

Faucon's guards issued curses, but Osbert lifted his hand to stop them. He reached toward her. "Give me the dagger, Lady Marguerite."

She would never be allowed to cross the small distance between them to hold the knife to Osbert's chest. The men would stop her before her first footstep landed on the rocky floor. So instead, she held it against her own throat. "I would rather die now than live with the burden of Darius's and Marcus's deaths upon my soul."

Osbert's eyes widened. The men behind her muttered to each other—some issuing encouragement for her to take her own life, others wanting the opportunity to take it themselves. Darius's captain lowered his hand. "If what you say is true, am I safe in assuming you have a plan to save Darius's life?"

Marguerite nodded but did not remove the dagger. She held the point steady against the rapid pounding of her pulse.

"I trust you not, but I see no choice but to listen to your plan. If you betray Faucon again, I will give you to the comte's guard." Osbert lifted one eyebrow and stared at her. "They will ensure that you suffer long and hard."

Marguerite's pulse slowed. She sighed in relief and lowered the dagger. She understood his threat. For a reason that was beyond her comprehension, Comte

Faucon had managed to create an image of evil for himself that extended to his men.

She knew Rhys. If any harm befell Darius, his brother Rhys would cheerfully see to her death. But it would be swift and clean.

His men, on the other hand, would not be so forgiving. She'd heard tales about the captain of Comte Faucon's guard. The man had a sick penchant for prolonged torture. It was said to be a highly effective manner of gaining information, except for one minor detail—the men who broke under his hand did not live.

Her plan would work. And if it did not, she would rather condemn her soul for an eternity by taking her own life than fall into the hands of Faucon's captain.

Osbert reached out, tore the dagger from her hand and tossed it back on the pile of weapons. "I am waiting, Lady Marguerite. What do you think we need to do?"

"Send a man to Rhys, quickly, before the earl and Bainbridge arrive in this cavern."

"Quickly? Lady Marguerite, we have already sent men to look for Comte Faucon. The Earl of York captured one of the men and took the missive the man carried to Rhys."

"Did the others escape the earl?" She prayed that they had. Perhaps that would hasten the comte's arrival.

Osbert shrugged. "As far as I can tell, they did. They have not yet returned to Thornson."

"Good. Then perhaps Rhys is already on his way here. Send another man to meet him on the east-to-west road."

"Why would you assume that to be the correct direction?"

Marguerite wanted to scream; they were wasting precious time with this discussion. "Was the comte not last seen at Brezden?" At Osbert's nod, she continued, "That is less than a two-day journey from here. If one of the men would but go to Thornson's village, my maid could secure a trustworthy guide all the way to Brezden's gates if need be."

"And if he is not still there, perhaps they will know where he headed." Osbert frowned, thinking the idea over in his mind. Finally, he admitted, "I agree with this much of your plan." He pointed at one of the men. "Pick up your weapons and go find the lady's maid."

"Wait!" Marguerite grasped Osbert's arm. "My son. Find and free my son first. Otherwise, I can say nothing to save Darius without risking Marcus's life."

The captain revised his order to the man. "Secure the boy's safety, then bring Comte Faucon here as quickly as possible." The man jumped to his bidding and slipped away through the tunnel.

Osbert then turned back to face her. "What else do you have in mind?"

She swallowed and sent a silent prayer for the ability to explain her plans to Darius's captain winging toward the heavens. "Surrender. As Darius already ordered, do not fight the earl."

Osbert closed his eyes briefly and shook his head. "Oh, aye, that sounds like a completely logical way in which to save Lord Darius."

Unarmed, carrying no torch or weapon, Darius strode toward Earl William and Bainbridge, defenseless in the dark.

At this moment his safety meant nothing to him. He

no longer cared if the earl took his life, or let him live. In fact, the latter might be a harder task than dying.

How could she do this to him? Why? For what reason would Marguerite betray him in such a manner?

He posed no threat to her or those at Thornson. He was certainly no threat to their son. Had he not proven himself time and again?

He should have put her and her men in chains for the traitors they were when he first arrived. He should have followed the king's orders and routed the smugglers that night, along with their leader—Marguerite.

Instead, he had saved the woman from Bainbridge's clutches and married her to keep her and their son safe.

Darius shuddered. He was too soft. He thought too much. If he somehow managed to come out of this alive, he would never make the mistake of caring too much again. From now on, he would make his life much simpler by just following orders to the letter.

He squinted against the garish light of the nearing torch and stopped his approach. This spot was as good as any to face death.

"Faucon, hold!" The earl's unnecessary shouted order bounced off the rock walls.

Darius lifted his hands to show William that he was not armed. "I am going nowhere."

Bainbridge laughed as he pointed his sword at Darius's chest. "I was correct. Faucon is in league with the smugglers."

Earl William slapped the side of his own sword atop Bainbridge's, knocking the weapon away from Darius. "Simply finding the man in a tunnel does not exactly prove his guilt."

"I am certain we will discover his men with the ill-gotten goods nearby."

Darius snorted at Bainbridge's excited certainty. Of course the man knew what they would find in the cavern ahead. "Considering you had help in this charade, I am sure you will find just what you seek."

Bainbridge's lip curled briefly before a smug grin worthy of Satan swept his mouth. "I know I will."

Earl William motioned Bainbridge ahead with his sword. "Feel free to lead on." He then looked at Darius and shook his head. The earl did not appear surprised, angry or even overly joyous at the discovery.

Darius frowned. There was much more afoot here than he'd thought.

At William's nudge, Darius turned around and followed Bainbridge, the earl at his back. In a whisper meant only for Darius, William said, "Follow my lead."

Had the earl actually said those words? Or did his ears deceive him in the same way as had his misplaced trust in Marguerite? Unfortunately, now was not the time to turn around and ask the earl to repeat himself. All he could do was to wait and see what happened.

When the three of them reached the entrance to the cavern, Bainbridge stood aside and nodded toward the Earl of York. "You first, my lord. Let this surprise be complete."

William muttered something that sounded suspiciously like a curse under his breath before stepping forward into the supplies-laden cave. Darius followed, keeping his gaze on the earl's back. He'd no wish to look any of his men in the eye—their concern for their lives would make him ill. And he had even less desire to ever again set his gaze on Marguerite.

With a huff of impatience, Bainbridge lunged in front of William and Darius. He stepped forward and took Marguerite's hand, drawing her closer. Darius took a step sideways, putting more than an arm's length between himself and the woman who'd placed him in this position.

"My dear, dear, Lady Marguerite." Bainbridge reached into the pouch hanging from his sword belt and pulled out an object that Darius could not see. "Since you have kept your part of our pact, let me reward you."

He placed the item in her palm, and Marguerite quickly curled her fingers around the object. Bainbridge then waved toward the tunnel on the opposite side of the cavern before saying, "You are free to leave."

To Darius's amazement, Marguerite ignored Bainbridge and dropped to her knees before William. "My lord earl, I beg of you, make no assumption of what you see here before listening to Faucon and his men."

William stared down at her. "In truth I can make no assumptions of any kind. All I see is a group of unarmed men standing around doing nothing."

Bainbridge raced to the closest crate and tore off the lid. "Nothing? Look in here and what do you see? Swords, daggers, axes, shields. All meant for a journey north and eventually to Empress Matilda's troops." He opened another crate. "Gold, gems, coins. Enough to fund months of battle."

The brightening gleam in the earl's eyes informed Darius that the goods in this cavern would never find their way to any location save Scarborough in York. Earl William would undoubtedly use them to replenish his own coffers.

Bainbridge glared at Marguerite. "You need leave

this place immediately, else harm may befall your son—"

Before Bainbridge could finish his snarl, Darius leaped forward and grabbed the front of the man's tunic. "Touch one hair on that child's head and I will see you in hell."

Faucon's guards surged forward as one, their curses filling the silence of the cave.

"Faucon, hold your men," William shouted into the rising voices.

Bainbridge pushed Darius away and swung his sword up for belated self-protection.

Darius raised his arm. "Osbert, hold."

Quickly, before the two men could be at each other's throats again, William moved around Marguerite and stood between Darius and Bainbridge.

"I demand satisfaction!" Spittle flew from Bainbridge's mouth as he shouted. "Put this traitor in chains and deliver him posthaste to his maker."

"No!" Marguerite rose and grabbed the earl's arm. "No, my lord, please, this is not his doing."

Earl William looked from one face to the other. If Darius didn't know better he would have the impression that the earl was uncertain what to do. That wasn't possible— William always knew what move he would take next.

Before any decision could be made, a group of approaching men drew everyone's attention to the tunnel. Darius glanced at Bainbridge and felt the hairs on his neck rise. What else had the man planned for this night?

The answer to his question appeared at the doorway. "My Lord Faucon, the men are ready to move the supplies into the boat," Everett called out just before entering the cavern.

Darius groaned. He could not deny one simple fact—Bainbridge had seen to everything.

Marguerite released the earl's arm and gasped. "What are you doing?" Her stare of disbelief flew to Bainbridge. "What have you done?"

Bainbridge shrugged. "My lady, of what do you accuse me? I have done nothing except made certain Earl William was present to see the traitorous level to which Faucon has sunk."

William sighed. "Faucon, I am left with no choice but to hold you in a cell until word can be send to King Stephen."

"Nay!" Bainbridge shook his head. "No. There is no need to wait for the king's orders. The man has been caught in the act of smuggling. He should pay for his treachery with his life—immediately."

"I do believe I hold rank here." The earl leaned closer to Bainbridge. "We will do this my way. I will not put a Faucon to death without King Stephen's knowledge."

While that statement brought Darius a measure of relief, he wondered why William had suddenly decided to hand over control to the king. It was a tactic the earl seldom employed.

Bainbridge's face turned an unhealthy shade of red. "This is not what we discussed."

William's focus swung from one side of the cave to the other before fixing on Bainbridge. "I am certain you are not blind. It seems to me that at this moment we are far outnumbered, and only Faucon's order to his men to hold has kept them from attacking." He stepped back. "However, if you would wish to battle Faucon and his men by yourself, I bid you good luck."

To Darius's amazement, Bainbridge appeared to actually consider the invitation. Darius's own hand itched to grab his sword and meet him man to man. Finally, Bainbridge backed down. "Nay. I do however request that Faucon be confined and not left to roam freely about Thornson."

At that request, William nodded. "Yes, I agree." He motioned toward Darius. "In fact, I think now would be an excellent time to return to the keep."

"No, wait." Marguerite stopped them. "Do you see that this was all arranged? Faucon was here to stop the smugglers, not to help them load the boats. With the threat of harm coming to my son, my task was to keep him and his men busy in this cavern long enough for you to catch them here."

"She lies. I did not need to use threats against a child to gain her cooperation. It took much less than that."

Marguerite looked to Darius. "That is not true. Until the man Osbert sent to rescue him succeeds, Marcus is held captive. I would never have put your life in danger for Bainbridge unless he had threatened my son."

Darius wasn't certain what to believe. Even if their son had been threatened, why did she not just tell him that? Why go through the motions of lying and ensuring he and his men be caught with the goods?

Marguerite pointed at Bainbridge. "This man would not tell you the truth even under the threat of death." She swung around and motioned toward Everett. "However, Sir Everett has been a coward for as long as I can remember. Twist his arm and he will spill all."

"Lady Marguerite, cease. Can we not continue this back in the warmth of the keep?"

"But—"

William cut her off by grabbing her arm and pushing her in front of him. "Go. I am chilled and wish the warmth of a fire and the taste of your wine." He called over his shoulder. "Sir Osbert, dismiss your men and escort your lord to the keep."

"My Lord Earl, I can bring Faucon along."

William laughed at Bainbridge's statement. "I wish the two of you to arrive whole and alive. You can escort Sir Everett to the Great Hall. He, too, must be confined."

Everett's cries of innocence could be heard all the way back to Thornson.

When they stepped out of the kitchen buildings and into the bailey, Bertha rushed forward, crying, "Lady Marguerite, you are safe!"

"And why would I not be safe?"

The maid looked nervously from Bainbridge to Marguerite. "I was told that you were being held captive and that Bainbridge needed Faucon's ring to gain your safety."

Marguerite groaned. "Where is Marcus?"

The serving woman pointed toward the stables, to where young Marcus was merrily playing with a stick in the dirt.

Bainbridge refuted her earlier accusation. "And you told these good men that I held that boy hostage. Now, my lady, who is the liar?"

Darius barely heard Marguerite's shouts following him as he let the earl lead him to the keep and away from any more of her lies.

Chapter Eighteen

Darius stretched out on the pallet, his fingers linked behind his head, staring up at the ceiling of this tower cell. In truth he had no complaints about his accommodations. This cell had a pallet, a bench, fire and a narrow window opening. He'd spent many nights in lesser rooms before.

He had no idea how this false charge was going to end. Would the king believe Bainbridge, or would he be allowed to speak in his own defense? He did not know. Nor did he know what Earl William was thinking.

They'd not yet had an opportunity to talk. The earl had ordered Osbert to lock him up in this tower room immediately upon returning to Thornson, and he had seen no one since then. Which, in truth, suited him well. It had given him the perfect opportunity to partake in some quiet, undisturbed sleep.

Darius stretched out his arms and twisted the kinks from his neck. He didn't expect the peace and quiet to satisfy him for long. Soon he would become bored to tears. Until then, he planned to take advantage of the time.

He pulled the cover back over his shoulders and rolled onto his side. Hopefully, with any luck, Marguerite would cease invading his dreams.

Marguerite paced the floor of her chamber. Not even the scent of the lavender in the strewing-herbs beneath her ever-moving feet helped to calm her.

She looked like the liar she'd been. It would have been better if she'd kept her mouth closed and simply done as Bainbridge had bade her. But no, she had felt compelled to defend herself before the earl and Darius.

A mistake she could not erase.

Had she remained silent, Darius and his men would not have known that she'd let Bainbridge con her into this horrendous act with lies of his own. He had not captured her son; he'd only managed to obtain the ring from Bertha with more lies. So now, even Sir Osbert doubted her word.

And Everett—by the heavens he had proven to be as much of a mummer as Bainbridge. The two men could not have timed his arrival with Thornson's men at the cavern more perfectly. And to enter acting as if they were there on Darius's command took either great planning or much luck.

She preferred to think it was no more than luck on Everett's part—she did not want to consider that he might actually possess enough intelligence to plan something that devious.

Bertha entered the chamber, interrupting Marguerite's musings. "Tell me, what is happening below?"

The serving woman shook her head. "Bainbridge is still spouting his lies and accusations to the earl."

"Ah, yes, but does it appear as if Earl William believes him?"

"I cannot be certain, my lady. At times it seems as if the earl is listening to every word, but at other moments it seems as if the earl does not even know Bainbridge is in the hall."

What was the earl up to? It was becoming increasingly apparent that he, too, had a plan. Marguerite shook the notion away. She had her own plans to worry about without concerning herself with Earl William.

"Where did they take Darius? What about his men? Who guards him?" She sat down heavily on the cushioned bench in the alcove.

"Lord Darius is in the rear tower cell. One of his men and one of York's guard his door. The rest of Faucon's men are not permitted into the keep."

Marguerite's heart slowed a little at the knowledge that Darius was at least guarded by those who would not seek his death in the night. "I wonder if I would be permitted to see him."

"Not without my permission." The earl had entered the chamber without either of the women seeing or hearing his arrival.

"My lord, forgive me." Marguerite rose. "I did not hear your request for entry into my bedchamber."

William shrugged one shoulder. "That is because I did not ask."

"What you lack in manners, you make up for in boldness." She wondered if now would be a good time to swallow her own tongue. "I apologize, my lord."

"No apology needed. You are concerned for your welfare and—"

"*My* welfare?" Marguerite's high-pitched question

cut off the rest of his sentence. "It is Darius's welfare that consumes me."

"I find that surprising, after you betrayed him so thoroughly."

"It was never my intention to betray him thus." Marguerite twisted a section of her gown in her fingers as she resumed her pacing. "I only thought to save my son, and help save my men."

"I think perhaps you need to explain that, because I find it difficult to follow your logic."

"My lady." Bertha dipped her head before heading toward the door. "I need see to the young master."

"Yes, please. Bring him to this chamber tonight, Bertha."

Once the maid left, Marguerite searched the myriad thoughts racing around in her mind. What should she tell the earl? How much should she divulge?

As if he could read her thoughts, Earl William grasped her arm and led her back to the bench. "Sit down. Do not plan what to tell me, just tell me what happened."

Marguerite shook her head; she did not trust this man. If she gave him information that would brand all of Thornson traitors, what would he do? If she admitted to withholding information from Darius, would it make her husband appear foolish?

The earl sat next to her and held one of her hands in his own. "Lady Marguerite, I know that you think Darius and I are enemies. That is so far from the truth that it is nearly laughable."

"Oh, aye, it has been apparent to all that you are fast friends."

"Granted, we hold no great love for each other, and to be honest, that is my fault. I have always gained much pleasure from goading the youngest Faucon. I am not certain what he resents more—my torment, or his own reaction to it. But I am as certain of his loyalty to his king as I am of my own."

Now she was even more confused. "Then why is Darius locked up in a tower cell?"

"We seek a greater threat to King Stephen and to Thornson."

"Bainbridge."

"Yes."

"Then why is *he* not confined? Why has he not been charged with acts of treason?"

"I did not catch him in the act, did I? It seems to me that I caught Darius in more questionable surroundings than I have Bainbridge."

"Darius was there to stop Bainbridge."

"So he says. At this moment, it is his word and yours against Bainbridge's."

She clung to a portion of his statement. "At this moment?"

Earl William sighed, echoing her own building impatience. "Eventually, Bainbridge will make his move. He thinks I am an overgrown fool so hungry for more power and gold that I will easily be led by he who offers more of both."

"Then Bainbridge is obviously the fool."

"Yes, he is, but unfortunately he is also a devious fool. Which makes him dangerous."

Marguerite tipped her head and looked up at William. "I fear you have only succeeded in confusing me more."

"I have permitted him to convince me of the wisdom of placing Thornson's men in charge of guarding the cavern."

"You *what?*"

He squeezed her hand and laughed. "He is eager to get his hands on those goods and to send them north to King David."

"So you will just let him?"

"Not likely. However, I will let him think I trust him. He will make his move, call in the waiting boats and load the goods onto the crafts." He paused to laugh again, the sound rumbling up from his chest. His lips curved into a smile and a gleam lit his eyes. "Too bad the men directing the vessels will be from York, Faucon and King Stephen."

Marguerite's heart stuttered with worry. "If Bainbridge so much as suspects what you are about, those men will die."

"We know this. As long as Darius remains confined in a cell and as long as I keep up the pretense of suspecting Faucon of treason, Bainbridge will remain content and unaware."

"Does Darius know this?"

"No."

Marguerite pulled out of the earl's grasp. "Then he should. I will tell him."

"Why? Because you think he will then forgive you for seeking to betray him with Bainbridge?"

She looked at the floor. "I need try."

"Lady Marguerite, what you did was wrong. You took desperate measures that could have ended your life and could have brought Darius and his men much harm. Even though I understand you were only seeking to help, you have lost the trust of the one man who loved you the most."

Had someone hit her with a sack full of grain she would not have been more surprised at his last sentence. She stared mutely at the earl, unable to give voice to the countless thoughts colliding in her mind.

He reached out and tipped up her chin. "Close your mouth. There is not one living soul in all of the kingdom who is not aware that my wife lived a year with another man. And now all wonder why I took her back."

"My God, you love her."

"That is such a surprise to you? Why? Because I am large enough and unrefined enough to be call *le Gros?* Because I am a man of power and strength who thinks only of his own pleasures?"

In all honesty, that was exactly what she thought. Instead, she asked, "You are the Earl of York, the Lord of Holderness, the Comte of Albemarle. How could someone of your stature suffer such humiliation in silence?"

"Silence?" William's laugh bounced off the walls. "I am sure Cecily would find that vastly amusing."

Marguerite could not imagine the woman having had any feelings of humor or amusement when she finally returned to Scarborough.

"As angry as I was, I could no more set her aside than I could give up my right arm. I believe you might call it love. I still think it is a sickness of the heart, but I have resigned myself to the simple fact that without her I suffer more."

She felt her lips twitch with a threatening smile. "Knowing that only makes you more human, my lord."

"Human? Me?" The earl rose slowly and towered over her, with a look on his face that promised death.

"Do not seek to tell anyone that I am merely human. You risk much by even having such a thought."

By habit, Marguerite flinched. Then she narrowed her eyes and stared up at him. "Why, you are as much a tease as the Faucons are."

"Guilty as charged." He patted her shoulder, the fierce glare leaving his face. "Do not mistake my confession for some high ideal of undying love. What Cecily and I now share came hard to us. It came with much shouting, many tears and countless nights of pain that we thought would never go away. You will find that at this moment, Darius wishes only to be free of you. I have heard his wish and have every intention of ignoring it—for a time."

Her stomach tightened as her heart squeezed in pain. "What about Marwood? My lord, I cannot leave Darius like this and go to another man's bed."

"Marwood?" The question hung in the air as if the earl did not at first know what she was asking. Finally, his frown of confusion cleared. "There is no Marwood."

"I beg your pardon? Then what was that all about?"

"I was but teasing Faucon. He does not know it yet, but his only true mission to Thornson was to marry you and raise his son as his own."

Marguerite's breath caught in her throat. She blinked rapidly, wondering what to say, what to think, how to react.

Earl William solved her dilemma. "The king has known for years that young Marcus was sired by Darius."

She shook her head slowly. How could he know? She and Henry had told no one; they had kept it a secret between them only. "No."

"Yes, my lady. He knew. And he had a request that he cheerfully swore to honor. If Darius were still a free man when Lord Thornson died, your hand in marriage would be given to Darius."

"How? Who made such a bold request?"

"Henry Thornson."

"What?"

"Lady Marguerite, I have the documents in my possession. The missive from Henry, the orders from King Stephen and a report from a cleric who visited Henry immediately after his request. The cleric confirmed Henry's admission that your son was indeed a Faucon. After seeing the boy myself, I can easily understand how the man came to that conclusion."

"The only cleric who ever came to Thornson was the one who performed Marcus's baptism. How would he know what a babe so young would grow to look like?"

The earl squeezed her shoulder. "The cleric was from Faucon—at Henry's request."

She stood and felt the floor start to sway beneath her feet. Marguerite put her hand against William's chest for support. "Why would he do such a thing?"

"I can only assume from his missive that he cared deeply for you, and that he wanted to be certain of your happiness should anything befall him."

"My happiness…"

"A treasure you may have squandered."

She moved away. "I need to see Darius."

"No." William grasped her arm, gently restraining her. "Comte Rhys has crossed over into Thornson's lands. After he and I speak to Darius, I will permit you a few moments."

"Alone?"

"No. I am sorry, my lady, but he wishes not to even speak to you. I will not permit you into his cell alone."

At her strangled groan, he added, "Give him time, Marguerite. Just give him time."

"Time? He has already asked that I be set aside. I do not *have* time."

"I will not grant him that wish until you also request the same. I am certain King Stephen will agree with me. And Darius will not go to the Church without the king's sanction first."

Her legs shook, her heart tightened. She felt the contents of her stomach threaten to escape and swallowed hard. "I will never request to be set aside."

"Then you have no cause for worry, do you." He helped her stand upright and headed for the door. "Just give him the time he needs to sort everything out in his mind."

Marguerite sank onto the edge of her bed. Time. How much time would Darius require before he accepted the fact his wife betrayed him?

She could blame the earl. After all, had he just told them why he was here and that he was planning to trap Bainbridge, none of this would have happened.

But in the end, it wasn't the earl who had forced her to plot with Bainbridge. She'd believed the man's threat against her son's life and she'd acted of her own accord, not letting her husband know what was afoot.

In her mind, that simple withholding of information did make her guilty of betrayal—and she was certain Darius felt the same.

Time. Dear Lord, let the time pass swiftly—before her heart broke completely.

* * *

Darius stared through the narrow window opening at the setting sun. He had been in this cell one night. One more night at Thornson and he could be gone from here. The thought of going home to Falcongate did not bring him as much peace as he had thought it would.

The reason was simple—he would going back there to live the same as he always had—alone.

All of the arguments his brother Rhys and the earl had tried had done nothing to change the facts. Marguerite had trusted him so little that she lied.

Rhys thought he was every kind of a fool. Perhaps his brother was correct. He was a fool. A fool desperately in love with a woman who had sought to brand him a traitor to his king.

Aye, he knew the story behind her actions. Earl William had forced him to listen as he and Rhys explained Marguerite's reasoning.

It made no difference to him. Had she trusted him at all, she would have told him what Bainbridge had done and said. She would have informed him of what was going to happen in that cavern.

He would never have done anything to put their son at risk. He willingly would have gone through with the charade—and ended up in exactly the same place. But he would have gone as her partner, not as an unwilling dupe.

Now, it was too late. Even though Rhys and William had tried, repeatedly, to convince him to talk to her, he'd held firm and refused. Not so much because he was angry, but because he was weak where she was concerned. He had no intention of talking to her until he was certain he could do so without his heart pounding, or his blood rushing hot.

He did not trust her enough to know that she would not use his feelings for her against him. That statement had made no sense to Rhys whatsoever. The earl had thrown up his hands in disgust and had, thankfully, given up.

But what he'd said was true. After all, she had counted on his love being so great that he would forgive her anything, even betrayal. She was wrong.

He would not forgive her, nor would he permit her the opportunity to try anything so underhanded again. No, he would never again be so weak where she was concerned.

In a way the entire situation was rather humorous. Years ago he had lost her to Thornson, and now, according to the earl, it seemed that Thornson had given her back.

Was he supposed to be thankful for Thornson's actions? He wasn't. He would have been more thankful had Thornson not taken her to begin with.

A sword hilt pounding on the door to his cell interrupted his whispered curse.

"Enter."

He turned and mentally shook his head at the look of concentration on his brother's face. Why did Rhys always feel the need to study him so carefully before speaking? Was he that much of a stranger to his own flesh and blood? Had his sire's actions on that long-ago day driven that much distance between him and Rhys?

The old Comte Faucon had disowned him, tossed him bodily out of Faucon with orders never to return. Rhys had been the one who'd asked him back once their sire finally died. So why now did Rhys treat him like a stranger?

"What are you thinking, Darius?"

He sat up on the pallet and shook his head. "Nothing."

"Do not do that."

"Do what?" As far as he could tell, he wasn't *doing* anything.

"The same thing you always do of late. I ask a question and you close me out."

"Just tell me something, Rhys. If Gareth had been here in my place, what would you have done?"

Rhys answered, "I most likely would have slugged him before telling him how foolish he had been." Ending on a half laugh, he frowned and asked, "What is this about?"

That was gist of his problem with Rhys. "Six years ago you would have done the same to me. So what is different now?"

"You are," Rhys stated simply. "You left Faucon an angry heartsore lad and returned a quiet, closed-off man. How do you wish me to treat you? As a boy whose sire just beat him senseless and cast him off, or as a man who keeps his distance at all times?"

"I wish you to treat me as Darius. As your brother. I cannot change what happened to the boy—"

"No. You are wrong." Rhys stepped closer. "Do you not see? You *can* change that. Everything that was taken away from you stands within your grasp, if only you would reach out and take it."

"If you are referring to my wife, I already tried reaching out for her." He spread his arms to encompass the cell. "And this is where I ended up."

"Well, by the Saints above, strike her dead for seeking to protect her son."

"There was no protecting to be done."

Rhys glanced up at the ceiling, then back. "She did not know that at the time. You are punishing her unjustly."

"Punishing *her?*" A haze of red fogged his vision. *"Her?"* He lunged up from the bed at Rhys's shoulder, shoving him out of the way as he strode to the window. "Oh, aye, she is being punished, all right."

Rhys grabbed his arm and jerked him back. "Yes, her. She has explained all to me and William. We have both told you everything she said. God forgive her, she was wrong. She made a mistake. But it was based on fear. She is not a man, Darius. She does not face the daily lies or treachery we do. While we are honed for battle, she is honed to keep her family safe at all costs. And thanks be to God, there is no shame in that."

"In case you have forgotten, I have already heard all of this. Now, let me go." Darius unsuccessfully tried to pull free. "Rhys, I am warning you."

"Warn me all you wish, little brother." Rhys stared down at him, his jaw clenched, his eyes blazing. "I am not releasing you until you finally hear what is being said to you."

Without thinking, Darius curled his fingers, swung his arm and landed his fist aside Rhys's jaw.

Rhys rocked slightly on his feet, then laughed. "Not bad. Want another try?"

The door to the cell burst open and Earl William quickly came between the two men, forcing them to step away from each other. "Stop this. Good Lord, what ails the two of you?"

Rhys hitched his thumb at Darius. "My little brother is begging for a good thrashing."

The earl shook his head. "Perhaps, but not by you."

"Then who?" Darius snorted before staring at William. "And you think you are man enough to try?"

"For the love of God," Sir Osbert said from the doorway, drawing his sword and slapping it against the wall. "Boys, cease!"

All three men turned and stared at him. He tipped his head slightly and backed out of the door, closing it behind him.

Darius bit the side of his mouth to keep from laughing. He shrugged. "My man can be quite effective at moments."

William gained his composure first. "There is a meal waiting belowstairs. I expect both of you to join me. We need talk about this night's activities."

Darius had to ask. "Will she be there?" He wanted to be prepared for the worst.

Rhys and William looked at each other. Finally, Rhys answered, "Yes. It is her keep and her men."

"Fine. I just wanted to know beforehand, that is all. What about Bainbridge and Everett?"

"I sent both of them to the village for the night." William rolled his eyes toward the ceiling. "Told them to keep a close watch on the comings and goings of the men there."

"We can only hope they take full advantage of the situation." In truth, Darius prayed they chose this night to act. Otherwise he would be here at Thornson longer than he intended.

Rhys assured him, "Oh, they will. They are far too greedy not to."

"Good." The earl headed toward the door. "We can finalize the plans over a meal and put everything in place. By morning it should be over and done with."

Darius waited until William and Rhys left before saying, "From your lips to God's ear, my lord." He wanted nothing more than to be gone from here as quickly as possible.

He took a deep breath. Tomorrow would come when it was time. Right now, he needed to prepare himself for his own brand of treason.

Chapter Nineteen

Marguerite's heart pounded so loudly in her ears that she could barely hear. The stone wall of the tunnel was cold against her back. The heavy, thick layers of the borrowed shirt, chain mail and wool tunic did not stop the dampness of the stone from seeping through to her skin, sending shivers of cold down her spine.

A pinpoint of a torch's light broke the darkness, bright in the distance. She sucked in her breath and pressed back into the narrow crevice behind her.

When the approaching men slowed their pace, she waited, silent and still. Finally, one man moved toward her alone, the torch held high, illuminating the blade held steady before him.

"Lady Marguerite?" Sir Osbert's near whisper seemed to reverberate like a shout in the quietness of the tunnel.

She released her held breath in relief before stepping into the light. "Aye."

"Are you ready?"

"Yes. My men are on the beach awaiting my signal."

Osbert motioned the men behind him to approach before tipping the torch forward. "After you, my lady."

Marguerite took the lead, guiding the men to a seldom-used corridor connecting the tunnel to the cavern.

Henry's overlong chain-mail tunic banged against her ankles. Had it not been for the slits front and rear, she would not have been able to walk with any ease.

Darius had seen to the cleaning of the armor. With the rust removed, the links moved more fluidly with her body. Osbert had brought the mailed tunic to her chamber, with orders from his lord.

She was to wear the protective links or stay and share the late evening meal with Rhys and the earl.

It had taken much wiggling and grunted assistance from Bertha, but Marguerite had donned the heavy tunic and followed the orders Osbert relayed to her.

While she could not deny the heaviness of her heart at the way Darius was handling this foray, at least he had included her. She refused to permit herself the hope that this meant anything more than what Osbert said—Darius had requested her assistance with Thornson's men; he wished not to take any lives unnecessarily.

Darius and his men hunkered low in the bottom of the boats. In preparation for this night, Earl William had seen to it that those manning the boats were from York and Faucon. Unknown to those men, Darius had taken action while Earl William and Rhys planned this attack over their evening meal.

Possession of the maps Marguerite had given him was a boon he could not ignore. While everyone thought he was safely ensconced in a tower cell, he'd been able to come and go with enough ease to meet with Osbert.

As much as Rhys wished to help him successfully complete this mission at Thornson, his own pride could not permit him to welcome his brother's assistance. Darius would see to the fall of Bainbridge and Everett himself. And with Marguerite's cooperation it would be done with minimal loss of life.

He ignored the sudden racing of his heart at just the thought of her. But nothing had changed—his men had packed their supplies and when this task was complete he would return to Falcongate.

For the moment, he needed to concentrate on the mission. His stomach threatened to rebel at the constant rocking and bobbing of the small boat riding the lapping waves.

One of the oarsmen offered, "My lord, do not look at the water. Focus on the shore instead."

It helped some, but Darius was unable to completely ignore the call of the sea and found his gaze wandering back to the water.

"There it is, my lord." Another of the men pointed excitedly to the outcrop jutting from the beach.

As expected, either Sir Everett or one of the other smugglers signaled to the boats with a torch. Darius motioned to the men in the boat next to him and they in turn motioned to the others.

Rhys drummed his fingers on the oak table. "How long do we wait?"

"Be patient." William polished off another goblet of wine and slammed it down on the table before helping himself to more of the roasted pig. "You know as well as I do where they both went."

"That is what concerns me."

"He is your brother, not your child—quit treating him like one." William drew the sleeve of his tunic across his mouth. "In case you have not noticed, Darius is a full-grown man." As an afterthought, he asked, "By the way, how fares your jaw?"

"Fine. Thank you." Rhys grabbed his own goblet and tossed down the wine, grimacing as he swallowed. "How do you drink this stuff? Good lord, William, it is near vinegar."

"You are far too spoiled by Faucon's vineyards. The rest of us find it…passable." To prove his point, the earl poured more of the dark liquid into his drinking vessel.

Rhys called for some ale, then sighed. "I cannot bear this waiting."

"You have no choice."

"What if something goes wrong?"

William shook his head. "Mother Faucon, they will succeed without our help."

"It would have gone easier if done according to plan."

"No doubt. But tell me, Rhys, what would *you* have done? Waited for your brother and his ally to come help you? Or taken the matter into your own hands?"

"He was supposed to have stayed in his cell. He never could follow orders."

William cleared his throat and asked, "How did you find Brezden's tower cell?"

The still-fresh memory of being held captive in his wife's tower grated on him. Rhys nearly snarled an answer, "Point made."

"Good. Now enjoy this fine meal."

Before Rhys could voice another complaint, the doors to the Great Hall opened with a bang and one of York's guards nodded to the earl.

Rhys followed William's lead and rose. To his dismay, the earl only ordered the table and benches be removed and the two high-backed chairs placed on the raised dais.

"What are you doing?" Rhys looked from William to the door of the keep.

"Sit down. We will wait here for Darius and his men to bring us the traitors."

In complete exasperation, Rhys nearly threw his long form into the chair next to William. "Now I remember why I no longer fight at your side."

"Oh, cease your endless whining and have some ale. You never could stand the wait."

Marguerite raised her hand, bringing the line of men behind her to a halt, before grinding the torch into the stone floor to douse its fire.

She did not need light to know Thornson's men were approaching to begin loading the supplies into the boats. She could hear their heavy footsteps and their voices as they neared the cavern from the main tunnel.

Silently, she thanked Henry for keeping this small, winding passageway a secret from all but her. From the main passage, this appeared to be nothing more than a long vertical crack in the stone wall, less than the length of two men from the cavern's entrance.

From here, she could watch and wait until the last man entered the cave, then lead Osbert and Faucon's men in behind the smugglers.

By now, Darius and the men in the boats would have received the signal and should soon be gaining the shore below. Once they landed, the additional men from

Rhys's group would join Darius from their hiding places along the cliffs.

Bainbridge and Everett would be trapped on all sides. When he was unable to escape, she had no inkling of how Bainbridge would react.

Her back tensed and her breath became ragged as the men walked directly in front of her. Osbert placed a hand on her shoulder and squeezed gently, offering silent support.

Once the last man had entered the cavern, she inched forward slightly, forcing her breath to slow. Darius had instructed she be patient and wait until Thornson's men had put their backs to their labors.

Soon, the men's chatter lessened. They began the taxing job of moving the heavy crates and sacks, laden with weapons and gold, toward the beach.

Certain they were busy at their duties, she rolled her shoulder beneath Osbert's hand and stepped out of the smaller tunnel. As silently as possible she stood at the entrance of the cavern. A quick glance over her shoulder assured her that Osbert and the others stood ready for action.

Marguerite entered the cave, shouting, "Thornson, hold! Disarm and live."

She then moved against the wall, permitting Darius's men free passage into the cave.

To her relief, all of the villagers dropped their crude weapons—pitchforks, spades and axes hit the stone floor with a clatter. Then they too moved to stand against the wall.

A few of Thornson's guards saw the wisdom in surrendering and followed suit, dropping their swords and daggers before lining up next to her along the wall of the cave.

Marguerite glared at them before ordering, "On your knees."

Changing their minds would be harder if they had the added burden of rising while wearing chain mail. To a man they dropped to their knees.

Osbert and his men made easy work of subduing the remaining men. Swords clashed, echoing off the stone walls briefly. Soon, the clanging of metal against metal faded to be replaced by heavy breathing.

Marguerite reached into a sack hanging at her waist and pulled out lengths of cut-leather straps. She stared down at the man kneeling next to her legs, handed him the straps and motioned toward the rest of Thornson's guards. "Secure their hands behind their backs."

While he saw to her orders, she turned toward the villagers. Her steady gaze had most of the men looking down at their shuffling feet.

Now that she had their attention, she stared at the tallest of the men. "John, explain yourself."

He stepped away from the wall, pulled his cap from his bowed head and held it before him. "My lady, I can offer nothing by way of explanation, except an apology for our actions this night."

"Who bade you help with this business tonight?"

"Sir Everett delivered Bainbridge's orders."

She sighed. "And you always follow Bainbridge's orders?"

"Aye, when Lord Thornson is not around."

Marguerite pinned each man, one by one, with a questioning look. "It will soon be time for harvest. Then winter will set in. Do you wish to remain at Thornson as honest working men, or do you wish to make your way in another manner? I will guarantee safe passage for any who wish to serve King David."

Each man's eyes rounded in surprise. They muttered between themselves and one by one stepped forward, cap in hand, before her.

John tapped his closed fist quickly to his chest. "I will stay at Thornson." The others immediately followed his lead.

Marguerite held back her sigh of relief. Let them think she was still debating the issue for now. She moved aside and pointed to the tunnel. "Leave here. Return home and await my word."

She then turned to Thornson's guards. Osbert had just finished tying the last man's hands and had stepped away. "Did you, too, take your orders from Everett and Bainbridge?"

Each man nodded.

"Darius of Faucon is your liege lord now. You have been aware of that fact since my marriage to him. All of you will retain your life, but will be sent north."

To her surprise, not one of them argued. They stayed stiffly in place, staring at the floor. "Fine, so be it."

Then one guard crawled forward on his knees. "My lady, forgive me. I would be honored to continue faithfully in your service."

That was more like what she had expected. She nodded. "You will have to discuss this matter with Darius." At his look of fear, she added, "I will vouch for you. But if you dare let me down, it will be my arm that severs your head from your neck."

Osbert ordered one of Faucon's men to stay behind and guard the prisoners. He then pointed toward the tunnel that would lead them down to the beach and the waiting activity with Bainbridge and Everett. "Are you ready, my lady?"

She finally released the sigh that had been trapped in her throat and nodded. "Yes."

He stepped behind her and said, "You did well."

From the beach, Sir Everett shouted at the oarsmen in the boats, "Be quicker. Put your backs into it."

Darius's lips curved into a sneer as he slid the hood of the mantle he wore up over his head. He would put his own back into it soon.

When the vessel came to a shuddering stop in the shallow waters, he joined the other men in pulling it farther up onto the beach.

Everett did nothing to assist except to pace wildly back and forth along the line of boats. He kept glancing over his shoulder, and Darius wondered who Everett sought. If he was looking for the men bringing the crates to the beach, he would be looking for a long time.

He had no doubt whatsoever that Osbert, his men and Marguerite had successfully seen to their end of this mission. With Osbert leading the men, Marguerite would not even think of doing less than her part.

Finally, Everett raised his hand to a figure striding down the beach toward him. Darius's sneer turned into a smile. His hand itched to pull the sword from the scabbard hidden beneath his cloak. With all of his being he wanted to run his blade through Bainbridge's traitorous heart and be done with it. Instead, he steadied his breath and waited.

Bainbridge surveyed the boats on the beach as he approached Everett and waited for the men behind him to catch up. At quick count, Darius saw only twenty or so men had followed Bainbridge. He turned his attention back to the two men talking. The wind easily carried their conversation to Darius's ears.

"All of the vessels arrived safely?"

Everett nodded. "Aye, all six are accounted for, my lord."

Bainbridge glanced toward the mouth of the cave. "The supplies should be arriving any moment now." He tipped his head toward the opening. "Go, make certain the men are not needlessly wasting precious time." He then ordered his men to spread out along the beach.

When Everett disappeared into the opening, Darius bit back a laugh. His men were attuned to his movements, and he motioned slightly at his side to hold—to wait for the moment that *would* soon be theirs. It would be soon, but the wait would only make the coming success sweeter.

Darius watched Bainbridge stride back and forth across the beach. The man gave away his nervousness by removing a dagger from his sword belt and flipping it in the air before slapping the short blade against his palm.

Against his palm. Darius frowned. The injury on Marguerite's palm had appeared to him to have been caused by a blade. She'd insisted that she'd gained it from scaling the cliff face. He wondered if perhaps the too-clean slice had been delivered by the weapon Bainbridge so easily toyed with now.

If his guess was true, then she had lied to protect Bainbridge on this matter, also.

Darius gritted his teeth. This constant wondering was what he could not abide. How could he go through life together with Marguerite when he would hold every word she spoke suspect?

He curled his fingers tightly into a fist and ordered his wayward mind, *Cease this insanity.* He needed to concentrate on the task at hand, not Marguerite.

Everett raced out of the cave as if Satan himself were on his heels. "Lord Bainbridge! We have been betrayed!"

Darius ripped the cloak from his body and drew his sword. He pointed it high in the air and shouted, "To Faucon."

His men on the beach followed suit, discarding their disguises and bringing their weapons to the ready.

William and Rhys's men, who had been hiding in the shadows along the cliffs, rushed forward, their weapons drawn.

Osbert, Marguerite and the others from Faucon emerged from the cave. Darius joined them.

While his men rushed the cliffs to do battle, Bainbridge twisted this way and that, seeking a way to escape. Darius laughed aloud when the man raced toward one of the boats. That had been the plan, to force the enemy toward the water and into the tender care of the earl's men waiting there.

He knew full well that Bainbridge would have nowhere to go, and so he turned his attention to another foolish man currently racing at him with bloodlust written plainly on his face. Darius's blade made short work of the fool.

From somewhere nearby he heard Marguerite shout, "Get me a sword." And without thinking he reached down to the man he'd just dispatched to his maker and tossed her that weapon. He was astounded when she caught it in midair, swung around and ran the blade through the back of a man seeking to kill Osbert.

Darius blinked. Obviously, Thornson *had* taught her well.

The rout on the beach was over as quickly as it began. Within moments, Darius's men had subdued the traitors who'd joined Everett and Bainbridge. When their fight was at an end, he called out, "Hold. Secure the prisoners."

Once the traitors were chained and yoked together in a line, they were quickly escorted down the beach. When Darius returned to Thornson, he would give them all into the tender care of William and Rhys.

A wild shriek from near the boats drew his attention. Obviously, Bainbridge was unwilling to meet his fate with any dignity.

Darius headed toward the ensuing scuffle. He would like nothing better than to have Bainbridge's blood on his sword, but had vowed to deliver the traitor alive.

"I said, shut your mouth."

Darius paused. That was Marguerite.

Quickening his pace, he sprinted to where the men held torches near the boats and pulled up short at the sight before him. Everett lay facedown on the beach, a dagger sticking out of his back. This would not please the earl or King Stephen in the least.

Bainbridge was on his knees before Marguerite.

She stood over him, the side of her sword against his neck. "You lied to me. You made false threats to harm my son."

"I need to make you see the right way of things. That is why I forced you to help me."

"You destroyed my marriage."

"I had to kill him. He held all I desired. His time was over, it was my turn to be in charge."

Marguerite paused. Darius froze. *Kill who...oh, my God, nay, not Henry Thornson.*

At precisely the moment her eyes widened in under-standing, she lifted the sword to take a swing at Bain-bridge's neck. Darius threw himself at her, clearing the distance between them in one movement and knocking her bodily to the wet sand.

She struggled beneath him. "Damn you, let me up. I will kill him."

Darius ripped the sword from her hand. "I cannot let you do that."

"Get off of me." She bucked beneath him, but the long chain-mail tunic hampered her movements and she was unable to throw him aside.

He sat up, straddling her, pinning her wrists to the sand, his ankles locked over her legs. "Let it go. You cannot kill him. Let King Stephen deal with him."

"He killed Henry!"

Darius flinched at her hoarse shout. "I know. I heard. I promise you, he will pay."

"Pay? He will pay? I will kill him with my bare hands."

He believed her. From over his shoulder, Darius barked a command at Osbert. "Get that piece of dung off this beach and into William's care. Now!"

"What about Everett, my lord?"

"If that sorry excuse for a man lives, take him along. If not, let the sea claim him."

"I hate you for stopping me." Marguerite snapped at him. "Revenge should have been mine."

Darius waited until most of the noise behind him died before staring down at her. He ignored the heavy

rise and fall of her chest, the tears streaking down her
face and the trembling of her lips. "I know you hate me.
You have made that quite plain, do you not think?"

She tried to pull her one wrist free. "Let me go. Go
away from here. Leave me alone."

"I will. As soon as we return to Thornson I will be
out of your life."

She stopped struggling and stared up at him. "Darius…"

Her voice was a whisper that tore at his heart.

"Darius, hold me once before you leave."

He had the insane urge to laugh. If he held her, could
he ever leave? He looked away, toward the waves lapping at the beach.

"Leave me with something to remember."

He closed his eyes against her plea. "You have Marcus. You have the only good thing between us—our son.
Every time you gaze on him, you will remember, Marguerite."

"Darius, do not leave. Stay. Stay and raise him
with me."

"I cannot." He released her wrists and sat up
straighter. "Every time you speak, I will wonder if you
lie. I will suspect each sentence that leaves your mouth.
That is not the path to trust."

"I will not speak, then."

Her unreasonable comment brought a smile to his
lips. "Oh, aye, that will last a moment or two." He
reached down and brought her injured hand between
them. "How did this happen?"

She frowned. "I already told you."

He let her hand fall, and fought to ignore the tightening of his heart. "Bainbridge cut you."

When she closed her eyes and turned her face away, he knew that he had guessed correctly, and that he had to leave.

Darius rose and helped her to her feet. The stoop of her shoulders and the hanging of her head let him know she was resigned to his departure.

As they crossed the beach, Marguerite asked, "Must you go so quickly?"

Darius swallowed past the dryness in his throat. "Yes."

"What will I tell Marcus—?" Her voice broke, but he refused to look down at her.

"Tell him I go to fight with King Stephen."

"So, you are asking me to lie to the child?"

He stopped and turned around. "No. Do not. Instead, tell him I went home."

"That will break his heart, Darius."

He resumed his walk, answering over his shoulder, "Then we will have something in common."

"Take him with you."

Darius nearly tripped on the smooth sand. "I beg your pardon?"

"Take Marcus with you. Take him to Faucon. Get him out of this place, away from the constant reminder of Thornson." Her breath hitched, but she continued. "I beg you, Darius, take him someplace where he will be safe and away from this battle between Stephen and Matilda."

He hated to admit it, but she had a point. However, as angry as he was at what had fallen between them, he could not do something so devastating to Marguerite. "You would be lost without your son."

"One day he will leave me anyway. It is the way of

the world. He will go to serve whichever liege lord you send him to. What matter if it is now, or in a few years?"

"Marguerite."

"Darius, I am serious. Give him the chance to know his father and his family before the world makes a man of him."

"I have not enough men with me to guard a small child."

"Then let Rhys bring him home."

He reached out and touched her cheek, and she leaned into his hand. "Rhys will remain here at Thornson for a day or two. If, at that time, you are still set on sending Marcus to Faucon, my brother will see him safely there."

He stroked his thumb across a tear. "But if between now and then you change your mind, Marguerite, I will understand."

"I will not."

Darius stepped closer to her. "I may not be able to bring him back to you for a couple of years."

"I know." She kissed his palm. "I know."

He leaned forward and placed his lips briefly against her forehead. "I will take care of him always."

"Of course you will. His mother will kill you if you do not."

Darius stepped back. "I would expect little else." He took her hand and led her to the horses tied to an overhanging root.

After mounting their beasts, they rode back toward Thornson in silence.

Once inside the gates, he led her to the stable and helped her down. Darius held her in his arms, not wanting to let go, yet not wanting to stay.

"Darius, do not make this harder for me than it already is. Go."

"Marguerite, I am sorry."

She did not even try to hide her tears. She looked up at him and stroked his face. "Oh, my love, so am I, so am I."

Chapter Twenty

❧❦❧

Falcongate, Early Fall, 1142

Darius tossed a pebble into the stream running swiftly by his resting spot beneath a large oak tree.

He smiled at the laughter coming from Osbert and Marcus as his captain trained the boy on the proper way to ride a horse. A horse would be one thing, but Osbert had the lad up on his destrier. Marcus's legs stuck straight out on the beast's wide back. But, as always, he appeared to be thoroughly enjoying himself. So, Darius left them be.

He thanked God every morning and again each evening for the opportunity to have his son here at Falcongate with him. And he always added a wish for Marguerite to be at peace with her decision.

"The day is not too trying for you, is it?"

Darius peered up at Rhys. "No, not really." He stretched his arms overhead before crossing them against his chest. "Idleness seems to suit me well."

Both men knew that was a jest. They'd been so busy

rebuilding sections of Faucon's walls before winter set in, that they fell into bed each night exhausted.

But Darius had risen this morning and flatly refused to do any manual labor. To his amazement, Rhys had readily agreed.

"I was wondering if you would do me a favor."

He looked away from Rhys and said, "I am not laboring today."

"It really is not anything overly hard. Joshua hurt his leg and there are only two more cottages to be inspected before we decide which ones to rebuild and which ones to tear down."

Darius sighed. "And the builder arrives tomorrow."

Rhys nodded. "Yes, of course."

"How is Lyonesse?" He knew the reason Rhys did not wish to inspect the cottages was that his wife had been so sick with carrying his child. Darius did not blame Rhys at all.

"Well, earlier this morning she seemed fine." Rhys scratched his head. "But she has been deathly ill ever since she dressed and ate."

Darius rose. "I will go. You see to your wife and watch over Marcus until I return." He waved Osbert and Marcus in as he asked, "Which cottages are left?"

"The two east of the falconer's hut."

Darius looked up at Osbert and Marcus when they stopped the horse a short distance from him. "I am going to inspect a couple of the cottages. You two tag along with the comte—I should be back at nightfall, or shortly thereafter."

Marcus, perched on Osbert's lap, asked, "Can I play with my sword?"

Rhys laughed and reached up to muss the boy's hair.

"Of course you can. I am sure one of the other boys will be glad to oppose such a fine swordsman as you."

Darius shook his head. "Have fun and try not to hurt anyone with that weapon of yours." Right now Marcus was too small to do much damage with a wooden sword, but the day would soon come when it would be otherwise.

Darius sat atop his horse on a hill looking down at the last cottage. His heart fluttered briefly as memories floated through his mind.

A small brazier provided light in the one-room hunter's cottage. They would supply their own brand of heat to warm the tiny chamber.

Her skin was so soft and smooth, like the fluffy softness of a rabbit. He stroked her naked limbs, reveling in the knowledge that she was his. She trembled beneath his touch, her nervousness making him feel bold and protective at the same time.

"For the love of God, cease." His words floated away on the breeze. This separation hurt more than the last. Weeks had gone by and he could not remember one day that his heart had not ached. Or one day when he had not wished he could take back his foolish pride.

Rhys had returned to Faucon a sennight after he had. Marcus had been with him, and Darius's first thought had been a useless wish that Marguerite had been bold enough to come, also.

But she hadn't.

How could he blame her? He'd lost count of the times he'd called for a cleric to pen her a missive, ordering her to Faucon. Somehow that did not seem enough. He needed to journey back to Thornson, but winter was due soon and he'd not subject their son to such a harrowing trip.

It would be nigh on impossible, but he would wait until he could smell the beginning of spring. And then, he had every intention of bringing his wife home. No matter what it took, no matter what he had to do, she was coming home.

Darius wondered if she ached for him the same way he ached for her. Did she lie abed nights, cold and alone, with only her memories to keep her warm?

Were those memories enough? Did they increase in intensity so that at times it felt as if a hand reached out and brushed against her cheek? Or as if lips pressed softly against her own?

He missed more than just the passion they'd shared. He longed for the woman she'd become. Years ago, he'd fallen in love with a girl. When she'd been taken beyond his reach, he'd pined for her until his pain became a familiar companion.

Once he'd found her again, he discovered a woman—full-grown and sure of herself and of her wants—instead of the girl in his mind.

His heart had recognized his true love at once. His body had quickly fallen in lust with the womanly curves and desires. But his mind had been slow to accept the adult she'd become.

It had taken leaving her of his own accord to realize how very much he missed, wanted and loved the woman she was now. He was drowning in a bottomless well of his own making, unable to save himself from the pain chasing him.

Only Marguerite held the cure to save him—and it

would be a long, lonely, cold winter before he could hold her and set things right between them.

Darius cleared his throat in an attempt to wipe away the madness. He had a task to complete and it would be best if he did it before the moon rose.

Darkness would only make the dreams stronger. They were near unbearable as it was. How would he survive the long winter?

He nudged his horse's side and slowly proceeded down the hill toward the cottage. A thin plume of smoke drifted out of the window opening—a sight that did not surprise him, since someone had also been using the cottage nearest the falconer's.

At this time of year it would be more odd if he found the cottages empty. Rhys did not begrudge anyone from hunting in his forests. He only asked that they use what they caught and not kill for simple sport. So far, nobody had taken advantage of the offer.

Darius's inspection would not take long and then the hunters could go about their business without interruption.

He reined in his horse outside the cottage, dismounted and tied the animal to a nearby tree. A leisurely walk around the outside of the small hut showed that it was not in disrepair. He would be glad to leave this building standing.

He knocked on the closed door. "Hail. I am from Faucon and only wish to inspect the inside."

Nobody answered his knock. Perhaps they slept. Darius pounded a little harder. Still no response.

He walked over to the narrow window and peered inside. He could see that the small brazier was lit, but he saw no sign of anyone.

What sort of imbecile would leave a hut with a fire glowing in the brazier? He crossed back to the door and pushed it open.

The heat from the brazier was nothing compared to the raging fire ignited by the sight before him.

She knelt on the dirt floor, wearing nothing but a thin under-gown and a stare so tormented, so full of hunger and pain that he found himself stepping toward her.

Darius dropped to his knees before her, afraid to touch her, yet terrified not to take her in his arms. "Marguerite."

She lifted her arms with her hands held out. Across her palms was a jewel-encrusted dagger. "I would rather die than live without you any longer."

He knocked the weapon from her hands and pulled her roughly into his arms. "Then live with me."

Darius buried his face in her hair, inhaling the scents of herbs and smoke.

Her fingers clung to his back, she held tight. "I am sorry, Darius. Please, please forgive me. I love you, I have loved you since we were children planning our future in this very hut. I swear, I will never lie to you again."

He nearly fainted from the shame of what he had done. He pulled away and grasped her face between his hands. Each tear that escaped her eyes made him despise himself even more. "Marguerite, there is nothing for me to forgive. I was wrong. I was angry and hurt and so very wrong."

"I lied. I betrayed you."

"To keep our son safe." Rhys's words rang loud in his mind. "You did what any parent would do. I did not fully understand that then, but I do now. You put everything on the line to save your child." He pulled her against his chest. "And you forfeited much for something that was never your fault. 'Tis I who beg forgiveness Marguerite and I will do so every day for the rest of our lives if only you will stay here with me."

Her soft laugh shuddered against his chest. "I will never leave you, Darius. We can both spend the rest of our days seeking forgiveness."

He traced a path along the downy softness of her back. "Or we could spend our days reclaiming our love for each other."

Marguerite leaned away from him. "I would like that much better."

A smile played at her lips, the pain receded from her eyes, and he made a silent vow to never do anything to put the hurt there again.

When she shivered, he rose, pulling her to her feet. "You are cold. Come let me warm you."

Cool air rushed against his own skin as he removed his clothing with Marguerite's help. They both burrowed under the covers, their arms and legs entwined.

Marguerite whispered against his shoulder, "Our last time in this bed did not end pleasantly."

"But all those years have led us back to where we started, my love."

"I am no longer that girl, Darius. You are no longer that boy. What if—"

He rolled on top of her and stared into her eyes. "You are the woman who gives my life purpose. I am the man who loves you beyond all else."

Darius lowered his lips to hers.

Many long weeks of hunger fed the fierceness of their kiss. Marguerite welcomed his demanding kiss with equal passion. He groaned under the assault of her nails raking down the flesh on his back.

No words broke the rhythm of their heated passion.

Darius touched, stroked and kissed the length of her body until she cried out for fulfillment.

Marguerite reveled in the power she held over him as she, too, touched, stroked and kissed the length of his long form until his own ragged cry echoed her need.

When Darius rolled onto his back, she rested her head on his chest, her fingers tracing patterns over his muscles. "How is Marcus?"

"He is fine. He misses you."

"Darius?"

"Hmm?" He fought to keep his eyes open.

"Have you enjoyed having him around?"

That helped in keeping him awake. He stared down at the top of her head. "Yes. Why?"

Marguerite reached across his chest and pulled his arm across his body. She then took his hand in her own and placed his palm low against her stomach.

"He will soon have a brother or sister, and I just wanted to make certain it was something you wished for."

Darius shifted onto his side and stared at her. He could barely think past the lump in his throat, let alone talk. Finally, he stated, "Wished for? My love, I am thrilled beyond measure."

She smiled and shrugged. "Good. Because I will not exactly be the most rational person for the next few months."

"With all that has happened between us and for all that awaits us in the future, I will take you as you are— forever." He kissed her forehead. "Marguerite, you are all I ever dreamed of."

She pressed a kiss to his chin. "Darius, you are all I ever desired."

He brushed his lips gently across hers, whispering, "My love," before pulling her close against his beating heart.

She settled easily into his embrace, brushed her lips against his chest, and whispered, "My life."

* * * * *

"He is insufferably rude and boorish. I have never met a man I would like less to marry."

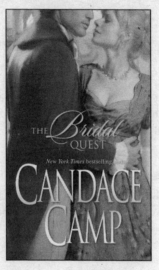

THE *Bridal* QUEST

New York Times bestselling author

CANDACE CAMP

Gideon, long-lost heir to the Earl of Radbourne, was a handsome, powerful man – and one who seemed bent on seducing Lady Irene Wyngate. As she reluctantly yielded to his attraction, wicked family secrets came to light. Secrets which would have devastating consequences for both Irene and Gideon…

Available 18th December 2009

millsandboon.co.uk Community

Join Us!

The Community is the perfect place to meet and chat to kindred spirits who love books and reading as much as you do, but it's also the place to:

- Get the inside scoop from authors about their latest books
- Learn how to write a romance book with advice from our editors
- Help us to continue publishing the best in women's fiction
- Share your thoughts on the books we publish
- Befriend other users

Forums: Interact with each other as well as authors, editors and a whole host of other users worldwide.

Blogs: Every registered community member has their own blog to tell the world what they're up to and what's on their mind.

Book Challenge: We're aiming to read 5,000 books and have joined forces with The Reading Agency in our inaugural Book Challenge.

Profile Page: Showcase yourself and keep a record of your recent community activity.

Social Networking: We've added buttons at the end of every post to share via digg, Facebook, Google, Yahoo, technorati and de.licio.us.

www.millsandboon.co.uk

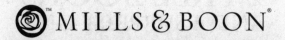

2 FREE BOOKS
AND A SURPRISE GIFT

We would like to take this opportunity to thank you for reading this Mills & Boon® book by offering you the chance to take TWO more specially selected books from the Historical series absolutely FREE! We're also making this offer to introduce you to the benefits of the Mills & Boon® Book Club™—

- **FREE home delivery**
- **FREE gifts and competitions**
- **FREE monthly Newsletter**
- **Exclusive Mills & Boon Book Club offers**
- **Books available before they're in the shops**

Accepting these FREE books and gift places you under no obligation to buy, you may cancel at any time, even after receiving your free books. Simply complete your details below and return the entire page to the address below. You don't even need a stamp!

YES Please send me 2 free Historical books and a surprise gift. I understand that unless you hear from me, I will receive 4 superb new books every month for just £3.79 each, postage and packing free. I am under no obligation to purchase any books and may cancel my subscription at any time. The free books and gift will be mine to keep in any case.

Ms/Mrs/Miss/Mr_____ Initials _____

Surname _____

Address _____

_____

_____ Postcode _____

Send this whole page to: Mills & Boon Book Club, Free Book Offer, FREEPOST NAT 10298, Richmond, TW9 1BR